Claire is an orphaned American en route to a career-defining international conference in the tropical White Sand Islands but is shocked to discover a travel warning for a killer named Amberly who looks just like her.

Local islander Kyle realizes his attempt at a peaceful new life is sabotaged upon Claire's arrival when the pair become shipwrecked and he believes Claire somehow holds answers why the notorious pirate, Amberly, killed his innocent brothers.

Meanwhile, Amberly unravels a sinister plot and sails through the islands to find her shipwrecked twin before she falls to more unbeknownst harm.

Claire, Amberly, and Kyle must face their pasts and make decisions about how far they will go for family and love.

White Sands Secrets
Copyright © 2023 Catherine Hazen
ISBN: 978-1-4874-3752-7
Cover art by Angela Waters

Published by eXtasy Books Inc

Look for us online at:
www.eXtasybooks.com

WHITE SANDS SECRETS

BY

CATHERINE HAZEN

DEDICATION

To Daniel – for your belief in me, and my stories.

PROLOGUE

The ocean licked his feet. A fresh spray of seawater hit Kyle's face with its familiar salty bite. He blinked, but the image of his struggling boat drifting further away was permanently imprinted in his vision whether his eyes were open or not. He could still hear the sound of his brothers' bodies hitting the deck. Lifeless. Alone. He should be lying with them now, already taken in by the island goddess, Iselle, to join the rest of his family.

Wet ropes bound his hands and feet. They slid clumsily over the deep mahogany deck. Compared to the large yacht protected in the cove, he knew his boat had no chance with nobody at the wheel. He watched as powerful waves swept dangerously over the railings and flooded the lower deck in the distance. The sea had always comforted him, but now he felt angry at its power.

Footsteps approached behind him. The buckles on the woman's boots hit the deck with a staccato clang. She was getting closer. He stiffened instinctively, forcing his bound legs to stand and tearing his attention away.

Fingers curiously fondled his wet and unruly brown hair. She pressed her lithe body into his from behind and ran her nose down his shoulder before standing before him, observing him with jeering hazel eyes. Kyle shook with rage at her sneering oval face, the auburn hair whipping around her. She peered so closely at him that he could see delicate drops of rainwater cling to her eyelashes, which were narrowed malevolently.

"You'll still get what you want." She moved her hands downward to seductively massage his upper thighs. "Well, eventually." He kept his shoulders high and his chest forward. He wasn't afraid to die.

"We could still get the boat, Captain," a gruff man's voice said behind him.

"No," the woman replied, her tone crisp. "We'll watch it sink . . . together."

Kyle grimaced as she pressed her body into his.

"So sad, isn't it?" Her soft purr whispered into his ear mockingly. He felt her lips upon his neck and recoiled in disgust. Greedy fingers quickly ran along his side and over his abdomen until he was locked in place with the perfect view of his boat being tossed violently ahead in the churning ocean.

"Watch." She sniggered, breathing into his ear, but there was nowhere else he could look as the boat listed to the side, the waves swallowing it whole until there was nothing left.

Kyle blinked angrily, his body involuntarily trembling. The man tightened the ropes at his feet. Choppy waves splashed around the yacht, the ocean's spray coating Kyle and the woman as they stood, rigid, pressed into the railing.

The woman let go of his hair, her slim figure moving away from him. The rain fell heavily on her striking features. It seemed cruel that she possessed such beauty while having no heart to match.

Kyle looked down to see the large rusty anchor securely tied to the rope that bound his feet. Lifting his head up slowly, the woman smirked and made one swift kick to his knees, catching him off guard as he buckled to the deck.

The woman knelt to his level and withdrew her knife.

"I can be merciful. You're making a terrible mistake," she whispered, examining her reflection through the knife's tarnished silver between the stains of his brothers' blood.

"I would never join you," Kyle spat out. "I want to die."

The woman's long, delicate fingers traced over the worn handle of her knife. She stared at him with a pitying expression for mere seconds before reaching up and slashing her arm through the air. Kyle hardly felt the pain of his pierced skin, only the warmth of his blood running from below his ear to the collar of his shirt. Her sadistic laugh rang in his ears as she sheathed her knife. Flipping her long auburn hair behind her, she stood and gripped her deck's slippery railing, observing the rolling ocean below.

"Toss him in," she said dismissively, abandoning the railing and walking out of sight. The clicking of her boot buckles diminished.

The sudden realization that he was about to join his brothers brought Kyle a welcomed sense of peace. His gaze moved to the area where their boat had vanished as he was plunged into the cold and stormy sea. The weight of the anchor pulled him further into the watery depths, engulfing his senses with darkness.

CHAPTER ONE

"I can do this, I can do this, I can do this," Claire repeated as she paced nervously in the empty conference room. Her black heels clicked sharply against the hardwood floor like the tick of a clock. Goosebumps crept up her bare arms.

"Deep breaths." She put her hand on her chest and listened to the exhale. She hated presenting when Mr. Gann was going to be listening. Because of his short fuse and lack of patience, she'd practically reduced her big project to an elevator pitch with a few leading examples. If she nailed this presentation, a promotion was sure to follow, and she could finally supervise herself. But only if this went well.

Claire turned to the dark window compulsively and stared at the glow of St. Paul's city skyline. The falling snow made it even more beautiful. In her reflection, her gaze roamed over her thin frame. She ran a hand through her short auburn hair, tucking any loose strands back into place. She frowned at her slouching shoulders and quickly adjusted her posture to fearless. With one last critical look, she smoothed her pencil skirt and turned to the clock on the opposite wall.

Eight-twenty-three AM. Seven minutes to go. Claire took several deeper breaths, running over the presentation in her mind as she flicked on the lights. She'd arrived two and a half hours early to practice, but she was starting to regret skipping breakfast. Her stomach grumbled in agreement. She chewed her lip and ignored it as her supervisor and the project manager, Jackson, walked in with the public relations manager, Neil, whose gaze was glued to his cell phone screen. She

4

stopped herself from snorting. It was amazing that Neil hadn't gotten fired yet, and comical to think he had *manager* in his title when he only oversaw his own childish personality. Jackson was his opposite, and today he looked particularly statuesque in his thin-rimmed glasses.

"Claire, are we ready to connect with Mr. Gann?" Jackson asked purposefully, his deep voice and confident appeal rendering Claire momentarily speechless, as he always did. She smiled, trying to catch his eye, but he remained focused on his work with the audio equipment on the table.

"I've already set up the video chat, but Beverly is still coming," she replied.

"This isn't anything we haven't seen before." Neil chewed his pen cap, casually leaning back in his chair with comfortable ease.

Claire stiffened, her smile slightly faltering as she watched Neil's eyebrows knit together with apathetic boredom.

"It's incorporating feedback from clients," she said. "These new designs reflected their changing needs. Navigational clarity is a big one, ease of use, appeal . . ."

"Yeah, but what do they know?" Neil rotated the pen in his mouth with his tongue before returning it to his pocket.

"Mr. Gann wants new ideas on our websites, and it's time for an upgrade." Jackson finally met her eye. As if on cue, her insides melted as the corner of his lip quirked upwards in an encouraging smile.

Despite his being her superior, watching Jackson's smooth movements always piqued her arousal. She felt her face flush but was grateful for the slight distraction from her nerves. It wasn't Jackson's fault that Mr. Gann micromanaged her through him, but Jackson had impressed Mr. Gann just shy of his six-month anniversary, and she was approaching a year.

I can do this, she thought to herself. But deep down, she heard voices of doubt. Gann, Inc. always seemed way too good to be true. She'd applied knowing she wouldn't get the job. Interviewing, she'd figured, would simply be a way to be in the same room with professionals. She could learn from them. Listen to their speech patterns and how they placed their hands on the table. All of it counted, and she wanted to master it to turn her life into something meaningful. She couldn't believe it when she got the offer. It was the end of her money anxiety. She would never be hungry again or have to rely on anyone but herself. No handouts, no scholarships. It was another step forward to freedom and strength. It became easy to play the part of a young professional, acting as if she belonged. She felt a gratefulness for her scheduled days, the safety net of her routine paychecks, and the flutter of her normal crush, but above all, the stability of her life was enough. No longer did she need to chase her old unhealthy highs. They were finally in the past, for good.

But the conference would decide her fate at the company. Despite her hard work on the new designs, it was clear that Mr. Gann was getting agitated. He'd halted hiring an additional designer and spent more time muttering to himself in the hallways than in his office, if he even bothered to show up at all.

Despite all that, she had to think positively. Today was the day her ideas would propel the company's image into this decade, and tomorrow she'd be off to the international conference to promote them.

The company's other web designer, Beverly, circled the table next to Jackson, her arms laden with glossy magazines. She briefly eyed Claire's opening slide on the screen before pushing the stack of magazines to the middle of the table. Claire observed the magazines, noting the title *The Isle Explorer*.

"Afterwards," Beverly said. Usually the chattiest person in the office, she was uncharacteristically quiet. Neil began casually texting while Jackson put the call through to Mr. Gann.

"How long is this supposed to last again?" Neil asked Claire without looking at her, talking loudly over the ringing noise coming through the boardroom's speakers.

"I booked us for a half-hour in case we have questions and want to discuss things," she replied. Neil grunted, squinting at his phone screen.

"The ideas are good, Claire." Beverly sat back and folded her hands across her chest. Claire gave her a small smile of thanks, for Beverly was always quick to judge, and her opinions were not always favorable to Claire's visions. However, the quick burst of unexpected confidence ended as the audio equipment stopped ringing. A moment of silence passed, but their company owner's face did not replace the black void on the video conference screen.

Suddenly Mr. Gann's booming voice spilled out of the speakers. "How the hell do you work this thing? Jackson! Did you set this up right before I left?"

With practiced calm, Jackson cleared his throat. "You have to hit the green button to turn on the video-chat feature."

Claire breathed deeply, willing herself to relax while Mr. Gann fumbled audibly. After a few minutes, his sunburnt face flickered onto the conference room screen.

"There. Finally!" Mr. Gann peered into his webcam. "Good to see everyone. I heard you're having another beautiful day there in Minnesota!" Mr. Gann thundered, pointing casually at the tropical blue skies behind him. "I'm almost envious. All we have here in the White Sands is sun, sun, and more sun. How many inches of snow are you supposed to get tonight? Actually, never mind. Just get to the airport early. Nobody's getting reimbursed for missed flights."

Forced laughter awkwardly filled the boardroom as the gentle snowfall outside began to increase.

"Get on with it, Claire. I have a lunch reservation here at the hotel's *Michelin Star* restaurant in thirty minutes."

Claire shifted her feet, her heart pounding a little faster. It was easy to remember how new she was to the company while under Mr. Gann's scrutinizing gaze. She picked up a laser pointer simply to have something to do with her hands, which were threatening to shake.

"Yes, good morning, Mr. Ga—"

"Afternoon for me!" he corrected her loudly, laughing at his own cleverness.

Claire nodded to the CEO politely. The dress requirement at Gann, Inc. was, above all, a forced smile. Mr. Gann fell silent, looking expectantly back at her. The tropical sun behind him caused silver streaks in his graying hair to shine. Recalling the exact words of her practiced introduction, she began with her head up and her arms at her side.

"As you all know, I've been working on a new design for our websites and have built four sample layouts. Although this differentiates a bit from our current brand, the layouts still correspond to our brand standards, and our competition has followed a similar formula that has generated proven success," she began, forcing her words to come out slowly as she gripped the laser pointer.

Mr. Gann frowned, showing early signs of disapproval in his pixelated form on the executive boardroom screen.

"The templates are responsive on multiple devices, have fewer links . . ." Claire's throat went suddenly dry. "There is less text, and our data shows that less time is spent on web pages, so the goal would be to increase click—through rates. With that in mind, I have designed—"

"Are you *serious*, Claire?" Mr. Gann asked.

"Yes!" Claire's voice rose to a higher pitch as the word came tumbling out. Time was running out for her to keep his attention. "The templates—"

"No, no, no, I don't like this at all!" Mr. Gann's magnified head had angry red lines of disappointment forming on his aging face. "We are not changing our formatting. I don't care what a few of your clients might have told you. We are not following any other standard but the one in place!"

The laser pointer's hard plastic slipped out of Claire's sweaty palm, no longer boasting the flawless grip the packaging had promised. Heat crept onto her face and neck. Claire looked at Jackson for support, but his face was impassive and offered no relief from the rising beat of her heart. Her stomach rumbled, and suddenly the room felt not like the familiar place she'd been practicing, but a suffocating prison of eyes staring at her.

"Sorry," she mumbled hastily, fumbling to pick up the laser pointer as a rush of dizziness washed over her. She mentally chastised herself for she had never heard Jackson or Neil ever apologize.

Her back grew the hottest as she stood up, adjusting her skirt. She couldn't even look her colleagues in the eye, for she feared they would see right through the facade she was desperately trying to conjure. Claire turned back to Mr. Gann's side of the screen, the room still echoing with his angry decibels.

"Mr. Gann," she began tentatively, forcing her words to sound natural while her heart thudded in her ears, "I think we need to take this risk, and I am prepared to answer any questions—"

"I don't want to hear it, Claire. I don't care *where* you read it, or who said what. We are not taking this type of risk with no guaranteed return! *Fix* it before you present this to potential investors this week!" Mr. Gann rubbed his temples and shut his eyes. "How could you let this happen, Jackson?"

Jackson cleared his throat loudly. "We will fix this, Mr. Gann," he said, matching Mr. Gann's volume. He shot Claire a regretful glance.

"You better. Cancel your ticket if you have to. I mean it. Get her under control," he thundered tersely. "You should have known better."

"But . . . this was my project," Claire stammered, unable to hide the hurt in her voice. "I'll take responsibility. I should be the one to stay here." Her legs trembled as she felt her dreams of a promotion disappear altogether.

"No!" Mr. Gann shouted, even angrier. Claire realized the entirely of her lower back was covered in sweat. There was no recovery now. Even her colleagues looked nervously at the screen.

Gann wiped his face and started talking calmly, facing the screen once more. "That won't be necessary, Claire. In fact, I want everyone here with me. Just fix this before the conference. I want a personal briefing on these templates after you land."

The video call terminated, but the vacant screen still intimidated Claire long after Mr. Gann's image had faded out. She felt the sting of his words as the room was bathed in uncomfortable silence.

Neil popped up out of his seat first. Jackson ripped out the sheet of paper he'd been writing on and tossed it in the garbage. Claire shakily placed the laser pointer back on the table.

"Take a magazine before you leave!" Beverly interrupted the silence with her usual joviality. "I thought it best we all have a look at where we are going so we can plan something for our free time!"

Neil doubled back to grab a magazine, curling it into his palm and whistling as he left. Jackson leaned into the table to shut off the connecting software. For the first time in a year, Claire felt nothing when facing him but shame.

"Start working on your revisions," he said. He looked as resigned as she felt. "I'll touch base with you tomorrow."

Jackson took two magazines and handed one to Claire.

"Thanks," she said quietly. A thousand apologies started and ended in her head before she was able to put one foot in front of the other and walk away.

She dropped the magazine at her desk when she heard Neil walk by.

"Well, that was a train wreck." Neil's voice was a whisper as he passed Beverly.

"Yeah, I don't know what she was thinking talking back to Mr. Gann like that," Beverly said.

Abandoning the magazine quickly, Claire turned back to her computer and opened her presentation. Her fingers pounded against the cheap plastic keyboard as she tried, in vain, to ignore them.

"How's Hayley? Did you guys finally get an exterminator?" Beverly continued in a louder voice.

"We were just texting about that," Neil replied indignantly. "She says it's my fault, and I should have caught the problem earlier, but she's home all day with Owen! She could have had the time."

"Oh yeah, when does he start daycare?"

"I dunno, maybe next month? Hey, wanna go out to lunch?"

Their low, rushed voices collaborated over shifting papers before they left. Claire couldn't believe that she would have to convert her templates back to the typical Gann, Inc. guidelines, undoing months of preparation for the conference and changing the pitch she had planned to investors. Even worse, she couldn't stop the meeting's reactions playing in her mind, each performance sounding more wretched than the last, the stares of her colleagues boring into her skull.

Claire ate an early lunch alone at her desk, focusing only on her work until the clock showed it was past dinnertime. A dull headache began behind her forehead. One by one, she could hear her co-workers express their goodbyes, voicing last-minute preparations before the trip the following day. Beverly unknowingly turned all the lights off, leaving Claire alone in the dark office.

Claire wearily got up and turned the offensively bright fluorescent lights back on, watching her mirrored reflection in the dark windows as she made her way back to her small desk. She knew she had to stop and finish the rest on the plane. She was spent, so she began uploading her unfinished presentation to the cloud storage.

With her bag carefully slung over her shoulder, Claire skimmed her email one last time while the upload continued. There was the latest update from Mr. Gann, who had sent a photo of his ocean view, boasting clear waters and a seemingly endless blue sky. She noticed a link to the hotel they would be staying at, The Ocean Royale, was pasted below the photo with links to news articles relevant to the company's arrival. Mr. Gann had spared no expense when it came to advertising for the conference, and Neil had spent the last year preparing press releases and contacting international business magazines.

The Ocean Royale's website was designed perfectly with simple text, sprawling tropical photos, and minimal links. Serene local music blended with relaxing beach waves in her speakers as the website slideshow changed photos. Incensed, Claire opened it in various browsers and checked its compatibility.

"My templates are even better," she muttered.

The accommodations were going to be the best she had ever experienced. Stunning ocean views graced every room, complemented by luxury amenities.

"One cannot miss the culinary experience of Istura, the Michelin Star restaurant featuring Head Chef Jaquarde Ponthieux and his pastry chef, Frédéric Pelletier. The restaurant overlooks the professionally designed gardens . . ." Claire read dreamily, her thoughts about the website naturally subsiding while she pictured herself there in twenty-four hours. She began to open the other links, admiring Neil's press releases for the representation that he gave the company. If she didn't know better, she would have been impressed with the professional edge of Gann, Inc. Opening the last link, her computer momentarily froze.

Page not found.

Claire frowned, looking at the source in the original link, and saw it was from a local island newspaper called *The White Sand Times*.

"Mr. Gann won't be happy about this." Claire clicked on the homepage, seeing various titles across the screen in French. She clicked on *English* and scanned the pages for their press release.

"*Temple set to be refurbished with taxpayer money . . . Yacht regulations cause tourist uproar — harbor commission to hold emergency meeting . . . Historic building renovations on Feulia Island . . . From the kitchen to street — Famed restaurant* Soixante Amours *kicks off annual Festival for Iselle* . . . where did you put it, Neil . . ." Claire muttered to herself and searched for Gann, Inc. until she found it, but her eyes were drawn to the headline reading LOCAL MURDERER AT LARGE on the sidebar.

"Murder?" Claire clicked it with curiosity and sat back in her chair. After a few moments, the page opened.

Claire put her hand over her open mouth as she saw the police sketch glaring back at her. The portrait was of a woman who had an oval face like Claire's, but with long hair and piercing eyes. It was all the same, from her delicate nose to the arch of her mouth.

Our mouth, she suddenly caught herself thinking. Claire leaned closer to her screen. The woman was identified as Amberly, with no last name; she was wanted for murder.

Squinting, Claire read the small text under the photo. The

travel warning was over a year old, followed by the name of the artist, Emere Marama.

"I hope nobody else here saw this picture," she mumbled. Claire searched the internet frantically for any additional information she could find, but the only new thing she learned was that the White Sand Island had a bounty of one million dollars for the woman Amberly's capture. When further text searching didn't work, she image searched the photo. Her breath caught excitedly in her throat when she found an article titled *Local woman only suspect in multiple-murder case*, but any further links were missing or broken.

Claire leaned back, nearly falling out of her chair. Her mind raced with possibilities. Could they be related? Could this person be her sister? Her heart beat erratically. Perspiration ran down her forehead and her back for the second time that day. Was the chance of finally finding her family worth overlooking the fact that she was a killer? Claire's hands shook at the truth of the thought. If there was someone out there who could understand her, even if she was a murderer, she had to know.

Claire recalled the year she turned thirteen when her curiosity about herself was at its highest. She'd spent months poring over court records, but they were all sealed.

Frustrated and shaken, Claire quickly closed the browser. She wrapped her burgundy pea coat around herself and turned the lights off. Her hands trembled as she thought about her sneering doppelganger engaged in criminal endeavors before morphing into Mr. Gann's angry face. The images did not leave her mind even as she stepped out into the shocking cold.

CHAPTER TWO

"Nathalie!"

Nathalie suppressed a grimace. Tom's excitement could barely be contained as he walked over.

"One second." She carefully slid her knife into the lemon, cutting the last wedge, masking the annoyance in her tone.

"Impressive," he said, sidling over to her. "I've never seen anyone work a knife with such magic."

Nathalie snorted, but gave Tom a small smile. "Nah, I just want to please that guy so he'll leave. He asked for more water, but he really just wants to stare at my ass." She dropped a lemon wedge into the ice water.

"Want me to bring it to him?" She watched Tom sit on the nearest stool. "That guy's been ogling you all night. It's disgusting."

"Don't worry, Tom. He'll be gone soon. Anyway, what is it you want to tell me?"

"Presley's Bar is staying open late for the carnival workers. Let's go have a drink after we go to the bank. The kitchen staff's already gone celebrating."

"That sounds fun after today. First, the fine *gentleman's* water." She winked at him sarcastically.

"No dawdling." Tom frowned after her.

She had barely cleared the barkeep doors when the man began jeering.

"Snowflake!" He tried to pull the loose dirty white shirt over his large stomach, but it only jostled the small silver cross he wore around his neck.

"We're closed, sir," she said firmly, handing him the water. "As you can see, you're the last one in here. Please finish that, and get home safely." She eyed the tarnished gold band on his ring finger and shook her head. "I'm sure your wife is starting to miss you."

"Don't got no wife no more." The man grasped the water with dirt-streaked hands. Five gulps later and he was finished, wiping the condensation on his stained jeans. He pulled a wallet out and threw two twenties on the table. Nathalie eyed it dubiously and took his empty water glass.

"Have a nice night," she replied coldly. She took the money and turned, but not before he had the chance to grab her exactly where he'd been staring all night—generously in her fleshly backside.

Whipping around, she glared at him as he stood. He didn't meet her eye while adjusting his stained baseball cap. He just chuckled before forcefully opening the door. It swung open to darkness, and soon, he was swallowed up by it.

"What an asshole." Tom walked towards the table and began wiping it with a rag. "Too many people like that come here during the carnival."

"Well, good thing Monica was available to help us today. Otherwise, we'd have drowned in customers," Nathalie replied, walking back to the bar. She jiggled her key in the cash register. It was the third time this week it had jammed on her.

"It's like that every year. Good old Village Carnival of Cedar Point . . . here, I got it." Tom eagerly took his apron off, folding his tip money into his wallet before pulling out his key, and opening the register drawer with ease.

"At least we're finally done," Tom said. His green eyes became alight with excitement, and his tousled blond hair gleamed in the restaurant's dim fluorescent light. She caught his eye and smiled in spite of herself, for he was handsome.

Stacks of neatly folded bills came into view, more than ten

times the earnings the restaurant brought in on a normal week.

"I'm buying you a drink on your last night here. No protesting! It's a shame you have to leave. What's Sweden got that we don't, anyways?" Tom wiggled his key free.

"The work abroad program that brought me here, Tom." Nathalie tried her best to smile at him gently. "But you don't have to get anything for me."

Tom shook his head and gently placed his hand over hers. It was warm and sent a curious tingle up her arm.

"I said no protesting," he said quietly.

Nathalie blushed again as a stray piece of hair fell across his forehead. Tom winked at her before pushing it away. She put the last several bills into the deposit bag, eyeing the clock discreetly.

"Time really flies," she replied slowly, zipping the bag closed. "I'll close up in here. You go ahead. I need to run to the bathroom before I go. They never clean the ones at Presley's Bar. Meet you out front in five minutes?"

Tom leaned in and kissed her cheek gently. "Don't take too long," he said, removing his brown coat from a nearby hangar and swinging his long arms into the sleeves. "I'll be sure to get the lights up front for you, too."

"Thanks so much!" Nathalie called after him, dropping the bank deposit bag into her satchel.

She picked up a dirty rag from the sink and placed it in the laundry basket. With the exception of the man's water glass, the dishes were cleaned and neatly stacked for the morning shift, and the overflowing garbage out back was proof enough of the surplus of customers. She smiled to herself and checked the clock. Shutting the bar's vintage lights off, she walked out quietly.

The cold stung her cheeks. Nathalie made her way down the hill alone, passing thick trees around the entrance to the harbor. She tried to ignore the chill ocean breeze and walked faster.

Except for the Presley's Bar, Cedar Point had shut down long ago, leaving her a lone figure on the path to the marina. Discarded plastic straws stuck to the cold blades of grass. Streamers were littered nearby, crunched with cold and the abuse of tires, and the sugary aroma of cotton candy and hot dogs still hung in the air. Three men conversed ahead on plastic chairs in front of a large trailer, the small orange pinprick of a cigarette hovering around one of the loud mouths. She walked away from them, keeping her head forward and leaving the pavement for a small gravel trail.

"Hey, it's Snowflake!" A familiar voice called mockingly as she passed, bolstered on by his friends' whistles and cat calls. Suddenly her footsteps were no longer alone on the gravel. "What's the rush, eh?"

Nathalie turned slowly and stared at the man from the restaurant in silence, carefully swinging her satchel over her shoulder. Hungry eyes raked over her body, the smell of beer and cigarettes clouding the air as he stumbled closer.

"This the one you gave a huge tip to?" One of his friends yelled, chuckling to his companion as they watched from afar.

"Hell yeah!" The man staggered closer to her, lifting his booted feet with difficulty. He grabbed the front of her apron and brought her nametag closer to his face. The glow of his cigarette glinted on the silver cross around his neck. "It's Nathalie, all right! Swedish chick from Langhammers Bar n'Grill!"

"Leave me alone!" She ducked out of the way, hastening to move from him.

"Aw, quit yer running, Snowflake. I thought of so many better uses for those pretty long legs of yours tonight." The man caught her wrist and tossed his baseball cap off to the side.

Nathalie let out a muffled cry as he dragged her off the path and into the woods.

"Catch you later, Nelson." The two men laughed at their friend. "Don't worry, sweetie, he'll take good care of you!"

She didn't resist as he caught her other wrist and smashed her against a tree, covering her body before forcefully finding her face with his own. Tree bark dug into her back, and the moon disappeared behind some clouds. Disturbed by the commotion below, a group of birds left their nest in the tree, flying towards safety. She saved her breaths carefully under his weight, just as she'd taught herself to do years before.

He breathed into her ear, an unearthly smell hinting at years of foul nutrition and neglect. As he pressed his waist against hers, she let herself relax. He laughed.

"Not even gonna put up a fight? I like it when they fight, you know. Makes it more fun."

His lips crushed hers with brute force. His chest knocked the wind out of her lungs as his hands wound tightly into her hair. Amidst the beer and cigarettes, she could taste the lemon she served him not half an hour ago. She tried in vain to turn her head.

"That's it, you foreign bitch, turn away," he muttered dangerously. "I don't want you to like it."

With a free hand, he began unbuckling his pants with surprising swiftness in his inebriation, pulling her hair roughly.

"Like it?" Nathalie breathed into his ear. "I wanted you to do this." He pulled her hair harder in response, a strange look of confusion crossing his face as her wig began to loosen.

"What the fuck?" he muttered as he pulled the blonde wig off. A curtain of auburn hair cascaded down her shoulders. She used the moment to catch his wrist while her other hand located the hilt of the knife strapped to her upper thigh.

His eyes widened in shock as her cold blade plunged deeply into his fleshly midsection, his dirty fingers gripping her arms in vain. Twisting the knife deeper into his stomach, she let out a sigh of unbridled pleasure.

She reached a hand to his neck and pulled at the cross until its fragile chain broke. Her bloodstained fingers lingered over the cheap silver as his mouth formed voiceless words and coughed bits of blood across her lips with his shallow, choked breath. She licked them slowly.

"Go be with your God now." She watched as his hands fell to his sides, his balance weakening fast. Savoring the bitter taste of his blood in her mouth, she spat it back onto his face before he crumpled into her.

"Hey! Hey! Get off her!"

The limp man was suddenly pulled away by strong hands, twigs snapping in the commotion. The moon appeared again from behind the clouds as Tom's face came into view. Kicking the man squarely in the back, he watched the motionless figure and looked pleased with himself while she hid her knife and tossed the necklace to the ground.

"Oh my God, Nat, are you okay? How far did he get?" Tom took her shoulders gently, but he didn't wait for her response. "I saw you walking down here instead of turning towards the bank, and I followed you . . ." he trailed off, frowning at her hair.

"Tom," she began slowly, watching his face rapidly turn from relief to confusion as he picked up a long strand of deep auburn. Tom glanced suddenly at the motionless man on the ground.

"He's not moving." Tom made to kick the man over, but her arm shot out to stop him.

"Leave him," Nathalie pleaded, but Tom didn't listen. He gasped in horror as he turned the man around with his foot.

She watched Tom carefully, his eyes wide with horror. His hands reached up to clutch his blond head in disbelief as he backed away, mouth open in shock as he made to turn around.

"Don't run," she commanded, dropping her fake accent. She grabbed his arm to steady him. He looked as if he was about to vomit upon seeing her bloody hand gripping his coat.

"Who are you?" he whispered in fear.

"Come with me, and I'll tell you everything," she replied. She took his shoulders firmly. "I could use someone like you, Tom. Someone willing to come after me, like you just did."

"Police . . . we need to speak to the police . . . Nat, let me go . . . *Nathalie!* Stop!"

"Don't choose death, Tom," she whispered silkily, keeping him steady. "And, make no mistake about me, I was never in danger from this man." She leaned into his ear, his hair tickling her nose. "Join me or die like him. I don't leave witnesses."

"Somebody *help!*" Tom yelled loudly, his voice echoing in the trees as the clouds drifted in front of the moon again. "No, Nathalie, *stop!*"

"My name," she whispered to him, her knife meeting flesh for the second time that night, "is Amberly."

Thick trees covered the shore as she dragged the heavy bodies behind her. She heaved in deep breaths from the exertion, angrily cursing the turn of events that had caused her delay. Her boots filled with cold water as she waded in the swamp.

"And who's going to miss you, drifting carnival worker?" She deposited the pudgy body unceremoniously at her feet and kicked thick fallen tree branches until she found the side of her hidden rowboat. Once she flipped it over, she ripped off as much of her wool stockings as she could, grateful for the cool air on her legs. Hoisting Tom up first, she dumped him in and heard a loud *crack* as something broke from the force of his fall, his lifeless, glassy eyes staring above. Throwing her bloody satchel on top of him, she swore at him for the extra trouble, heaving the other man in on top, the scent of beer still clinging to him in death.

Quickening her movements, she eased the boat into deeper water, giving it a solid push before jumping in. The ocean breeze took strands of her long hair behind her. The waves lapped around her as she grasped the wooden oars and cut through the water until the familiar white hull appeared.

The deep mahogany deck of *The Duchess* shone in the moonlight at the private dock. She'd kept it hidden all these months after a hefty payoff from the dock's owners. That was what she loved about rich snowbirds; as long as they got more money, they never asked questions as to how their property was used. She never even needed to meet them face to face. Svante took care of that.

With swift, expert knots, she tied the rowboat to the small ladder on the stern. Her fingers ran over the railing as she climbed aboard with the stealth of a cat, her footsteps quiet and her satchel close. The chill air had made her knife cold against her leg, the once warm blood on it now turning sticky.

She stared at the familiar sight of her captain's cabin. She had seen the view a hundred times before, but she always savored the quiet moments before leaving port, especially when she'd been away for so long. She left her position and turned to the stairs as Svante's figure appeared below her.

When bathed in the moonlight, she could see the familiar tattoos of Svante's former life gracing his muscular arms and neck. He eyed the bloody contents in the rowboat and discarded blonde wig with a slight smirk. Her focus never left him as he climbed up the railing and joined her on the upper deck. A cold breeze whisked across the yacht, but neither of them flinched. She watched him gaze shrewdly over her bloodstained clothes, the nametag hanging off her apron, the cold water still leaking out of her boots, and the tattered remains of the wool tights hanging like wet socks around her ankles.

"Well?" Her booted foot clicked the deck impatiently.

"Got as much as expected," he said coldly, yet the warm tones of the White Sand Island clung to his every syllable. She relished the rich sound; it had been months since she'd heard anything but ugly American accents. She placed her hands on his hips and drew him closer, smiling.

"Perfect," she whispered. "The restaurant was good to me tonight." She smirked at the thought. "We can refuel in the morning and go even further north. A few more small scores like this, and we should be clear to move on to something bigger."

Svante took a large swig from the flask he kept in his back pocket, his eyes averted. Annoyed, she dropped her hands and shot him a questioning look.

Svante placed his flask back in his pocket and withdrew a sheet of paper. She grabbed it forcefully and opened it so fast it nearly ripped in half. Her eyes narrowed to slits.

Every detail was accurate. The wind in her hair, the angry eyes that had seen too much, the malice that traced the corners of her own mouth. She drank every detail in the wanted notice until her hands shook. She glanced at Svante before gazing outwardly at the moonlight ocean, lost to a wave of memories that fueled her anger.

"Emere," she whispered viciously.

"I was told it was all over every coastal town, even further north than this." Svante took another swig from his flask. "You think Jaquarde put her up to it?"

"It doesn't matter," she whispered. "She just won't stop betraying me."

Amberly watched the moon's jarred reflection in the gentle waves before turning abruptly, taking Svante's flask and drinking deeply. The gin burned her throat like needles, coating it thickly with a bitter taste. She paused as she let the drink permeate her senses.

"Take care of the rowboat and bring the bodies aboard. We'll dump the fat, dirty man later when we're farther away, but I want to keep the handsome blond. Now I have plans for him and Emere."

"Yes, Captain," Svante said obediently.

"We cannot afford any more mistakes." Her eyes narrowed dangerously. "I did not leave The White Sands to see my face on a wanted sign."

"No, Captain," Svante agreed.

She nodded and turned, about to head back to the helm.

"Amberly?"

It had been months since she'd been addressed by her real name, but still, she didn't turn around.

"It is good to see you again."

Amberly remained frozen, feeling his eyes on her back. Any other time his words would have melted her insides, but not now. Her fists tightened further around the crumpled notice.

"Jaquarde and Emere will pay for this," she stated woodenly. "We have no choice. We're going home."

CHAPTER THREE

Claire sat up in bed. She'd already gotten up several times for water, warm milk, relaxing music, and covered her body in lavender lotion. She looked at the clock. It was two a.m. Her flight left in a few short hours, and try as she might, sleep remained elusive in the wake of her day.

She fluffed her pillow, inhaled the lavender on her skin, and tried as hard as she could to let the day go and forget about the upcoming trip. Something must have worked. The milk, or even the lavender, but her mind finally drifted.

It was her eighteenth birthday and the last day of her senior year. She saw his face, clean-shaven, as he began writing on the black-board. Her body relaxed further. He hated shaving, he always joked about it to the class, but she knew he did it because, as he said, it would be smoother on her thighs when he finally licked her until she orgasmed. The thought made concentrating on the final exam impossible. When the bell finally rang at the end of the school year, Claire sank into her familiar pattern, sidling up to his desk as the other students left. His sincerity would melt her, enough to ignore even the tiniest gut feeling of warning.

The scene dissolved, and she was staring at him across a table. The college scholarship letter she shared with him was close to the eighteen candles still smoking on the square sheet cake. A single spot of frosting was missing. It tasted sweet on Claire's tongue. He had put it there, his finger lingering over her lips as she licked it off.

She was less nervous than she thought she would be when they arrived at the motel. Nobody had ever made Claire feel this way before — made her ache and burn with desire. How did he manage to be so sexy while locking the door and tossing his keys on the bed? She caught her breath and smiled — today, all of her fantasies would become real. She was an adult and would be a woman shortly. She didn't know how she'd waited until tonight, but he'd insisted. He looked at her and pointed to the coffee table, a wink in his eye. She obliged and leaned on the edge, letting him caress her panties under her skirt. It was a yellow skirt, pleated, his favorite color. Would he notice she was wearing the perfume he always complimented her on?

It was hard to control her cry as he slipped off her panties, letting them dangle at her ankles. He pushed her back on the table and buried his face into her, tenderly licking the delicate folds between her legs and squeezing her hips, pulling her further into his greedy mouth. He was right — it did feel better when he was unshaven. On and on, he drank her wetness, at some point lifting her onto the bed, and when she felt she could take no more pleasure, he entered her. He stifled her cry of relief and pain by crushing his mouth over hers.

He ravaged her vagina, digging into her hips with his.. Her legs naturally opened. Should she tell him he was pushing too hard? She was unable to voice her thoughts. What if they upset him? She didn't want to risk anything that would take her away from this pleasure. Her legs trembled from the excitement. She moaned when he touched her small breasts. She came as he did, eager to feel him continue to throb inside of her, but he gave a short, concluding sigh and pulled out. Her orgasm faded quickly, leaving her confused and longing for more as Aiden left to clean himself. Claire closed her legs awkwardly, doused suddenly by a cold wave of confusion. Her legs shook and crumpled beneath her as she got up from the bed she'd soaked. Aiden wordlessly wiped his mouth. The hollow feeling in Claire's heart worsened when he answered his ringing cell.

It was her, his fiancé. This was finally their night, and all he wanted to do now was say how much he missed his fiancé? How he couldn't wait to be done with work and make love to her? Jealousy and anger clouded Claire's thoughts. She felt sick. She turned her head to hide the tears rolling down her face.

Claire woke with a start. She was drenched in sweat, her heart racing with anxiety. That was ten years ago. How could he still make her feel this way? She closed her eyes against the uneasiness in her heart, cursing herself for the nightmare. She counted her breaths in and out for several minutes. She listened to the whirr of her tiny bedside fan and focused on relaxing her body, limb by limb. The body he'd devoured, her mind countered.

She glanced at the clock. Three-fifty. Only a few more hours until the trip. "The trip." She reminded herself aloud. "*Your* trip. No Aiden. *You* support you now." She made the mantra repeat in her head. She counted her breaths again until she finally slowed her heartbeat, but she knew sleep was not coming back.

Claire fidgeted with the scarf around her neck. Part of her wanted to stay on the plane instead of facing Mr. Gann or thinking any more about the *wanted* notice. But she marched forward regardless and hoped her colleagues wouldn't notice her shaking legs. She inhaled deeply, the breeze carrying the salty scent of the ocean while nearby palms swayed lazily. She stared at her phone for what felt like the hundredth time, still unsure whether to text her last foster mom. She feared her dreams of Aiden and her old life would get worse if she didn't. She stared at the empty open text box but knew what Cindy would say to her.

"Claire, we've given you all the information we have. You can talk to the agency again, but what are you looking for in the past when you have such a better future?"

But this time, I have some proof. However, they have proof, too. They'd only bring up the conference and how successful they feel I am now. Not that they deserve any credit for that. I was their charity case.

"Hurry up, Claire!" Neil barked at her impatiently.

"I'm only three steps behind you," she retorted, but he was

checking his phone and ignoring her. She sighed in irritation and decided to think about texting Cindy later when she was on the charter boat to the conference. In an effort to clear her head, she looked towards the famous white sand. It was only just visible ahead on the shoreline. A large flagpole rose from a grassy area near one of the many oceanfront airport parking lots, surrounded by palm trees. Claire followed the pole up to the huge light blue and orange striped flag of the White Sand Isles, the fabric looking glossy and proud in the sunshine. She squinted at a small logo of a wave and half of an outline of a woman's silhouette face.

"Let's eat before we catch the boat," Beverly insisted, walking towards a restaurant surrounded by unlit torches, radiant tropical red orchids, and more towering palm trees. Claire looked up and read the restaurant's sign, *The Blooming Orchid,* which was carved ornately out of wood. Beverly let her carry-on bounce loudly against the wooden steps of the deck while Claire watched the hostess frown at this carelessness. Her dark skin, the same chestnut brown as the table she leaned on, crinkled into a scowl as they noisily approached. Reluctantly, she pulled out menus for the group.

Claire lagged behind on purpose and quickly scanned the available pamphlets at the entrance. She took one about the history of the White Sands flag and the Beach of the Isles, which had piqued her curiosity through the many advertisements on the plane TV, as well as posters in the airport.

The group wove in between the cramped tables, settling in a shady corner surrounded by purple and white orchids. Fruit stands and art sat propped up on small carts outside of shops filled with swimwear, their outdoor hangers flapping in the breeze. It was a fairly busy day, with accents of multiple origins coming together to form an audible blend of different languages. Fisherman and tourists calmly walked the serene harbor line. Claire couldn't help but feel a slight pang of jealousy as she watched young children excitedly clutch their parents' hands, eagerly guided along as they took in the street vendors with wide eyes.

"Clarion Charter Tour is next," Beverly said, spreading the itinerary upon the table to review and breaking Claire's train of thought. "See? Right there. It was really a nightmare getting them on the phone. Apparently, they book very fast."

Claire read her menu, seeing choices of freshly caught fish, salads, sandwich, and drink specials.

"That hostess forgot to give me a knife." Beverly folded her napkin across her lap grumpily.

"You have thirty-two small knives in your mouth," Neil said. He stretched his arms at length, narrowly missing a waiter carrying a precarious amount of empty plates.

Beverly threw Neil an irritated sneer. Claire turned her attention behind her bickering coworkers, where men began pounding large steel drums near the beach. They were accompanied by chanting from a small group of people. One of them raised a small White Sand Island flag, and the tourists nearest raised equally small ones in tune to the beat. Turning back to the table, Claire looked at the pamphlets she'd taken moments ago and paged through the one on the White Sands flag.

The Goddess Iselle

Hundreds of uninhabited years passed on what we now call the White Sand Islands. Flora and fauna were abundant and untouched before it became a temporary trading post or resting location for Polynesian tribes and traders alike, advantageous due to its shielded rocky coves and expansive shaded areas inland. The many shores were perfumed by exotic flowers and miles of beach made up of black volcanic sand, earning the nickname dark paradise, *according to records found by European travelers. The island changed from a resting point to a permanent residence for tribes, and generations of native-born islanders soon began to revere the black sand.*

According to legend, the rains of a terrible hurricane was the will of a goddess of the sky, Iselle. She brought the glittering white sand to ease what was once dangerous night passages through solid black rocky shorelines as the people of the White Sand Islands explored neighboring islands. These explorations often led to clashes between tribes.

As trade routes were established in the region, more islands were discovered before it was officially christened The White Sand Islands. It became a port that drew in many from neighboring countries. Over time, the perception of the islands shifted from fear to one of good fortune, from the deity of Iselle.

The island retains this early influence today; as long as the islands remain white, Iselle continues to protect them.

Please visit the White Sands History Museum to learn more about island history, the Goddess Iselle, and the tumultuous relationship between the people of the White Sand Islands and the settling Europeans that ultimately led to the construction of the Temple of Iselle. A special exhibit featuring rare early stone carvings of the Goddess are displayed until April 10. The White Sand History Museum is located at 6 Manroro Street, Nusa Via. Open 9 – 5, Monday through Saturday.

The steel drums continued their steady beat as passersby stopped in the street to watch or dance. Closing her eyes for a moment to soak in the information she'd read, Claire began counting the beats in the uplifting melody.

"That music is annoying," Neil commented, but Claire ignored him and watched as a group of young Europeans passed by, chatting audibly and cheerfully. Their eyes were alight with the excitement that came with a carefree attitude. A pair of beautiful women in bikinis broke away from the group and sidled up to the outdoor bar. Jackson's eyes quickly glanced up and down, taking in their fit, deeply tanned bodies.

"Wow, damn." Neil sniggered, elbowing Jackson. "Good

time to be single, huh, Jacks?"

Claire felt her cheeks grow hot as she watched Jackson trace his fingers over his chin, watching the women avidly and smiling sheepishly at Neil's remark.

"Did you guys read about when the white sand appeared hundreds of years ago?" she blurted out lamely, hoping Jackson would glance her way. He didn't, and nobody else responded.

"It's because Iselle protects the islands . . ." Claire fell silent and wistfully looked down at the napkin in her lap.

"And a good afternoon to you all! Are we all set?" A tall, dark-skinned waiter smiled widely down upon them all. Claire let the waiter's voice mull over in her mind, fascinated by his musical tone. He made a show out of getting his pad and pencil out of his pocket as everyone nodded. Claire experienced a strange sense of relief when she saw the women in bikinis leave the bar, even though Jackson followed their path towards the harbor.

"Let's start with this lovely lady." The waiter turned towards Claire. "And what will—" he stopped suddenly, his black eyebrows raised as he caught Claire's eye.

"What is it?" she asked uncertainly.

"I'm so sorry, miss, you gave me a slight fright." Claire was suddenly aware that everyone was watching her.

The waiter continued. "You see, we have a notice"—he pointed to a sign, barely visible over the register—"about a woman, wanted for . . . some issues."

"Issues?" Claire tried to maintain a confused look even as the uncomfortable thought hit her and turned her face bright red. She exchanged a knowing look with the waiter that confirmed her suspicions.

"She's a local woman," he continued. "A modern-day, shall we say, pirate? You have her eyes, her face. It's truly uncanny, the resemblance. They say she's very beautiful, as you are . . . luring men into her boat before . . ." He mimed sticking a sword through someone, catching the eye of the neighboring tables. Beverly frowned, and Claire felt Jackson and Neil shake with silent laughter next to her. Claire felt sweat begin to bead along her forehead. The waiter leaned into Claire but spoke loudly enough so that her co-workers could hear.

"She's the seductress of the sea!" He finished with a dramatic flourish, and Claire felt as if her face would be permanently scarlet. The steel drums thundered a finale down the street, and vigorous applause followed before another beat resumed.

Beverly's eyes narrowed further. "Can we resume with ordering, please?" She shot Neil a reproving look as he visibly shook with giggles.

"Of course." The waiter sank into a deep bow. Claire forced her fingers to fumble for the menu even though her appetite had vanished.

Once they concluded ordering and the waiter left, Neil let out a final laugh and turned to Claire, poking her in the ribs. "Got a secret life down here, Claire? Mr. Gann wouldn't like you killing people for sport in your spare time. Or is that how you get your website ideas that nobody likes?"

Claire took a steadying breath, rubbing the tender spot on her side Neil had poked. She intended to meet his eyes but instead looked up and focused on two men with the same dark island skin tone as the hostess and waiter, seating themselves at the table nearest. The taller of the men had a strange tattoo on his neck, but she barely glanced at it before feeling his gaze on her. It raked from the end of her heels, up her slender legs, and rested on her breasts before meeting her gaze. A playful tug at the corner of his mouth formed into a smirk, but Claire knew her body was already at the mercy of his fantasies. She swallowed, averted her gaze, and struggled to compose words. "It's just a silly coincidence."

"Don't worry about it, Claire," Jackson said kindly. She shot him a thankful glance, but Neil still shook his head with laughter. None of her colleagues paid any attention to the two men.

"Really, you all need to grow up a bit," Beverly snapped. "He only kept going because your laughing encouraged him. He probably just wants a bigger tip."

"Lighten up," Jackson said suddenly. "We've had a long day, and we're about to have a long boat ride."

Beverly's lip stiffened, and she gently clasped her hands on the table with a deep breath and exhaled, surveying Jackson with determined politeness until the food was brought by their waiter on a large tray. Claire inhaled the group's choices of pastas, local fish, sandwiches, and artistic salads, all featuring a single orchid placed appropriately on each dish. Foreign spices unfamiliar to her traced through the air in a succulent aroma.

Noticing the tension, the waiter was quick and gave Claire the slightest bit of a wink before leaving. The group began to eat quickly. Claire moved her own pink orchid and bit into her sandwich, appreciating the vibrant sauce drizzled over the thick bread and bold seasoning on the local fish. Unfortunately, the food wasn't enough to distract her. The waiter's comments still rang in her ears, and she felt unnerved. After a few meager bites, she set her sandwich down.

Glancing around to take a breath of air, she noticed the two men staring in her general direction. Their expressions were identical, determined, and fearless, like they owned the place. They exchanged words too far away for Claire to hear.

They looked like criminals to her. Maybe it was the tattoos that seemed to cover every inch of the bigger one, or maybe it was the furrowed eyebrows and dangerous way they seemed to drape their bodies casually over their chairs as if accommodating hidden weapons. Or, maybe she spent too much time watching movies after long work days. Claire shook her head and turned back to her sandwich, mentally chastising herself for being so immediately judgmental about them.

"I can get the tab with my card," Neil said, pulling his wallet out.

"No, I've got it." Beverly got up from her seat and made to walk towards the register.

"Actually, I have to get it," Jackson said, placing his napkin on the table. "Mr. Gann thought it best if I cover food expenses. He sent me an email last night."

"That makes no sense," Beverly said as Jackson pulled out his wallet. "It shouldn't matter who buys what. We all have cards."

Jackson shrugged at Beverly.

"I'll come with," Claire said quickly. "How about if I get us all some waters for the boat ride?"

"Whatever," Beverly replied dismissively, while Neil stuffed the rest of his sandwich in his mouth and tossed his orchid aside.

Jackson paid the hostess and scribbled in the twelve and a half percent tip as per Gann, Inc. guidelines in his scrawling loopy signature on the receipt.

"Four waters, please." Claire stepped up to the register and snuck a quick look at Jackson, but he was facing the other way. His finger tapped cheerily against the counter to the beat of the steel drums.

"Bag?" The hostess asked in a bored voice.

"Yes, please," she replied.

"Fifteen dollars," the hostess said, as Claire handed over her own company card.

"Good call about the water," Jackson commented, squinting into the sun.

"It's not working." The hostess abruptly handed her card back, while Jackson hastened to get his out.

"Did you activate it?" Jackson questioned.

Claire turned back to the hostess, who looked slightly irritated. "Yes, of course," she said, but the hostess was already running Jackson's through her machine.

"No worries," Jackson said, signing another receipt as the hostess handed Claire the bag of waters with less than a friendly expression. "But look into it when we get to the island. You're going to need that card, especially when you take your clients out for dinner. Mr. Gann doesn't reimburse cash transactions or out-of-pocket expenses."

"Right," Claire said.

"Let's go over your presentation together on the boat. Are you done yet?"

"Almost. It shouldn't take more than an hour. It's on the Gann cloud now, but I'll email you a copy when I'm done too."

"That's a smart idea. We won't get any service on the water, so let's put the spare copy on my flash drive. I could come over later tonight and help you with them if Mr. Gann wants more changes?"

"It's a date," Claire said, not realizing the double meaning behind her words until they hung in the air before her.

Jackson gave her a kind smile that she returned tentatively. They walked back to the table, where Neil and Beverly had already assembled their luggage.

"Where's my sandwich?" Claire demanded, staring at the crumbs on her empty plate.

"I thought you didn't want it." Neil dismissively picked his teeth with a toothpick. Beverly was already outside on the veranda with her bags, clearly ready to take the lead down to the boat docks. Claire scowled at Neil's back as she followed him onto the hot pavement. They passed several multicolored signs to the harbor, shopping and music districts, and the Temple of Iselle.

"I've made a reservation under Gann, Inc." Beverly informed everyone as they walked to the harbor in a staggered line. Claire was thankful for the breeze for the heat emanated from the pavement, and it was more of a relief to step onto the cool wood of the dock. The masts of the many sailboats and yachts moved with the wind. Their lines hit the poles like a harbor wind chime chorus. Flags snapped in the air as they walked amongst the docks, passing endless tourist tours, charter fishing trips, and large, privately owned yachts.

"I found it," Neil called, pushing through a throng of people in wetsuits exiting a deep-sea diving boat. *CLARION CHARTERS* was painted in large block letters on the side of the boat. Claire noticed it was the biggest boat in the harbor; its decks were already full with passengers.

"Ahh, yes," Beverly said, doing an awkward about-face in her heels to catch up with Neil. A short line had formed by the boat, and the departure time was listed on a sandwich board on the edge of the dock. "This is their last boat of the day," Beverly informed everyone. "With our late flight, we were lucky to get reservations."

Claire got in line with the others and watched azure waters float in a mild current beside the dock. Maybe on the boat ride, she could relax a little.

"Next!" The attendant gestured Claire forward. Claire grasped the handle of her carry-on, passing a promotional sign from the boat's company on the dock, and lifted her luggage over the ramp.

"Company and name, ma'am?" The attendant wore a light blue suit and an expression of haste. His large hands grasped the clipboard.

"Gann, Incorporated, I'm Claire Vaughn. I'm the last of them." Claire pointed at Beverly's back.

He frowned at his list as Claire made her way forward, but the attendant put his hand in front of her. "Please wait one minute," the man said, holding his hand out to block Claire. "We don't seem to have you on the list."

"What's going on?" Beverly turned around. "What is it?"

"I'm sorry, ma'am, but she's not on the list. We have strict rules about our passenger limit, and it cannot be exceeded. We've already reached maximum capacity."

"I can't believe this!" Beverly exclaimed. "I know I made the reservations right. I even had a phone call yesterday confirming everyone's name!"

The attendant seemed unconvinced. "Ma'am, I do apologize. We print the lists immediately before boarding so they're ensured to be up to date. Do not be concerned. There are plenty of other charters that can take the young miss to her destination today." No sooner had he finished than the rumble of the engine began.

"Please, I need to get to the island with my co-workers for a conference. Can we work something out?" Claire's face burned for a second time that day. With rising panic, she saw Jackson had already reached the end of the ramp and boarded, with Neil two steps behind.

"I'm sorry," the attendant said with finality. "We'll help the young miss find another ride," he said to Beverly.

"Do what he says, Claire," Beverly said contemptuously, never taking her eyes off the attendant. She haughtily snatched up her suitcase and stalked up the small ramp behind Neil, who was shrugging off help from the attendant at the top of the ramp.

Claire's mouth gaped slightly open at the realization that she wasn't going to board. Her stomach flipped again as she half considered running past the man and up the ramp, but she didn't know what that would possibly achieve outside of making a scene.

"Ma'am?" the man in the light blue suit said. "Start at the D section of the harbor. That's straight ahead and to your left. Most charters leave on a thirty-minute basis. You will, I'm sure, find someone to take you to Sunavae Island. Now, if you'll please step back, we have to get underway. Good day to you."

With a tip of his hand, he signaled to the upper decks and walked up the ramp himself. Claire stood frozen as the two crewmen on the dock quickly roped off and secured the ramp.

The boarding door was closed. Claire watched, dumbfounded, as the other passengers meandered onto the upper and lower decks to watch the view. Neil waved to her from the lower deck. Jackson appeared next to him, staring down at Claire with a confused expression before taking his company phone from his pocket and began texting. Her phone buzzed in her dress pocket, and she took it out quickly.

You HAVE to get to the island. Gann is expecting you to have the new templates finished. He told me if you don't, you'll be fired. I'm sorry. I was going to tell you 2nite.

Claire's legs were wobbly and unable to support her without shaking.

Fired.

She was about to reply when the bellowing honk of a horn startled her. The boat slowly backed away from the dock, right on time as a clock in the distance chimed the top of the hour. The *Clarion* eased its way out of the harbor. She barely saw Jackson once the boat began turning.

"D section," she muttered to herself, and she turned with urgency to find the dock.

"Looking for a ride?"

A finger traced her upper arm and rested on her elbow. The man's jagged delivery immediately told her English was not his first language.

"Ahh, no thanks," Claire replied uneasily as he crept closer to her. She instantly recognized the bulkier man from the restaurant. Muscles rippled under his dark skin, and his shoulders were hunched menacingly, accentuating the open-mouth shark tattoo under his chin. She felt like prey as she stared at the rows of spiked teeth running across his jawline and collarbone. Claire tried to turn away, but he grabbed one of her wrists roughly.

"Let go of me!" Claire shouted, trying to wriggle free. His grip tightened, and she breathed in the scent of cigarettes and whiskey.

"He won't unless I tell him to." The slighter man appeared at his side, a wicked grin encompassing his face as he licked his lips. His accent was smoother but not without the timbre of the islands. "Don't make this harder for yourself."

"I'm not the pirate woman," Claire stammered blindly.

Both men laughed. She slipped off her heels and took a short breath.

"Is there a problem?" An attendant in a red jacket called from an adjacent charter.

"Just helping the young miss with some directions to her hotel," the shorter man called.

Claire felt the grip slacken slightly and took advantage of it. Within a second, she brought her arm upward and twisted the man's strength against him. Forced to let go, he did not attempt to grab her again with the attention of the attendant.

Claire picked up her carry-on and ran as fast as she could into a group of tourists departing a scuba diving tour. She ran back to the dock she'd come from before sneaking a glance behind her and saw the men approaching fast. Claire ran further away from the tour boats until she reached the next dock. She tripped on a fishing net and fumbled with her carry-on, the delay losing her precious seconds. Shouts from behind told her that the men continued to roughly shove tourists out of the way.

An awful ache began to form in her side. Inhaling quickly, she ignored the smell of dead fish emanating from the surrounding boats. The end of the dock was in sight. Claire skidded to a halt.

There was nowhere to go but the ocean, unless she tried to make it back to the turning point in the dock system that would take her down another row of fishing boats.

"Shit." Claire cursed her stupidity and turned as a woman screamed.

The men pointed their guns at anyone in sight, making the tourists around them break apart so they could get through.

Panic spread through the crowd as Claire whipped her head towards the closest boat. Sweat clung to her palms and trickled down her back as she used pure adrenaline to throw her carry-on over the railing. Without looking behind her, she climbed over the railing, landing awkwardly amidst fishing gear and life jackets. She crawled to the door that she assumed led to the lower cabins. It opened easily. Shoving her suitcase ahead of her, she moved as quickly as possible. The narrow staircase was darkened from being underwater. She could only hope she was alone, and no one had seen her sneak aboard.

Claire's blood chilled as she waited. The buoys that shielded the boat from the dock bounced at a pulse reminiscent of the current below. Still, it wasn't enough to drown out the turmoil she felt inside or the continued shouts on the dock.

Headlines of *Tourist Murdered* floated through her head as she waited in the shadow behind the door, frozen in fear. Suddenly, footsteps thundered from above.

The movement rocked the boat from side to side before beginning the descent down the stairs. She held her breath and bunched her hands into fists, shrinking into the corner as much as she could.

A person entered the dark room, shrouded in shadow. It stopped near the tiny bathroom off of the stairs, then turned to the bunk beds parallel to each other and flushed to the wall. The figure glanced at each of them quickly without pausing.

Her heart beat so loudly in her ears that she was sure the person would spot her behind the door. But the figure moved out of sight. Claire let out a sharp intake of breath.

A large hand covered her mouth as her body was pulled to the floor, pinned. The cold tip of a knife pressed against her throat.

CHAPTER FOUR

Blinking back fear, Claire opened her eyes.

There was a hard edge to the man's face that only seemed to worsen the more he searched her eyes. Even in the dark, she could see his dark skin was the same complexion as the two men, but his hair was a shorter mass of windswept curly brown hanging above his shoulders.

"What are you doing down here?" he demanded, his voice low. Claire felt her heart pound erratically, the panic causing her breath to catch in her throat and rendering her speechless. Seeming to realize the effect he was having on her, he eased his grip on her shoulder and instead knelt before her on the floor, removing his knife from her throat but still pointing it.

"There are two men . . ." Claire stammered, never taking her eyes off the knife. "They're following me. They had guns. I ran in here to hide . . . one had tattoos. I should call the police!"

The man snorted. She felt as if he were staring into her very soul. Blinking and looking away from his piercing gaze, she rubbed her sore arm and looked at the red imprints his fingers left before glancing at the knife again.

"I saw what happened on the docks." There was no sympathy in his eyes. "The police will do nothing. Luckily those men didn't hurt anyone yet. But you . . . I'll never forget that face," he uttered threateningly, his voice rich with the island accent.

Claire felt her dread multiplying. His deep brown eyes were almost a refreshing change if they weren't so angry.

They stared at her with unwavering force, making her more uncomfortable with every second that passed between them. Swallowing dryly, she had a grim idea dawn on her as she recalled the waiter at the restaurant and his initial look of fright.

"I have nothing to do with that pirate women!" she snarled. "I've seen the notices, too. I'm not stupid."

The man straightened his shoulders, his gaze narrowing shrewdly, but he seemed to accept this logic with a heavy dose of distaste for her regardless. Claire let out a breath of relief as he sheathed his knife.

"Could have fooled me," he said in a dangerous tone. "Especially if you're being followed. People are still searching for her. Including me."

"Look, please, I need help," she blurted out, hiccupping on her short gasps of breath, determined to meet his eyes with the same ferocity. "I need to get to the island Sunavae. I just got here from America. I've never been here before."

"Why Sunavae?" he asked, his nostrils flaring.

"For a conference," she snapped back, her voice clearer. "This day has been a complete nightmare and just seems to be getting worse."

He stared at her. "What happened to your shoes?"

Claire looked at her dirty feet. "I left them at the edge of the dock so I could run faster."

"What's your name?"

"Claire," she responded. "What's your name?"

A slight smirk played at the corner of his mouth.

"Kyle." He continued to stare at her. She bit her lip, waiting. She guessed he was probably older than her by a few years.

Finally, Kyle spoke. "Okay, Claire. I'll give you a ride for six-hundred American dollars, including meals."

Claire's mouth dropped open. "That's twice the cost of the

charter I missed!"

"I'm cutting you a deal, as only a few charters go that way. It's an elite island few can afford to stop at. I have other guests joining me within the hour. Paid guests. On vacation."

"Still too expensive." She stood shakily and made for the door. "If you can direct me, or walk me to another boat when it's safe out there?"

"No." He leaned so close that she could smell him, a potent combination of sunscreen mixed slightly with sweat and fish. She wrinkled her nose as his hard gaze moved to her forearm, momentarily glancing at the red marks he'd left. "If you're being followed, you'll be found. Stay down here until we depart. You'll be safer."

"Do you know those men?"

"No. I'm not friends with criminals." He turned to leave. "Like I said, you'll be safer here. Take the bed with the yellow quilt tonight. The blue and green ones are the other customers, and I'll sleep in the wheelhouse. Pay me later."

Claire looked up at him in shock. "I can't stay overnight! I have to get to my colleagues today."

"I already told you, I have paying customers who made reservations long before you stowed away. I have to honor them first."

Claire wrung her hands together. "I need to tell my colleagues where I am."

"Good luck. No reception this side of the docks. When we get out to sea, come find me."

He disappeared upstairs, closing the door behind him.

What a mess she'd gotten herself into. She rubbed her sore eyes and peered out the tiny window, watching the sea breeze ruffle the palm trees along the harbor. She could barely see them, or the sun, above the water line. Charter boats floated lazily beside her, and the window dipped underwater as Kyle's footsteps moved the boat. The murky underside of the dock stretched ahead. Claire watched tiny fish skirt around the beams of the docks and through seaweed crawling up from below. Her heartbeat returned to normal, and although she didn't want to admit it, she did feel safe.

She checked her phone, but Kyle was right. There was no reception. She heard more voices, happier ones, above her on the boat sometime between staring out the window, twisting her fingers in agitation, and running to the tiny bathroom several times out of pure nerves.

A rumble of the engine startled her as the boat vibrated to life. It eased its way slowly out of the harbor. The window rose above the water line. For what was likely the hundredth time, Claire searched all along the docks for the two men. There were families, fishermen, passersby, and she even saw a plane take off overhead, but the men were nowhere to be seen. Only when the people on the docks looked like ants did she dare go up the stairs to open the door.

The cool breeze and smell of sea spray and wind momentarily took her breath away. Despite the peeling paint and the vibration, the railing was cool to the touch. Claire suddenly felt in awe of her surroundings, for the ocean seemed huge when seen in its entirety and truly was magnificent.

The loud motor propelled the boat through the waves, and Claire let her body adjust to the undulation while staring ahead at the beautiful view until Nusa Via became no more than a dot on the horizon. Leaning deeply over the railing, she looked at a school of fish passing rapidly beyond the boat and took several deep breaths.

"Oy there!" a man shouted in a thick Scottish accent.

Claire turned to see a teenage boy and what clearly looked like his older brother approaching, due to their identical face structure and copper hair. The older one extended his hand toward Claire. "We weren't expecting anyone else to come with! Please tell me you're the first mate?" He was fair-skinned and muscular, probably in his late twenties. A wide brilliant smile emerged, seemingly employed on a regular basis due to the lines on his youthful face.

"Cut it out, Paul, or I'll tell Justine on you," the younger one said.

"I'm Claire," Claire responded, taking his hand. It was gentle and kind. Claire felt herself relax further.

"I'm Paul, and that's Henry, the little brother." He gave Henry an affectionate slap on the back once they all stood on the lower deck. "I'm a bit older as Henry was, well, not planned," he said, giving Henry a slight punch on the shoulder. His younger brother rolled his eyes.

"Not so little anymore," Henry added.

Paul's smile was wide as he soaked in the sun, a slight harbor breeze whipping his hair behind his head.

"Are you fishing, too, lassie?" he asked, eyeing her dress dubiously.

"No, no, I'm going to a conference on Sunavae, and the Clarion Charter tour . . . lost my reservation . . ." she trailed off and paused for several moments as the boat roared further to life, cutting through the waves faster while spewing a diesel scented cloud of black smoke into the wind. Claire watched it dissipate.

"Luxurious Sunavae Island! We looked into going there, but it got pretty pricey."

"So I've heard," Claire replied. "Are you guys on vacation?"

"Sort of," Paul said. He gave Claire a shifty smile. "I'm getting married on Nusa Via Island when we return."

"Congratulations!"

"Yes, Justine, my lovely betrothed and her family are flying in in two days. Just us boys for now." Paul grinned. "Henry and I don't get to spend too much time together, so I wanted to do this for him. He loves fish."

"I was thinking about doing a fish conservation program this year in Florida," Henry added. "You're American, aren't you?"

"Sure am," Claire answered. "But I'm from Minnesota, not Florida. Well, I'm a foster child, but I grew up in Minnesota."

"Ahh, the spacious Midwest," Paul said appreciatively. "I have a friend in Chicago. I visited him a couple years back. *Bitter* cold weekend, and that wind!"

"Well, I won't be in your way for long," Claire said apologetically. "I had to take this ride."

"Oh yeah, Kyle's been great to us, too." Paul gestured to where the captain had disappeared. "He offered us a great deal. Couldn't beat it."

"Yeah, he . . . got me out of a tight spot." Claire stared woodenly out at the sea, not meeting Paul's eye.

"Well, you're welcome to fish with us if you like. Henry and I don't bite," he winked.

Claire shook her head as he raised his copper eyebrows in disappointment. "Thank you, Paul, but I think I'm just going to rest a bit. I've had a long day. Just flew in this afternoon."

Paul and Henry waved as Claire turned and went back towards the small stairs. Vertical fishing poles above Claire bounced in their holders, and buckets jostled on the deck as they picked up speed. She heard Paul's voice whooping with joy and noticed the light blue and orange flag of the White Sand Isles overhead on the upper deck for the first time. Its fabric snapped purposefully in the wind. The empty chairs next to her rattled loudly. For the first time in the last hour, she began to feel a little comfort knowing she was that much closer to her co-workers, and further away from the men and the accompanying terror they brought.

The boat's speed picked up again, triggering more of a breeze through the lower decks and whipping stray strands of hair around her face. Claire wobbled her way down the stairs. Balancing herself with one hand on the wall, she moved towards the tiny twin bunk beds and thought of the only other time she'd been on a boat, when her elementary school took a riverboat cruise field trip. She remembered eagerly staring out the window, marveling at the noise of the boat engine and clutching a chaperone's hand, feeling badly that hers was so dirty. Carefully Claire climbed up towards the top bunk with the yellow quilt, collapsing on top of the small, firm mattress, bracing her hands against the wall. She was terrified just thinking of Mr. Gann's reaction when she showed up late to the conference the next day. The feeling of being powerless to do anything about it caused her to feel sick.

Trying to push her thoughts from her mind, Claire slowly exhaled. She focused on the bedding, which smelled freshly laundered yet still carried a hint of suntan lotion. Sand deep in the sheets tickled her toes. She regretted not washing her dirty feet as she closed her eyes, matching her breath to the cadence of the boat moving.

CHAPTER FIVE

The cool water swirled with oils that perfumed the air with velvety bergamot. Despite the jacuzzi being large enough to fit at least six people, Amberly thought of it as her personal bathtub. She stretched her legs, enjoying the feeling of her muscles loosening, and observed her slim figure with pleasure as she followed her thoughts. Thousands of miniature white bubbles swirled away as she floated, facing the deep mahogany ceiling and the tips of the several potted palm fronds that surrounded the bathtub. The water enveloped her in a blanket of the only comfort she had ever known. She closed her eyes, embracing the solace and the control. Her long lashes dripped pearly drops of the perfumed liquid gently back into the tub.

"You will never own me, Jaquarde," she murmured to herself. The phantom feel of his touch on her skin still clung to her like an imprint a thousand baths would never erase.

A knock at the door interrupted her thoughts. She opened her eyes and sat up.

"Enter," she called crisply, gathering her long hair to one side of her face.

Svante walked in, followed by a tall, weedy young man with blond hair.

"This is Dev." Svante pushed the young man forward roughly with one of his heavily tattooed arms. The thin man stumbled in, his eyes jerkily surveying the room before him. Amberly watched him with interest. He had a pallid look; even his hair was bleached of color. Perhaps he needed to eat more or get more sun. Either way, he was exactly what she was looking for. She stood slowly, the luminance of the oils sheathing her body in a sultry glow. Bubbles slowly cascaded down her naked body as she stopped to pick up her knife. She watched as Dev's eyes widened and his gaze darted over her, his feet shifting as she stepped elegantly out of the water and onto the top step that led to the jacuzzi. She descended down the three steps with poise, moving with her back straight and chest forward, never taking her eyes off the newcomer. Water dripped from her long auburn hair, down the outside of her legs, and pooled at her feet.

"Well done, Svante," she purred.

Dev averted his gaze from her body.

"Look at me," Amberly said quietly.

His eyes took several seconds to dart to her face. They were full of bewilderment, yet hinted at a streak of boldness she would have to draw out of him.

"Speak."

Amberly caught his chin with her hand, spraying him with drops of water from her arm and forcing him to hold her gaze.

He cleared his throat and his gaze found her face, his mouth struggling to move against her hand grasping his jaw so tightly.

"Svante said you were looking for a new member," he managed with difficulty.

"Correct," Amberly murmured in a low voice. She let go of his chin and circled around him, observing his lanky frame and nervous, hunched shoulders, "You are my crew. You will call me Captain at all times."

He quickly nodded as she stood before him again, this time inches from his face. She clucked her tongue at his shaking hands, crossing her arms while still gripping her knife.

"You sound European. Am I right?"

"Norway, originally, but not since I was ten."

"Why?"

"Runaway."

"Interesting. Now touch me," she commanded, her voice still low.

Dev looked up at her in great surprise, but he seemed unable to meet her fully. She watched as one of his hands shook at his side, but he only brought it to her left hip, grazing it lightly with his fingertips before withdrawing quickly. Amberly scowled. His attention darted over her shoulder again to avoid looking at her directly.

"I don't like nervous people." She was insulted. Nobody had ever treated her with such trepidation, not even Svante. "They are weak and become a liability. If I give you a command, you will obey it."

"I'm not nervous," he said suddenly, looking at her and trying to regain her favor.

"Really," she stated quietly, fingering the collar of his shirt as she pulled him close. "There's only one way to check." Her hand reached for his belt and pulled him forward. Smiling at the element of surprise she had over him, she swiftly let go of his belt and pulled his shirt over his head. He fumbled as he came out of it, his lanky frame awkwardly trying to regain his balance. Reaching down into his pants, she watched as Dev met her eyes this time, shocked at her groping.

"Either you're nervous, or you don't like women," she said in a dangerous tone, but despite that, she was enjoying fondling him as he cowered under her gaze. "Which is it?"

Dev's face flushed, but he kept his chin up and remained frozen in place. "I like women," he stuttered quietly.

"Good," she breathed. "Because nobody looks at my body as long as you have without reacting." Pulling her hand out of his pants, she stepped back slightly.

"Your posture tells me all I need to know," she said, suddenly louder and as if addressing a group of more than just

Dev and Svante, who still stood by the door. "A lifetime of following orders, until one day, you snap, despite your bravery in running away. I can see it in the way you lean forward, not meeting my eyes, and the way you keep your shoulders inclined towards your chest. Let me guess . . . petty crimes was where you started, and then what? Something . . . bigger?"

"Arson," Dev confirmed, the flush on his face starting to disappear.

"Excellent." Amberly reached to the back of his neck, running her fingers through his hair, and turned to lead him up the three steps to the bathtub. At the top, she pressed her body firmly into his back, running her hands deep into his scalp before gripping his greasy hair. Without preamble, she kicked out his knees and thrusted his neck downward into the bathtub until his head was fully submerged.

"Time for the rebirth," she muttered. "Come here, Svante, I want a word. Hold his other arm down."

Svante was by her side in an instant. Amberly picked up her knife and traced a line along the back of Dev's neck from shoulder to shoulder. Blood poured instantly from the deep cut as Amberly pushed his head further downward, letting the bath water soak into the wound. Dev's hands found the sides of the tub as he scrambled to get to his feet again, but she prevented that easily. Several large bubbles of air escaped from his mouth and popped at the surface.

"Why did you choose him?" Amberly asked calmly, pleased at the fight Dev was putting up.

"He was available, Captain, and willing."

"Good." Amberly watched the blood from the deep cut in the back of his neck run into the water in rivulets, swirling with the oils. "So much easier to mold the lost and vulnerable."

Amberly set her knife back down and pulled Dev out of the

water. He coughed violently, his eyes blinking from the sting of the oils. She gripped his wet hair firmly while Dev shook with the effort to breathe and control his balance.

"You passed, and now, we'll bathe in your blood." She gestured to the bubbling water stained in crimson streaks. Dev nodded, heaving for breath.

"There are no clothes here." Amberly released Dev. "They cover true intentions, and I will tolerate nothing but truth. See how your hands already shake less?" She observed as he tossed his pants aside. "You will learn to control that, or you won't last long. Never show such hesitation with me again."

"Yes, Captain," he said between deep breaths. Long lines of blood and water ran down his body, but he seemed determined to not let her see his pain.

"Get in," Amberly ordered, and Dev did just that as the jets turned back on. Svante placed his clothes on a nearby chair and climbed in after Dev. She hungrily followed the line of tattoos down Svante's back and arms that she'd seen so many times before, yet they always excited her. She paused at the top stair to appreciate the scene she'd successfully created. Stepping her feet in gracefully, she submerged herself to her neck and let several moments pass as she observed the men before her, waiting for her to speak. She smiled as a fresh wave of blood left Dev's neck and joined the water.

"Our mission is simple," she began. "There's an artist that needs to be taken off of Sunavae. That's where we'll start. She keeps the company and bed of my former employer. We will reach Sunavae in two days' time, or sooner, if Iselle is on our side . . ." She paused and raised her knees, swinging one leg to rest atop the other, admiring how sleekly sculpted it was as it dangled above the water. She reached to the side of the tub, finding the long-necked glass bottle of purple oils and poured it in.

"We'll try their residence first. If they're not there, we'll keep searching. They won't be hard to find," Amberly said. The men's attention followed the liquid's dispersion in the force of the jets. Amberly set the empty bottle aside.

"You should know, Dev, that many have come and died over the years, but Svante has been with me the longest. He's very hard to kill." She turned towards Svante. "Now, tell me what news you have of the notice."

"As you may recall, Captain, there were three men on the boat that day."

"Yes, yes, go on." Amberly looked at her nails dismissively.

"They were brothers. The two you killed on the boat washed ashore within a week. They were survived by one— the one we tossed overboard with the anchor. Perhaps he's the one cooperating with the White Sands government and put the notice out, with the help of Emere? He would have described the ship to the authorities."

Amberly paused in spite of herself. She stared at the mahogany ceiling beams and felt her mouth form a thin line, her teeth gritting together before she let out a sadistic smile. "He lived," she whispered in a dangerous voice. "Impressive, really. But I'll not abandon another ship. We will be very careful."

Svante nodded curtly.

"Whether it was Jaquarde or the brother, it doesn't really matter. We'll find the answer when we reach Emere."

Amberly turned to Dev sharply. "Are you prepared to do whatever it takes to follow my orders?"

Dev sat up straighter upon being directly addressed. "Yeah. Yy-es. Yes, Captain."

Amberly clucked her tongue. "Do not be so eager to please that you choke on your own tongue, Norwegian. You still have much to learn . . . but we'll give you your first lesson soon enough."

"Looking forward to it, Captain," Svante said, inclining his head towards her while Dev nodded. Amberly smiled and began tracing small circles in the palm of her hand with her index finger.

"As am I. Emere, Jaquarde, and that brother will all die. As will any witnesses."

Chapter Six

K yle carefully flaked the mahi mahi fish and added it to the steaming pot of strawberry tomato soup. The contents swirled with his wooden spoon.

Was she telling the truth? There were just as many criminals as tourists in these parts. Ladling the soup into a serving bowl, he placed cubed cucumbers and fresh parmesan cheese on top. A small loaf of sliced wheat bread and apple butter from the farmer's market was already on the tray. Once he added cutlery and cloth napkins from the monthly community garage sale, all looked ready.

Kyle glanced out the window as the sun began to sink into the ocean. His thoughts lingered on the last time he had seen that face, the menace lurking behind the cold eyes of the woman.

"Come on! Let's just go home, okay?" Jake yelled, shaking damp black hair out of his eyes. A nervous hand ran over his unshaven chin. The fishing rods from the day lay soaking on the deck.

"We shouldn't take our chances with them, not with the increased looting in the area," Nick, Kyle's youngest brother, agreed. He abandoned untangling the nets as the sleek yacht sped closer, negotiating the increasing winds with the expertise of a skilled sea captain and matching Kyle's ability to do the same.

"There is still a chance they need help," Kyle replied, knowing that they had mere minutes before the clouds would open up and shower them.

"Well, it's up to you, Captain," Nick said, and Kyle nodded in

thanks, having only been christened with the title from his brothers mere hours earlier.

"I think you're right!" Jake pointed towards the back of the yacht. "A woman's waving a white flag! They need help!"

But saving was the last thing she needed. Kyle closed his eyes at the memories and forced himself to focus. He had paying customers, a hot meal to bring to them, and a woman to question.

He closed his cookbook, but the sight of it made him recall how excited Jake used to be when he talked about cooking.

"I finally paid the deposit for the class!" Jake had boasted. "Should be easy after working at Istura. You're going to be a better boss than Jaquarde."

"I can't compete with a head chef at a Michelin restaurant," Kyle remembered teasing him. "Anyway, people don't rent a charter for the food. All they want to do is catch a fish big enough to brag about in their offices back home."

"No way! We'll definitely have more repeat customers because of my cooking, not because of your fishing lessons!"

Kyle ran a hand through his hair, still damp from fishing with Paul and Henry. The old boat had been prepped with a full kitchen because Jake had planned it all out. The shelves had been organized with pots, pans, blenders, and even a homemade ice cream maker.

Kyle grasped the tray and slowly made his way out of the boat's tiny kitchen. He sighed as the cucumbers sank slightly to the bottom of the soup, but the parmesan melted perfectly.

Kyle recalled his matronly cooking instructor, Emmy Fioni, as they prepared their masterpiece meal for the final exam.

"Presentation is important. It's just as important as the meal itself. People want to be pleased by aesthetics."

Although he knew he didn't have even half of Jake's talent, Kyle found he didn't mind cooking as much as he thought.

"Excellent, Kyle," Emmy said. Tasting his zucchini chicken gazpacho brought delight to her eyes, her aging face smiling and causing her glasses to rise on the bridge of her nose. She reminded him so much of his own mother. "You'll go far with this talent, if you let yourself. Excellent choice to top with plain yogurt. Jake would be proud of you."

She was a visiting instructor to the small community college on Nusa Via Island, but she'd made more of a difference than he could have imagined. The kindness about her helped him believe he could try his luck again and not give up.

Kyle carefully balanced the food up the deck's stairs. Paul and Henry looked so content and relaxed on their chairs, chatting excitedly about their day in the water. Henry was still in his swimming trunks, and Kyle smiled in spite of himself. Henry seemed over the moon to be spending so much time with his brother. Claire, however, was nowhere to be found.

"Claire coming up for dinner?" he asked, in what he hoped was a casual voice.

"She was on the yellow bed last I looked," Paul said, shaking water out of his damp hair. He leaned forward in his chair, his t-shirt ruffling slightly in the breeze. "Smells delicious!"

"I don't think she wanted to bother us." Henry immediately helped himself to the soup.

"Hm," Kyle grunted, unsure what to think of his sudden disappointment. He masked the emotion by swiftly handing everyone napkins. "Has she come up at all since leaving port?"

"Only once that I saw." Paul helped himself to a bowl. "Got the weight of the world on her shoulders, that one."

Henry began shoveling bites of soup into his mouth, ignoring reproving looks from Paul. Frowning, Kyle turned towards the stairs, half hoping she would magically appear so he wouldn't feel obligated to have to check on her, but the stairs were empty of anyone.

"I'll check on her." He walked back down the steps and took a moment to observe the ocean to collect his thoughts. The sea was serene and calm here, waves peacefully lapping against the side of his boat. Dusk was falling, casting the sky with pink tones. Dozens of uninhabited islands lay off in the distance, and his White Sands flag barely stirred in the calm breeze.

He'd spent the last hour not just preparing dinner but also preparing to face her once more. Really, he knew he should've been happy. The money would assist with his much-needed boat repairs, and it wasn't even that much out of his way to take her to the island. Could he manage to look at her and not see his brothers' killer?

Locals constantly told him to feel lucky for being the only known survivor of the woman, the only one who'd stepped forward with a clear image of what she looked like — but he felt far from lucky. She still appeared to him in his dreams, dancing in front of him just out of reach with a triumphant sneer.

Kyle entered the lower cabin. The door was open, as it had been all afternoon, but he couldn't see or hear any movement. It was slightly dark with the setting sun, but after living in it for a year, he could get around with his eyes closed.

Kyle grasped the handle of his knife. Frowning, he eased forward and saw her atop the yellow quilted bunk where he usually slept.

Her short auburn hair had fallen around her forehead and was draped over the small pillow. She was curled around the yellow blanket delicately and still clothed in her flowery dress. One of her hands clutched the book he'd forgotten to remove from his bed. The exhale of her breath was sweet and soft. There was too much kindness in the silent face, and perhaps even sadness under the exhaustion that claimed her. This face could never mimic the woman's glare, and he knew it, even if they shared the same hazel eyes. Her eyes were different — kinder, and with deep, dark bags of worry etched underneath.

There had to be more to her story. He ran a hand over the scar on his neck before carefully easing his knife back to his side.

"Better hurry," Paul said, gesturing to Henry. "This kid's got a hollow leg. Can't stop eating."

Henry grinned and watched as Kyle sat down and helped himself to the strawberry, fish, and tomato soup.

"Did you wake her?" Henry asked.

"No," Kyle replied quietly. He forced a smile, finding it wasn't too difficult when confronted with paying customers. Patience with the public had to be rekindled if he wanted to earn a living, even if the vision of Claire and her familiar face remained branded in the forefront of his mind.

"I saw some black sand today," Henry said, between a mouthful of bread. "I was trying to get close to some fish when we were snorkeling, but I scared them off. The sand was underneath them."

"Iselle wouldn't like to hear that." Kyle carefully dipped bread into his soup. "Some people believe that if you see black sand, it's bad luck, but really, it's just volcanic rock deposits brought in by the tides."

"That folklore is awfully prevalent here." Paul stretched his arms behind his head before resuming eating. "I love the idea of a beautiful goddess making these islands white."

"Why's the sand white?" Henry asked Kyle.

"Parrotfish," Kyle explained, chewing thoughtfully. "They have beak-like teeth, which is why they're called parrotfish. They eat algae on the coral reefs and wind up eating the coral and rocks too, ultimately pooping it out, and that's what makes the sand white."

"Hold on a second. The White Sand Isles are actually the . . . poop sand islands?" Paul frowned, and Henry suppressed a laugh as he swallowed his food, his eyes wide with humor.

Kyle smiled. "Their teeth grind up the rocks and coral and create tons of sand. Maybe we can see some tomorrow. They're hard to miss because their colors are incredibly vibrant. You can actually hear them eating when they scrape their teeth against rocks."

"I'm going to look them up in our guidebook," Henry said excitedly.

"I really preferred the story of the goddess," Paul replied.

"When you look at your book, be sure to read up about how they change genders, too," Kyle said to Henry, whose eyes widened again.

"Now, really." Paul wiped his mouth on his napkin before placing it on his empty plate.

Henry laughed, and even Kyle couldn't help letting out another smile at his youthful earnestness and bond with his brother.

"I have a book on parrotfish if you want to read that, too." Kyle gestured towards the pilothouse behind him. "Help yourselves to anything in there."

"I saw that bookcase. Very clever touch," Paul said.

Kyle nodded in thanks, watching the sun sink further down the sky before Paul continued.

"Have you had a lot of business? You're certainly an excellent cook, my god. If you want to experience your first winter, please come work for me at our inn in Scotland."

Kyle felt his chest strangely constrict as he thought of Jake again before unconsciously scratching his scar.

"I've always wondered what snow it is like. People come

here escaping it all the time, so it must be bad."

"Oh, you have to see it. Although, it's really the cold that's the problem," Paul said.

Henry spoke with his mouth full of bread. "It seeps into every crack in your house, chilling you to the bone."

"Coming here is like being awakened from that cold," Paul continued. "At the very least, we can shed the pounds of clothing and try not to look so pale."

"That's not a good sales pitch," Kyle said, laughing. "I might just prefer the parrotfish."

After Paul and Henry finished, Kyle set about cleaning up the dishes. As he brought the last dish into the galley, he noticed Iselle had filled the sky with her soft hues of sunset pink and yellow. There was still no sound from Claire, not even the whisper of a footstep or the creak of the beds. He wasn't sure how to continue to question her with Paul and Henry on board.

Kyle walked up to the wheelhouse and checked his instruments and the boat's position for the night. He could see Henry playing a small hand-held video game while Paul read a thick bound book about the founding of the port town Mo'Tewa in the late 1700s.

Settling himself in his chair, Kyle listened to the stillness of the sea and the sounds his boat made when interacting with it. The gentle lapping of the waves on the side, the tranquil swaying of the current.

"Time for your cradles and my rocking chair," his father said. His voice was weary as he addressed Kyle and his brothers. It was a long day of keeping the children from tossing each other overboard. "You kids are going to send me to Iselle to join your mother if you don't stop all this roughhousing. Bed. Now!"

Kyle ran a hand through his hair and smiled briefly at the

memories. The current was calm, but for the first time, he felt uneasy on his own boat.

CHAPTER SEVEN

Claire awoke with a start, bolting upright and promptly hitting her head into the ceiling above her. The nightmare of Mr. Gann firing her slowly subsided as she became aware of the yellow sheets twisted around her legs. A book page stuck to her cheek. She picked up the book and ran her long fingers over the glossy cover of a western American landscape. *The Potter's Ranch.* If her memory was right, she recalled it being a best seller some years ago. She set it down and saw the blue quilted top bunk nearest to her looked haphazardly made, as did the green one below it. Gently shimmying herself down the small stepladder, she went into the bathroom and looked at her bleary reflection.

Claire splashed some cold water on her face and took a deep breath, willing herself to put Mr. Gann's screaming face out of her mind. She climbed the steps and opened the cabin door to a gorgeous fresh day.

The water glistened in the sun and magnified the colorful fish below. Ocean stretched so far off into the distance that it seemed it was all there was to this world.

Her anxiety didn't feel as if it belonged in this world, even with the peeling paint and rust covering the screws on the boat railings. The air she was breathing was fresh with ocean breeze and a familiar faint smell of sunscreen.

Taking a deep breath, she looked behind her into the enclosed cabin that held the galley and a few lounge chairs. Seeing nobody but smelling the faint aroma of coffee, she wandered up to the sky deck. The captain was sitting in his chair.

He looked relaxed and serene, a lazy hand on the wheel yet an alert eye on the unmoving horizon. Fabric from his t-shirt stretched along his back as he leaned forward to watch something out his window. Binoculars were within arm's reach, as was a coffee mug with steam emitting small tendrils of heat into the air. Maps were neatly rolled and labeled along windows. Faded golden curtains were velcroed back to reveal sunbeams, tinting through the smudged glass and glinting on various navigating instruments.

His view was majestic. The bow of the boat pointed like an arrow into the vast expanse of ocean. She knocked awkwardly against the side of the door frame. He turned and looked surprised to see her, but not as surprised as she was when she saw his brown eyes reflect warmth before disappearing to the hard gaze he'd pierced her with the night before.

Claire felt a slight shiver at that and averted her eyes, seeing a bookcase to her left full of an assortment of boating guides, tourist pamphlets, paperbacks, and hardcovers in varying stages of wear.

"I started that book on the bed," she said, venturing tentatively. "Do you like to read?"

"Sue Holstrom was my mother's favorite author." Kyle twirled a rubber band between his fingers before rolling a map carefully closed.

"Wow." Claire raised her eyebrows. "I didn't realize she had a following this far south. *The Potter's Ranch* was a huge hit in the States."

"My brothers and I were all named after the male characters in her past books."

"What did your character do?" she asked.

"Scaled a snow-capped mountain and survived an avalanche for fourteen days. He never gave up, my character, even when all seemed lost. Mom always loved to read books in winter settings. She'd never seen snow."

Claire raised her eyebrows. "Have you?"

"No."

"You should."

"That's what Paul and Henry said last night."

"There are no mountains or avalanches where I'm from, but the cold might bring you close to your character."

"Other events have brought me closer to my character." Kyle looked her in the eye, and Claire flinched slightly.

"Okay," she stammered quietly. She rubbed her eyes and stepped fully into the captain's quarters, the tile feeling cool against her bare feet. A figure bobbed out the nearest window.

"Is that Paul?" she asked.

Kyle leaned forward and looked out his window. "No, it's Henry," he said. "Paul had the blue goggles."

"Fun. Um, what time is it please?"

He looked down at his watch. "Just around eight o'clock," he said.

Claire let out a resigned sigh, knowing the conference was already well underway. It was hard to believe that she had slept through dinner and all night.

"Are we, uh, taking off soon? I mean, moving . . . soon?"

He glanced up at her briefly, not hiding the exasperation in his eyes. "Soon," he said. "This trip isn't about you. I'm not done asking you questions, either."

Claire felt her shoulders sag as she digested his words, feeling a slight sting at the effect they had. "Well, when will we get there?"

"A few hours. There are some leftovers from breakfast for you in the fridge," he muttered indifferently.

"Guess I'd better eat." Claire turned, not waiting for a reply. She went back down the stairs and reached the small kitchen. Orange juice, fresh fruit, and milk sat on the top shelf of the fridge, and a plate near the back was wrapped. She peeked inside and saw the breakfast.

After locating a fork, Claire stepped out onto the deck and watched as Paul and Henry, yards apart, waved to each other in their diving gear. Their heads were bobbing in jubilation. They slipped underwater once more before swimming to the boat. Kyle came down the stairs to greet them as they swam closer.

"Did you have fun?" he called, swiftly tying a looped knot in a piece of rope. He attached it to the nearest beam and tested his weight against it while Paul and Henry swam to him with powerful breaststrokes. Catching the rope, Henry was the first to come aboard, beaming.

"That was so much fun!"

"Aye, aye, Captain!" Paul called from the water, removing his goggles. His hair stuck out in odd angles, the last parting gift from the goggles' elastic band. With a splash, he grabbed the rope as Claire hovered with her plate behind one of the beams and slowly edged her way forward.

"If it isn't sleeping beauty!" Paul cried, spreading his arms out welcomingly. His chest was full of springy red hair that clung to his body. He stepped forward, swim trunks dripping as he took Claire's free hand and kissed it. She felt her cheeks heat from a blush.

"I do believe slumber has made you more beautiful." He winked.

"Paul! Oh, hi, Claire! I saw black sand again!" Henry appeared, wrapping a navy-blue towel around his waist.

"Cool." Claire envied his enthusiasm and wished she could skip the conference and go diving underwater. "Well, I didn't intend to sleep so much."

"Jet lag, darling." Paul winked again. "Got enough room inside you for all that food?"

Claire felt her face flush again but smiled nonetheless. "I

promise I do."

Paul and Henry made their way past Claire and into the galley. Kyle remained standing nearby and watched her, but he seemed to be uncomfortable and quickly went up the stairs. The action was followed by a rumbling of the engine and a large puff of smoke coming from the back of the boat.

Coughing, Claire quickly turned and walked into the galley to join Henry and Paul. The propellers spurred into action and jostled her footsteps. Setting her coffee mug down, she closed the sliding door to the outside and protected them from the billowing clouds of smoke.

"That looks healthy, eh?" Paul observed in a deadpan voice.

Claire watched the cloudy air through the small window. "My old car used to do that once and awhile."

"I also have fond memories of the first junker," Paul said. "Well, I'm sure it'll all be sorted out soon, after all, you wouldn't want to be late for your conference! What time does it start?"

"Last night, technically," she replied dryly, lifting her coffee mug to her lips.

Paul raised his eyebrows. "You don't strike me as the fashionably late type."

Claire raised her empty glass in a toast. "First time for everything, Paul."

He laughed and looked towards the doorway where Henry stood, watching the water. "Let's go, Henry, come on. You make a better door than a window. Let's have a look at that fish guidebook, too."

No sooner had they left than Kyle walked through the door.

"Is the boat going to be okay?" Claire asked, fidgeting with her coffee cup.

"You mean the smoke?" Kyle asked, refilling his own

coffee. "That's normal. *Emmy Fioni* is reliable, which is more important that being pretty."

"And my conference?"

"We'll be at Sunavae's port in about two hours. There's a storm scheduled to blow through about midday. Radio says we can skirt around it, but we need to wait a bit longer to be safe."

"Thank you." Claire looked at him as she spoke.

Kyle didn't return her gaze.

"Bring your food up to the skydeck. I want to talk." Kyle turned and left without another word.

Claire sighed. "Yes, Captain," she muttered sarcastically, following him carefully while balancing the leftover plate. When she reached the skydeck, she watched the majestic White Sand Islands flag billowing proudly behind the boat, overlooking the endless blue ocean.

Claire closed her eyes, and the breeze played over her face. The sun was steady and warm, so unlike the cold bitterness of home or the personalities of her colleagues. The conference was undoubtedly filling with professional small talk at this very moment. She could almost see the bustling of business suits and feel the endless sea of handshakes amidst the artificially cooled air of the hotel.

She wistfully looked down at her bare feet as a long bug flew near her. The bug hunkered its wings down to avoid being carried off by the breeze. Claire set her plate down and tried to ease it near her foot so it was sheltered further when a scent of sea and suntan lotion was upon her. She turned, distracted, and the bug was blown away.

"Were you trying to save that bug?" Kyle asked, his usual indifferent tone hinting at surprise.

"I guess," she replied stiffly, sitting beside Kyle.

"It was a glassy-winged sharpshooter," he said, seeming to forget his own train of thought. "That one has probably been with us since Nusa Via. It'll get off on Sunavae. They usually do."

Claire closed her eyes and rested her head in her hands. "Look, I want to find out more about this woman, too. I saw the notice online before I left, and I've already been mistaken for her twice." Looking up at him, she watched the brown eyes harden.

Kyle frowned and let out an exhale, briefly glancing ahead at the boat's path in the water. The boat floated over a fresh set of waves, the undulation causing her plate to slide slightly across the table. She caught it but suddenly felt queasy, and clutched her stomach.

"Is this your first time at sea?" Kyle asked quietly, his tone more mellow.

Claire nodded, suddenly wondering if she should have stayed below deck to eat.

"Keep your eye on the horizon. Find a spot and focus on it."

"You must never get seasick." Claire took a deep breath.

He shook his head. "No. I've spent my whole life on a boat."

Silence passed between them. The boat continued to bob forward in the waves.

"I was thinking about asking the artist . . . about the sketch or . . . something," Claire said. "I wonder if she can help me."

Kyle looked out at the ocean before running a hand through his hair, but the breeze swept his curly hair back into his face once he stopped.

"I have two more days scheduled with Paul and Henry, and then I'm dropping them off in Nusa Via. I'm not sure I can trust you, but if you really have no known connection to the woman, then you shouldn't do this alone. I'll come back to Sunavae and take you to the artist Emere."

"You don't have to. I can handle myself," Claire said.

"Look, I just want to find out more about who she is. All I know is her name, Amberly."

Kyle snorted. "Don't think finding out more about her will help you."

"How can you say that?"

Kyle's face hardened as he looked back at her. "Because that woman killed my two brothers and left me to die. Nothing can change that, even if she's ever found."

CHAPTER EIGHT

Claire shut the tiny sink faucet off while her reflection stared back at her in the mirror. Slowly she imagined her face changing into the sultry glare of the women as the boat listed to the left.

"Focus," she whispered to herself.

Putting the conversation with Kyle out of her mind was proving to be impossible. She stepped out of the small bathroom. The garment bag covered her light powder blue dress like a straitjacket, and it took an effort to free it.

Nervously, she rubbed her shoulders before she undressed. The boat's cadence suddenly picked up and she almost lost her balance, catching herself in front of a faded map featuring the many nearby islands that had been clearly bleached from the sun at some point. How absurd it felt to be getting into such dress attire here, in a cramped boat among bunk beds, about to face the conference she was extremely late to, her colleagues, and Mr. Gann himself. She thought of the day she'd bought the dress and matching jacket at the upscale department store. It was a perfectly clean fit in the dressing room mirror. Light jazz was playing over the speakers. It gave her a feeling of confidence, and she liked the professional look it gave her, like she was really in control. Claire smoothed the fabric over her torso, fumbling slightly out of nervousness as she adjusted the buttons. A good five inches was added to her height as she stepped into her nude heels to complete the outfit.

"I can do this," she said quietly to herself in the sink's

mirror. A stray bit of glitter fell on her cheeks as she finished applying eyeshadow. "Maybe they'll actually be worried about where I was?"

Her calves protested against the extra height of her heels as she ascended the stairs. Claire expected the gorgeous ocean view to refresh her. Instead, a growing dread filled her stomach when she was welcomed by an eerie white mist.

She heard voices from the skydeck and carefully walked up the second set of steps to join the boys, steadying her heels on the slick surface. The condensation glittered all over her new jacket. She heard Henry ask a question but didn't hear what it was.

"The instruments do that for me." She heard Kyle replying from inside the wheelhouse. "We're really close to another island, Ildetache."

"Can't even see it," Paul commented.

"There's a lot to see when you're on it," Kyle replied darkly. "People love spending a day on the white sandy beaches."

"Can we check it out?" Henry's boyish voice piped up excitedly.

It was a few moments before Claire heard Kyle respond as she slowly made her way up the last step. "Maybe on the way back. She's a beauty, but uninhabited, so we'd have to stay on the shore. The inside has poisonous snakes crawling through the loncue trees."

Kyle casually flicked a switch and the windshield wipers began doing their job with a loud squeak, but only to present more fog beyond.

"Have you spent a lot of time on that island?" Claire asked from the doorway, with a sinking suspicion that she already knew the correct answer.

Kyle nodded and didn't turn around, but Paul did.

"Wow," he exclaimed, staring at Claire. "You look great."

Paul gestured Claire into the cabin.

"Very professional," Henry added.

"Thanks," Claire replied. "What happened out here? It's like we're in a twilight zone."

"The kid radioing the weather update to me was new." Kyle didn't mask the irritation in his voice. "We're heading straight into a storm."

"Be glad you missed what Kyle said to the kid's boss," Paul whispered. "He won't have a job tomorrow."

"He shouldn't," Kyle said loudly. "The weather is nothing to mess around with. People die out here."

Claire raised her eyebrows and exchanged a look of dubiousness with Paul. She took a step forward and let go of the railing. A loud squeak told her that her foot was slipping out from under her as she fumbled with her step.

Claire winced as her shoulder collided with the slippery deck. Her head hit the metal floor. One of her heels flew off, hitting the bottom of the wheelhouse door.

"Seriously? Are you okay?" Kyle asked, his voice vacillating between anger and irritation. Claire blinked to see his horizontal form hovering in the doorway. Seeing her lone heel right below him, her eyes widened. He followed her gaze and picked up the heel.

"Yes." Claire's face blanched white with shock, and she held her hand out for her heel, but Kyle frowned before tossing it aside. Slowly he reached down and pulled the other heel off her foot.

"Don't put these on until we reach land," he stated gruffly.

"I'm sor—" Claire stood but felt her words cut off by a loud gurgling noise coming from the engine. The boat lurched forward as the engine made disturbing coughing noises below. Claire grabbed the doorframe of the wheelhouse, stepping inside. Kyle swore to himself and gestured at Paul. He adjusted his controls, and the engine purred an octave lower before ceasing altogether.

"You shut the boat off?" Paul asked Kyle.

Kyle didn't answer and instead pointed at the wheel. "I need you to steer in this direction while I check my fuel filter. Just keep the wheel steady." Kyle darted past Claire and was downstairs in seconds.

Paul took the wheel and didn't move it. Henry cast a furtive look at Claire, who walked closer to Paul and stared at the heavy fog in the distance. Only the squeak of the windshield wipers routinely removing the condensation broke the uneasy silence.

"This is bad, isn't it?" Claire asked worriedly.

"Seems to be," Paul replied.

Kyle returned several minutes later, running a hand over his face. He checked his instruments carefully and turned the engine on. It choked.

Kyle shook his head. "I emptied the dockside fuel tank in Nusa Via yesterday when I filled up. Must have gotten some dirty fuel from the bottom. Steer us away from the storm, Paul. Edge along the clouds to the left here. I'm going to change my filter as fast as I can. I need this boat at full throttle." He disappeared again.

Claire peered closely through the windshield. She could see patches of blue in the sky and a faint light from the sun trying to break through. Kyle came back faster than she expected.

"The wind is picking up." Kyle frowned at the white horizon. He restarted the engine, which responded with a puff of acrid black smoke expelling from the rear of the lower deck. "I don't have time to change the filter. We need to find shelter now. The storm is coming faster than predicted."

He turned the wheel, but the boat seemed to protest any change in direction. He muttered something incoherent but she couldn't hear what it was, only that the tone sounded somewhere between a curse and a prayer.

"Look!" Henry yelled.

Claire looked up to see several large black rocky outcroppings looming ahead of them between the intermittent patches of fog. Slight waves splashed against the deck, and Claire felt the boat begin to rock from side to side.

"We're getting blown off course," Kyle said calmly, but Claire could hear the unease in his voice. "The boat can't keep up with the current, so we're heading towards these shoals and rocky jetties.

"Take the wheel again, Paul. Steer over here—that's it. Claire, Henry, I want you to take this radio and switch it to forty-eight, the emergency channel and say mayday, tell them we have a jetty dead ahead and we're on the northeast side of Ildetache. I'm going to drop anchor and try and stop us from getting any closer."

Claire felt her heart drop into her chest and shared a frightened look with Paul, who grasped the wheel as Kyle ran out of the room again.

Claire took the radio and braced her shaking hands. The boat pitched forward with an incoming larger wave, bringing them closer to the nearest black rock. Henry switched it on as Claire found the station, only to be greeted by static.

"Mayday!" she called into the speaker.

"Say *over* afterwards," Henry said nervously.

"Mayday, this is the *Emmy Fioni* on the northeast side of Ildetache, over," Claire called again. Paul's hands shook on the wheel beside her.

Claire repeated her message, but there was no reply except static. Within minutes, the heavy white fog lifted and floated dreamily away, showing angrier gray skies further above. The boat lurched awkwardly as the anchor dropped, but it still swayed dangerously towards the rock. Claire, Paul, and Henry breathed sighs of relief. Claire didn't realize she'd been holding her breath.

"That was so close," Henry whispered.

A powerful wave swayed the boat. Claire's stomach turned slightly with the movement. She looked out the window, her heart pounding with the intermittent static of the radio. Great rolling waves cascaded upon themselves, creating white foam on top that tipped into the deep valleys underneath. Turning in fear, Claire saw quickly approaching rocks all along the side of the shore. She heard Paul take a steadying breath beside her.

"We're going to hit that rock," Henry whispered in fear. "The boat is moving again."

Claire grabbed the wheel with Paul. Kyle burst through the doorway just as the boat crashed into the rock, not once, but twice in succession with the incoming wave. The force and angle of the collision cracked the windshield. The radio shorted out with a quick *zap* as the next saltwater wave sprayed over Claire. Struggling to regain her footsteps, she felt her arm collide with Paul's leg as she fell. The carpet squished beneath her with the incoming water through the windshield as Paul helped Henry up. Kyle steered and pointed to the bench that sat behind his captain's chair.

"Grab some life jackets out of there, now," he said firmly.

Claire's pulse raced with apprehension as Paul helped her to her feet. The underside of the bench had at least a dozen lifejackets, varying in size.

"Take this one." Claire handed the smaller life jacket to Henry, his expression mirroring the look of urgency Paul had. Claire grabbed one that luckily fit her perfectly, although very tight due to her business attire underneath.

Warm seawater sloshed around the cabin. The boat crashed into the same rock again.

"Hurry," Kyle called as he tried in vain to maneuver the wheel. "We're going to sink. I'm trying to angle us to give us more time."

Shaking water out of her eyes, Claire blinked and moved further down the stairs, Henry right on her heels. The sea was roiling with black waves, licking the sides of the boat with a furious hunger, and Claire had no desire to get into it.

"Keep going," she heard Kyle yell. "Get ready to jump off."

The deck was filled with several feet of water. Remnants of Kyle's fishing gear floated in it, knocked from their holsters. She stepped into the warm water, dodged the fishing poles, and followed Paul, hearing Henry just behind her.

Claire's eyes widened in terror as the boat pitched again, tilting dangerously forward. She braced herself as the wave passed and looked at the beach ahead, the wild surf crashing onto it. Kyle came down the stairs, stopped next to her, and pulled the anchor up.

"What about rocks ahead?" Claire yelled over the wind.

"There are no other rocks ahead. They're only out here. The current will take you to the beach. Stay near the shore and be prepared for a massive downpour and heavy winds." Kyle talked so fast that Claire felt sure she misunderstood. She could barely move her arm in her new jacket, and knew she couldn't ever swim like this. Quickly she untied her life belt and swung her shoulder to free herself of it. Kyle looked at her incredulously as the group adjusted their footing to a smaller wave that lurched the boat forward.

"We don't have time for that!" he snarled.

"I can't swim with these clothes on!" Claire shouted back. She shed her constricting jacket and hastily stepped out of her dress until only her purple satin slip covered her. She fumbled to put her life jacket back on and saw Kyle's brown eyes, full of concern for all of them.

"Get to the island safely. Wait for me on the shore."

Paul extended his hand to Claire. She took it and climbed onto the railing. Kyle disappeared back up the steps as she awkwardly swung herself over the railing and sat on it. The water danced on her toes as the boat rocked downward. Another patch of fog appeared ahead, rolling ominously across the waves.

"On three!" Paul stood on the outside of the boat, his free hand clutching the railing strongly. "One!"

Henry followed Paul's example, easing his legs toward the outside of the boat until he was standing facing the island.

"Two!"

Claire struggled to keep her feet on the slippery boat, gripping Paul's hand.

"Three!"

Her feet left the familiar cool metal of the boat deck as she tumbled into the turbulent water. Paul's hand slipped out of her fingers as she struggled, her senses soaring with the shock of submersion. Her slip found its way up to her elbows. A wave took her forward as she kicked and bobbed back up to the surface. Blinking the stinging sea water out of her eyes, she turned to see that boat was yards away. The front was splintered, and the hole allowed vast amounts of water inside. Kyle was nowhere to be seen. Paul and Henry bobbed several yards to her left.

Claire kept her eye on the white sand ahead and swam as fast as she could muster, powerless when the current pulled her this way and that, propelling her faster than she could ever swim towards the shore before enveloping her underneath the water. Panic caused her limbs to flail pointlessly until she resurfaced, gasping for air. Although her eyes stung with seawater, Claire saw the white sand was getting closer. The curling waves wrapped up in themselves before breaking with a crash on the shore, spitting white foam into the air. She looked for Paul and Henry again but was only allowed a moment's glance before a large wave grew behind her and swallowed her.

She relaxed her muscles, letting the water twist her this way and that, until she suddenly felt sand beneath her toes. She half swam, half ran forward until she reached the beach and collapsed on her back, desperate for rest. Her body shook with adrenaline as the sea pulled over her in a liquid blanket, breaking at her chin and filling her ears with rushing water.

Claire began unbuckling one of the fasteners on the life jacket to allow her breath to expand with her rapidly rising chest. The white sand reflected the grey clouds above and became dulled with the rapidly approaching fog. Palm trees loomed ahead in shadows.

Claire turned and searched the shoreline, but there was no sign of Paul or Henry anywhere. Her heart skipped a beat. She looked into the distance of the water and didn't see Kyle on the boat, still angled lopsidedly with the rocks. Within minutes she was completely surrounded by fog. It eclipsed her vision and brought with it an unsettling sense of blindness.

"Paul? Henry?" she called loudly over the crashing waves, standing awkwardly after her swim. Fear moved her legs forward. The palm trees served as poor reference points, for they all looked the same, and she couldn't be sure how far she was going in relation to Kyle's boat.

Before she knew it, the sky opened up, showering her and dissipating the fog with a new sense of obscurity. Without preamble, Claire ran into the jungle, desperate to find cover.

CHAPTER NINE

Loud waves consumed the hull of the *Emmy Fioni*. Kyle wiped his forehead of sweat. He threw the last secured cooler of food overboard, watching it sink to the bottom, leaving a trail of white bubbles in its wake.

"There she is in that slip ahead! Yeah? Whatchya think? Such a great deal, right?!" Jake exclaimed.
Kyle mouth dropped open as he stared at the boat.
"You're right," he agreed, and both brothers laughed joyously. "She's perfect! With her shape and hull, we'll cut through chop or fly across wide open spaces!"

The creaking noise from the boat transformed into a wretched moan as the hull cracked open. A wave cascaded into Kyle.

"You curse me, Iselle," Kyle said to the familiar waters.

He joined the wave as it spilled back into the sea. His muscles strained with the effort to propel himself under the powerful capping waves. The depth and lack of oxygen was constricting his chest. When at last he resurfaced, all that was left of his ship was the White Sands Flag, limply floating on the surface of the water. Soon it too was dragged down, his dreams becoming wreckage before his eyes.

Deep breaths came and went. Kyle heard them as if watching himself from above. He squinted where the sun should have been, desperate for light to fill the darkness of his mind. It had only been a year since he'd last found himself on the beach ahead, left for dead by the woman.

The rain began. Sheets fell from the sky and evaporated on the hot surface of the island's jetties beside him as he swam.

I won't question why this happened, Iselle, although I don't understand it. He propelled himself further through the water.

He would never forget the jeering hazel eyes of the pirate woman, nor how he recoiled at the way she ran her bold, questing hands over his body before commanding to have him tossed overboard. Why did she drop him so close to an island? Her yacht could have taken him to the far depths of the ocean or out of White Sands territory. None of it made sense.

Kyle swam until the white sand grazed his fingertips. Then he stood. The saltwater and rain stung his eyes as he took a deep breath and lumbered towards the beach. Waves crashed heavily beside him, punishing the shoreline with fury when the rain stopped. He saw someone dash in the water towards him.

Kyle raised his hand as high as he could, and the figure waved back frantically.

Henry's smaller frame kicked up sand as he ran forward, clearly exhausted. His face was in a panic, and he ran over the waves clumsily until he reached Kyle.

"Where are the others?" Kyle asked quickly, suddenly realizing the hoarseness of his voice from swimming and the seawater he inhaled. He'd barely finished asking when Henry gripped a shaking hand on Kyle's arm.

"Paul! Have you seen Paul? I've looked everywhere." Henry's eyes were wide with fear. Dirt and sand streaked through his hair and over his clothes. "I can't find Claire, either. We got separated. We were together when we jumped, I swear, but when we got to the shore, there wasn't anyone. The rain and waves came so fast, I couldn't find anyone else. It's been at least ten minutes—"

Henry stopped as Kyle placed a hand on the boy's

shoulder. It was stronger than he imagined, full of muscle even though his face still held traces of youth. Kyle felt the boy's pain, the fright of being away from his family, and the uncertainty of what was ahead.

Kyle looked into the dense greenery beyond the shore. "Come on. We'll start looking for them now."

CHAPTER TEN

The rain had stopped, but the water collected on hundreds of palm fronds still dripped steadily over the thick jungle. Claire lost track of her footprints and her resolve to stay close to the shore as she meandered about the deep rivulets forming in the sandy dirt.

A loud crashing sound erupted somewhere in the distance, and Claire froze, listening intently.

"Kyle?" she yelled. The rain-soaked earth was cold under her feet. She raced through the greenery, towards the sound. Hopefully, it was towards the shore. Her feet tripped on an exposed root that caused her to dive headfirst into a large tree trunk. Claire gripped the base of the tree. She shakily regained her footing, brushed the dirt out of her eyes and looked downward into a small clearing that she'd missed by mere feet.

The drop couldn't have been more than six feet down, but it was covered with tiers of layered rock. Water cascaded down them into a small pool and formed wild tributaries that ran deep into the luscious greenery beyond.

Claire carefully slid her body over the edge of the precipice, gripping the nearest root in her hands. Her body hugged the rocky wall as she carefully made her way down. Rainwater fell into her eyes and mouth, and the dirt and sand stung her eyes. Her slip caught on something and she heard it tear, the lace fabric shredding easily until her feet found purchase on the rocks below.

Claire moved towards the waterfall and felt the spray of

the water on her face and legs. She crept closer, her focus solely on keeping her balance over the slippery moss-covered rocks.

"A cave!" she whispered.

She peered further and saw the crawlspace behind the waterfall. Thankful it would at least keep her away from the dripping water above, Claire took a deep breath and crawled forward through dead, wet leaves. The waterfall pounded into her shoulders heavily. Carefully she slid forward on the hard rock until she was out of reach from the water's power.

Claire collapsed uncomfortably into the slippery rock. The momentary rest was needed after her swim and escaping the rain. Wet hair was plastered around her face and her tattered slip hugged her body, streaked with sand, mud, and dirt and provided no warmth whatsoever. The sound from the water echoed underneath the rock. It was strangely difficult to bring her shaky legs closer to her chest, and she knew why.

Cold. A bitter, bone-chilling cold. It was as if her skin was suddenly made of pure ice. Her body shivered with it. She tried to cover her legs with parts of her slip.

"I have to get back to the beach and the others," Claire muttered. Carefully inching herself out of the cave, she turned and scanned the area around her. An eerie humid mist was forming. The precipice she'd climbed down earlier was barely visible.

There seemed to be nothing she could see that wasn't covered or permeated by water. She was no exception. Her vision blurred. She heard a strange noise below her, a rhythmic clicking of sorts, and she looked down to her knees and hands, seeing nothing until she realized the sound was coming from her own mouth as her jaw chattered uncontrollably.

Frightened by the foreign sound and her body's automatic response, her focus settled on the nearest brown tree several feet to her left with plentiful large fronds. Could one be used as a makeshift blanket, she wondered? She ripped a frond and saw a green coil around the trunk.

She froze.

The green snake quickly disappeared back up the trunk to hide under other palm fronds, and her fears were momentarily replaced by relief. She backed away, wiping water out of her eyes when she felt something slimy touch her wrist.

It happened so fast. The snake hissed and struck her cheek. Claire slipped as she backed away and clumsily picked up the frond she'd dropped.

The venom pumped into her body, and each step took longer than the one before. She felt colder. Strange shadows muddled her vision. Her heart beat wildly. She touched her face, and there was blood on her hands.

"I need to wash this," she said. Her voice sounded strange and far away.

Claire closed her eyes as she set her palm frond down upon the cool stone by the waterfall's cave. Ringing filled her ears and drowned out the rushing water. Everything looked blurry and made her dizzy. She closed her eyes and breathed deeply, trying to stay calm.

When she opened her eyes, the cave was gone. A familiar face floated in front of hers. When he smiled at her, the numbing cold she felt was replaced with warmth. Wooden desks, covered in initials and old gum, appeared around her. She was in science class, and it was the last semester of high school. She turned to the face, questioningly. The handsome features caused her heart to skip a beat. Adjusting his tweed coat with his strong hands, he regarded his students and rubbed his clean-shaven face. She remembered now, it was the new teacher, Mr. Hartman. He'd just graduated from some ivy league university and would only be here for a year.

"Mr. Hartman is my father," he announced to the class. "Call me Aiden." She felt his eyes linger on her face longer than the other students. He wrote his name on the cave wall with white chalk. With his youthful look, he could have been one of them. He looked like he'd

just started shaving! Claire laughed at the thought. Her voice echoed across the wet walls.

She stumbled weakly to his desk and stared at a small framed photo. An average-looking woman with a fat face stared back. Aiden claimed it was his fiancé, but it had always felt more like a prop to a lifestyle he could commit to. It didn't matter anyway. She knew him better than this woman ever could.

Claire removed her lifejacket and slip. Aiden watched her naked body slowly expose itself. The classroom disappeared. A dimly lit motel lamp made him appear as a shadow. She felt his gaze on her the whole time. She heard the chattering of her teeth as Aiden's hand reached from the shadows to touch her face. It left her skin smoldering for a moment, then pleasantly numb. The feeling gradually spread to her lower jaw and deeper into her body.

"It will only hurt for second, but you're tough. You can handle it. I believe in you, Claire. Besides, doesn't it feel good to be my girl?"

She could sense his disingenuousness, but her body was reacting too fiercely. Every cheap word he said made her skin tingle. Her vision swirled and she fell to her knees, scraping the skin off on the thin motel coverlet. His hands quested for her breasts, massaging her nipples gently. He pulled her top off. She gasped with pleasure. He really knew what he was doing.

Her eyes found his face as she rolled onto her back. He was naked. It was much more powerful to see it in person than to see pixelated photos of him on her phone. Now, no detail escaped her eyes — the way his hipbones curved, the splay of hair on his chest, the sight of his hard penis. For her. The sight of it made her feel a drenched wetness and ache welling deep in her body, well beyond her vagina.

"That's it," he said, laying her down gently. The buttery yellow glow of the lamplight bathed both of them. "Show me that beautiful body."

He was above her now, finally taking her virginity. The sting of pain was nothing. Compared to the yearning she felt for him, she barely registered it. The feel of him sliding in and out of her drugged her senses to anything but wanting more.

"Happy birthday, my love," he cooed in her ear. "Do you like it? Does it feel good?"

"Yes. Go harder," she whispered, biting his ear. He laughed, while she inhaled the scent of his aftershave until he obliged. She could still smell frosting from her birthday cake on his cheek. The look of joy on his face made her happy, or maybe that was also the glow from the words he wrote on the birthday card he gave her. Claire grabbed it and threw it into the air. It turned to dead, wet leaves as they hit the ground, but she didn't care right now. He cared enough to press himself into her body, enough to touch her face. That was all that mattered.

Claire turned and stumbled, hitting her head against the cave wall, hair separating from her scalp. She felt fingers curl into a tight fist and tug her back into pleasure. Her panties dangled at one of her ankles.

"You like it rough, don't you?" he whispered. Aiden grabbed her waist roughly and took her from behind on the bed. He ignored her initial cries of pain, for she felt sore, and ached from how long he took the first time. But part of it still felt good.

"God, I love your tight pussy. It's even better the second time around." She heard the motel bed protest against the dark carpet, leaving a long black mark. His hands found her hip bones, still jutting out with her youth. They bruised her with his possessive grip.

Her face dug into the hard ground, but when she lifted it, she took in a lungful of water from the nearby falls. Her body convulsed as she choked, her face stinging with every breath.

Aiden disappeared. Claire instinctively tucked her legs to her chest and curled into a ball. Her body felt ravaged, and her chest was constricted with the feeling of being utterly alone.

"With an ass like that, I can see why he'd want some of it!" Hollers and catcalls came from the football players who began to appear around her.

She rolled over on her side and turned to face them. "How dare you say that to my face," she said, her legs shaking. They pointed at her and laughed.

"You're right," they agreed. "We should be saying it to the back *of your head like he probably is."*

"Have you seen his cock? Is that why you got an A?" a classmate whispered in her ear. Claire turned to her other side, the cold rock of the cave digging into her back, and she stared at the girl. The girl's shoulders shook with giggles at her own remark. The ends of her perfect blonde hair swayed tantalizingly across her shoulders and sounded like wet leaves thrashing against bark. Claire braced herself on the rock, failing to control the rage building at the girl's sneering face. How dare they violate her memories of feeling beautiful and wanted by someone?

She swiped through the waterfall and took the girl's hair in her fist, ripping some of it out. Her wet arm butted up against the cave's ceiling as she reared back and punched, over and over. The sound of thunder echoed in the cave. Rough hands of football players grasped her shoulders and she was pulled away, her head hitting the black rock. Claire trembled with fear as her hands fell to her sides, bruised and bleeding. The girl lay on the linoleum floor, unconscious.

"Talk to God," a classmate whispered. Her earnest eyes burned into Claire's under a mop of unkempt hair. "He will forgive you. I'll pray for you, too. You've done really bad things. You'll go to hell for this."

Backing away, her elbows scrambled on the wet frond, but she couldn't get up. She waited for Aiden's eyes to return to her, but they never did. The frond curled under her grip. She looked down, seeing her foster parents' kitchen knife in her hand.

Was college really that important? Why wouldn't he just call her back, after all they had shared, all the promises he made?

Claire checked her phone again. Her flowery screensaver stared back at her, devoid of anything but the time and date.

He said he loved me.

She succumbed to abandonment and breathed deeply, tears leaking down her face.

CHAPTER ELEVEN

"You are absolutely sure they made it to shore?" Kyle asked Henry. They walked back to the beach for what felt like the hundredth time. Darkness was imminent, and another storm threatened on the horizon.

"Yes!" Henry insisted. His breath was ragged from anxiety. His shaking hands twisted his t-shirt into a ball as he wrung out the water, wiping his hands on his swim trunks. "I was close to Paul the entire time, even as the fog rolled in, and we could touch bottom by then anyway. Claire was further down, but I swear I saw her, too. I want to keep looking."

"We'll find them," Kyle stated calmly. "Chances are both Claire and Paul found cover in the jungle."

"I know Paul got here," Henry assured himself. His voice became more high-pitched and nervous. "Claire couldn't have been too far behind. I know it. It's getting dark. It's— "

"It is. Keep looking for the matches," Kyle said gently.

"I can't find anything, Kyle." Henry moved back toward him, his expression etched with fear and concern.

"Okay, I'll keep looking." Kyle pointed towards the edge of the trees. "See that tarp washing up?"

Henry nodded.

"Grab it, please, and bring it back here. I'll make a shelter for us."

"A shelter? What about looking for Paul? Claire, too?"

"Go get the tarp," Kyle instructed, keeping the same calm tone. "There's another storm brewing. Iselle isn't done with us for the night, and it's important we take cover."

"Why not just go in the trees just there?" Henry asked impatiently, pointing to the jungle.

"Trees will fall." Kyle pointed too as a flash of lightning forked across the sky. "Coconuts will also fall from the trees, and believe me, with a high wind that's dangerous. Trust me, Henry. We're no use to Paul or Claire if we put ourselves in danger."

Henry looked unconvinced, but Kyle made no move to persuade him any further. Years of arguing with his brothers taught him that much. He continued to search the many haphazardly stacked contents from his boat in various stages of disarray on the beach.

"Finally," Kyle muttered to himself, locating a waterproof bag of emergency items that was being jostled around in the light surf. He turned back to look at Henry. The young boy still appeared on the verge of darting into the trees alone until a loud crack sounded in the air. The open ocean only enhanced the sound into a booming echo that reverberated towards them and shook the trees. Henry's eyes widened, and quickly he darted towards the tree line to collect the palm fronds.

It was easy enough to locate fallen branches from the storm. Kyle secured them into the wet sand just away from the waves. The long sticks stayed firmly rooted in place, and by the time Henry returned, Kyle had managed to rig up a rough lean-to, triangular in shape and only big enough for the two of them to huddle or lie in.

"It doesn't seem like much." Kyle took the palm fronds and sawed one of the final sticks with the knife at his side. "But it's simple and will help us when it starts to rain. Sleep might be hard to come by, but we need to do all we can to recuperate. We need to be ready when the rain stops to start looking for Paul and Claire."

Henry nodded and grabbed the end of his damp shirt,

wiping sweat off of his entire face. Kyle could see he hadn't lost the worry, which was etched deep into his features. Henry pointed behind Kyle.

"Another cooler?"

Kyle turned and felt relief course through his body. "Just as I planned," he murmured. It was the most important cooler he had, for his small ax was inside. Henry was at his heels in moments to help him drag it out of the water.

"I threw as much of the essentials overboard as I could," Kyle explained. "But this one . . ."

"There are clothes in here! Snacks, too? Can we eat them?" Henry dug through the items.

"Those are protein bars. Yes, go ahead and have one."

"There aren't many of them." Some of the worry lifted in Henry's voice. "Will you have one, too?"

"Not now." Kyle took the small ax and pointed back towards the trees. "I'm going to get a few more small branches so we can finish rigging up our shelter. I want you to put that stuff back in the waterproof bag, and get this cooler and the others that washed up in a pile. Cover them with more palm fronds, and get anything that can be set up for rainwater to collect. If you move the contents around and get an empty cooler, that'd be perfect."

"You sure we can't stay further under the trees?"

"No, the water will wash us out. This is the flattest place for us to stay."

"Okay."

Kyle breathed a quiet sigh of relief, for he didn't have time to explain further. The clouds were approaching quickly. He put the finishing touches on the small shelter until the drops of rain began.

Henry successfully moved the coolers and set one up for water collection. Kyle nodded in approval.

"Now comes the hard part," he said to the younger boy.

They crawled into the small lean-to. "Patience."

Henry shivered slightly beside him, but the small shelter was effective at keeping most of the rain out.

"I hope it stops soon."

"Usually I love the rain," Kyle explained, more to himself. "Especially when on my boat. It was nice to listen to it as I fell asleep. Storms sound so different out here."

"How often did you sleep on your boat?" Henry asked.

"I lived on it," Kyle replied quietly.

"Really?" Henry sounded surprised.

"Really."

Henry shifted his weight in the sand. The wind switched, and the lean-to rustled slightly. "I suppose that's not much different than Paul. He lives above the inn." Thunder cracked above them. Blowing raindrops flew into their faces, and a branch from the lean-to fell.

"That's bound to keep happening," Kyle said dismissively, fixing it before any more rain got in. "We aren't going to stay completely dry, but this will keep us somewhat from the wind."

"Your home is gone then," Henry said, not listening.

Kyle adjusted the top of the lean-to and twisted another vine around the sticks holding it together. "Yes," he said.

"I'm sorry," Henry ventured tentatively. "Do you have family to stay with? When we get back?"

"I'll be fine, Henry." Kyle lay down and shook the rain out of his eyes. The lightning seemed to ease slightly, but the rain was persistently coming down in sheets.

"Paul's getting married in a couple days." Henry's voice wavered with exhaustion.

"When the rain stops, hopefully by first light or before, we'll look for them." Kyle closed his eyes. "I promise."

"Justine's going to freak out," Henry said. "That's Paul's fiancé. She's nice and all, but—"

"Relax," Kyle interrupted. "Try not to follow your worries."

"Okay." The younger boy ceased speaking. The pattering of rain continued. Kyle closed his eyes, savoring the heavy feeling taking over his body.

It seemed as if no time had passed at all, but Kyle's eyes snapped back open as he heard another crack, thinking it was thunder.

Kyle sat up and caught the broken part of the lean-to just as it was about to fall on him. Blinking, he pushed the wet tarp out of the way and saw that the sky was a brilliant purple and pink, the yellow early morning sun on the verge of combing the beach.

Henry stirred beside him. Like Kyle's, his clothes were damp and matted to his body. Sand was folded into all creases of his shirt and shorts. Kyle stood and walked towards the woods with his ax, shaking the damp sand off and observing the cooler of rainwater as he passed. It didn't take long for him to find what he was looking for amidst the fallen leaves, branches, sticks, and shorter plants.

"Coconuts!" He leaned down and examined the fallen fruit. He picked one up and saw Henry peering out at him from the lean-to, his eyes bleary.

"Another good reason to carry an ax," Kyle said, carefully placing a coconut between the nearest rocks. Grasping the handle, he swung down hard, cracking the shell. Several birds from a nearby tree took flight. Kyle gestured Henry over. "Carefully now, there's lots of milk inside."

Henry walked forward, looking stiff from sleep. He drank heavily. Kyle cracked the shell of a second one for himself with practiced precision. He lifted it to the sun, drinking the liquid that poured out.

Henry put a small piece of the white stringy flesh in his mouth. "Tastes . . . different. Feels kinda weird to chew."

"It can take getting used to," Kyle said. "But for now, I want to save those protein bars I had in my emergency kit, at least until we find Claire and Paul."

"I'm really not hungry. I thought I was, but . . ." Henry paused, setting the coconut on his knee.

Kyle looked at his half. "I'm not either, but keep your strength up. Eat one more piece, and we'll start to look for them."

Henry nodded. After a few moments, Kyle walked purposefully into the thick greenery with his emergency bag, hearing the young boy behind him.

"Don't we need the compass from the bag?" Henry called, easing a large green frond out of his way.

"It's in my pocket," Kyle said, looking around. "We have a lot to be thankful for with the storm. We got fresh water, and some food fell naturally, which would have been a lot harder to come by had it not stormed."

"I guess," Henry said.

"I want to go towards the water to look for Paul and Claire," Kyle said.

"Back to the beach?" Henry asked quizzically, swatting a leafy plant out of his face.

"No. There are several waterfalls and a long river on this island, and chances are they were looking for cover under the rocky bluffs," Kyle explained.

Despite a year having passed, the island looked the same; quiet and still, save for the occasional bird passing. He'd walked every inch of the place, and being back was like being in an eerie dream. The tall palm trees swayed gently above him as sunlight broke down through the trees. The lagoon had to be getting closer. He could almost feel the cool water on his skin from when he'd dived into it, washing the blood and sweat off.

"I hear water," Henry said after a few minutes and hasted

his steps in the terrain.

"Careful!" Kyle reached a hand out, but it was too late. Henry tripped over a large, deep brown root and the contents of the emergency backpack spilled out of the bag. Henry's half-eaten coconut flew out of his hands and rolled further down the steep incline. A change of clothes, matches, a lighter, and a long wooden whistle fell with a splat in the nearest puddle of mud.

"Are you okay?" Kyle knelt down as the young boy rubbed his ankle.

"Fine," Henry said stiffly. He shakily brushed off the light brown mud that was smeared all over his swim trunks and picked up the muddy clothes.

"Don't worry about those," Kyle said, watching Henry's face redden as he put the matches back in the bag with the whistle. "They'll dry in no time in the sun. We can brush the mud off later. These are roots of the loncue trees, and there are a lot more of them the further in we go."

They walked in silence for several steps. The sound of water grew louder and they reached the waterfall within minutes, stopping just before the drop below to the rocks. The stream was heavier with rainwater, but Henry wasn't looking at it. Instead, he pointed towards the left of the waterfall.

"Look at that weird tree down there. One leaf is missing, like it got torn off."

"That's a really young loncue tree." Kyle frowned, looking around. "Maybe Paul or Claire did it."

"Paul?" Henry called loudly, but was greeted only by several small animals' footsteps skirting away from his loud voice.

Kyle and Henry carefully swung themselves over the drop with the help of an exposed root to support their weight. Kyle walked closer to the young tree, examining the missing palm frond and the large snake coiled high above him. He swallowed, imagining the worst. "Claire? If you guys hear me make noise!"

Henry froze. Kyle scanned the area carefully. A gentle breeze lifted some raindrops from nearest trees, sprinkling them from above. The sound of the waterfall drowned out any other noise, save for Henry shifting beside him uneasily. Kyle watched the white, bubbling water topple over the black rocks. A flutter of a yellow bird's wing caught his eye and flew past an orange color jammed in the rocks just below them.

He squinted. It was a lifejacket. One of the smaller ones he'd bought for the *Emmy Fioni*.

Kyle barely lifted his finger to point when Henry nodded beside him.

"I see it!" Henry yelled, walking closer to the streaming water and heaving the emergency bag over his back.

Kyle pulled the lifejacket out of the rock, feeling the material in his hands. It was Claire's.

"Someone's stuck!" Henry had crawled ahead of him, peering into the crawlspace behind the waterfall. Dousing half his body in order to get behind the waterfall, Kyle eased his balance on his knees while Henry wobbled behind him on the slippery, uneven surface. A sour smell met Kyle's nostrils as he saw a still figure ahead in the shadows.

He couldn't tell if she was alive or dead. Claire had managed to curl into an awkward ball and was completely naked. In the moment it took him to reach for her thin wrist, he felt a pang of guilt unlike any other. This was not the woman who deserved death. This was not the woman capable of murder. Kyle saw an unrecognizable, swollen face under her short, dirty hair. A large purple lump contorted her ashen white face. Her eyes were closed. He felt sick as he pressed into her thin wrist but breathed a sigh of relief to feel the faint flutter of a beat on her cold skin.

Kyle carefully placed his hands on her ankles and pulled gently, uncurling her position.

"I'm taking her out, Henry," he called, his voice echoing in the dark space.

Henry climbed out from the waterfall while Kyle dragged Claire to the edge of the entrance as gently as he could, planting his feet firmly against the rocks. He stood under the waterfall, holding his breath as he got covered in waves upon waves of water in order to keep her from it. His shoes slipped as he carefully pulled her towards the edge of the water until he was able to grasp her waist. Stepping out from the waterfall, he pulled her further towards himself, lifting her into his arms, and felt her head flop into his chest.

"Grab her clothes and the lifejacket, please," Kyle said calmly. Henry obeyed instantly, climbing deftly back behind the waterfall. Kyle carried Claire to the edge of the stream towards the wet sand and dirt. The path was anything but even as he moved slowly across the rock.

Claire's arms flopped to the ground lifelessly in the sunniest spot he could find. Kyle protected her head from doing the same thing, carefully lowering her into the wet dirt. Large fern plants scratched gently at his calves as he tried to arrange Claire in a natural position. Her face looked grotesque. He stepped back and took a deep breath.

"Is she . . ." Henry's voice trailed off as he shook water out of his eyes and hair, dropping the remains of Claire's slip next to her.

"Not yet," Kyle whispered, kneeling to inspect her face. "She's been bit by a yinnoc snake. They can be deadly, if left untreated."

He glanced momentarily over the rest of her body, scanning only for more damage. Dried blood caked under her fingernails, and her knuckles were bloody. Kyle inspected her hands curiously and lifted her index finger. Several auburn hairs stuck to the blood there.

Henry shifted nervously beside him. "Why did she take all her clothes off?"

"She was probably in a fever." Kyle gently put Claire's hand to her side.

"I've never seen a naked girl before," Henry whispered, as if Claire would wake up any minute. "Other than anatomy textbooks, anyway." Henry knelt beside Claire and searched her swollen face, and Kyle noticed him fighting back tears.

"The snakes hide out in the loncue trees," Kyle said quietly. "She must have scared this one when she pulled off the palm fronds. The venom causes fever and delirium as a first reaction . . . but the fever appears to have broken," he said, carefully removing his hand from Claire's forehead. "We have to squeeze some of the venom out right now. I don't want it getting worse."

"What if Paul is somewhere in the same condition?" Henry's voice cracked again slightly, and Kyle put a hand on the young boy's shoulder.

"We need to wash this out once we drain her face," Kyle said, not answering Henry. "We'll take her downstream."

Henry nodded and suddenly took his shirt off. "Take this," he said insistently. "She might be embarrassed."

"Thank you," Kyle said, as Henry handed it to him. "I was going to ask which one of us would be willing to sacrifice a shirt."

"It's still wet," Henry pointed out.

"Doesn't matter. It will dry."

"Paul would know what to say to make this funny," Henry said. "He was always cleverer than me." His face looked troubled again.

"You are clever and smart, too," Kyle said firmly, fitting the shirt around Claire. "You saw the palm frond Claire ripped out before me."

"Yeah, but you found her," Henry said sullenly.

"This isn't a competition," Kyle replied, more sternly than he meant. "I've been to this island before. I'm familiar with some of its secrets. There are more waterfalls with similar caves, some big enough for the four of us to stand comfortably under." He trailed off, thinking of the one he'd found not far from here, the one he'd lived in for days before moving to another part of the island.

"Maybe Paul found one of those then," Henry said, standing suddenly, looking panicked. "I need to go. I need to find Paul. I can't just sit here while you're helping Claire."

"Henry, we're not going to split up. This island is too big," Kyle said testily. "Wait until Claire's a little more stable, and then we can go."

Henry's eyes rested on Claire again as he bit his lower lip stubbornly. "I'm going. I'm not waiting around if Paul is like this, too!"

"It's too dangerous!" Kyle stood and took Henry's shoulders. "There are more things on this island than poisonous snakes, Henry. There are sinkholes, bats, and waterfalls with strong currents and sharp rocks. Old dead trees and coconuts fall by the minute. You don't want to get lost in here!"

"You aren't my brother!" Henry burst back, throwing off the bag of emergency supplies from his back. It hit the ground, its contents clanging together under the waterproof mesh.

Kyle stepped back, stung, and his chest constricted with the unexpected argument. He kneeled and grabbed his bag forcefully. Without a word, he thrust the wooden whistle at Henry.

"You're making a mistake," Kyle insisted, not meeting Henry's eyes. "But you're right. I can't stop you."

Without a word, Henry took the whistle and ran off into the woods. Numerous plants stirred as the young boy ran, his bare, determined shoulders soon lost amongst the curving greenery that made the island so well known for its beauty. Sinking down to his knees beside Claire, Kyle closed his eyes, trying in vain to be sympathetic to the young boy, and recalled his own desperation when he knew he'd lost his family.

"Except I knew they were gone forever," he whispered to himself.

Suddenly he felt a soft touch on one of his hands.

"Hot," Claire whispered. Her voice sounded several octaves lower. "My body . . ."

Kyle paused, momentarily taken aback at the slender fingers questing his calloused palms. She stirred, but she didn't open her eyes. Her fingers were gentle and probed for reciprocation. He watched them, his brow creasing at the unexpected delirium she seemed to be in. He took her smaller, cold hand and squeezed back carefully. Claire sighed and sank her arm slightly into the dirt and sand.

"Are you in pain?" he asked her quietly, turning to rifle through the emergency bag for the medical supplies.

"Yes," she whispered, her voice cracking. Claire turned her head slightly to look at him, but the movement seemed to cause her great effort. "I can't feel my face."

Leaning closer to her, Kyle took a deep breath. "I know," he said quietly, drawing his knife to Claire's face. Within seconds he located the tiny holes the snake had made. Carefully he pressed into Claire's cheek as her eyes fluttered closed. He ignored Claire's quiet moans as the deep green poison oozed out of the pulpy flesh. He focused his ears on the waterfall behind him and the jungle beyond, but there was no sound of Henry. A strong breeze brushed past the rain-soaked plants, causing them to dispose of the droplets they'd been clinging onto since last night. Several rolled over his knuckles.

"Am I going to die?" Claire whispered. Kyle looked down at her infected flesh.

"No," he said quietly. "I won't let you."

"Promise?"

He brushed stray bits of dirty hair away from her wound. "I promise."

CHAPTER TWELVE

Amberly felt the sweat burst through the pores on her forehead as an orgasm erupted between her legs, spreading to her entire body and clearing her senses. It suspended her awareness of anything but pleasure for several seconds until her ears rang. Heaving, she took her knife from the bedside table and pointed the tip at Svante's throat, raking her gaze down his tattooed chest.

"Finish."

His breath came in ragged spurts, his sweaty hands grasping her hips so hard she felt her nerves tingle uncomfortably. He grasped her tighter and brought her down on him as hard as he could muster.

A tiny droplet of blood appeared at the tip of her knife. Svante tensed beneath her as she felt his release. She pressed the knife further until his face creased with euphoria.

Amberly lifted herself away to rest on the silk sheets.

"Get out," she commanded.

He did not. Instead, Svante lit a cigarette and enjoyed a long inhale, blowing smoke into the mahogany ceiling and casually wiping the blood from his neck.

"I said get out," Amberly repeated, a dangerous edge slipping into her tone. Svante blew another smoke ring into the air and glanced at her with a slight frown.

"I should come with you," he said.

"You already did," she replied crisply.

"You know what I mean." Svante stared at her. His hands were gentle, but even the tenderness could never elicit the same feelings as her former lover.

"I have to do this, Svante. You know why."

Svante reached for his pants. "I have my reasons, too."

"Jaquarde won't hesitate to kill you himself if he sees you, especially since he thinks I already did it years ago."

"How could I forget," Svante replied dryly. "You think he won't do the same to you? This is risky."

Jaquarde's grotesque smile, lined with chew and smelling strongly like whiskey, floated to Amberly's consciousness. She swallowed. "I need to be able to be in a room with him and breathe before we do anything," Amberly whispered. "I need to catch the vibe of this whole situation before we do anything else. No one will recognize Dev, and you know how good my disguises are."

"Just because he got the conference schedule doesn't mean Dev's ready."

"He's ready," Amberly said firmly. "Stay here, Svante."

"I should be with you." Svante looked her straight in the eye. "I owe it to you."

"No," Amberly replied vehemently. "We keep to my plan. We make sure Jaquarde is busy, then when we know Emere is alone, I'll kill her. After that, we'll deal with Jaquarde." Amberly caught a tiny fresh drop of blood on Svante's neck, and smiled. "I've never led you astray, Svante." She crossed the length of her quarters on her bare feet. Flinging the door open, she pointed her knife towards the deck.

"True, Captain," he said, exiting her cabin.

Amberly slammed the door shut and strolled purposefully to her closet. It held enough evidence to convict her of over a dozen crimes of theft and murder that she'd been unable to resell due to the wanted notice—stolen trinkets, expensive electronics, designer clothes, and rare jewelry.

She pulled out a silk blouse and skirt, complete with pockets long enough to cover the knife she planned to strap to her leg. She looked at her various wigs. Curly, long, blonde, brown, and she settled on a long brown and fastened it on with numerous pins on her dresser. She picked up a pair of sunglasses and placed them on top of her head. Approving of her reflection in her full-length mirror, Amberly sat and began the long make-up application.

Amberly left her cabin an hour later. *The Duchess* faced Sunavae's bustling port. Business people were arriving for their anticipated meetings. *The Duchess* blended in among the other yachts with ease at these docks, just as she expected. No one would find them here, or think she was foolish enough to show up. She sighed confidently. The warm sea air refreshed her face.

She signaled Svante at the helm and adopted a brilliant smile for passing yacht owners and boat enthusiasts alike. Dev had changed into a pair of black pants, a buttoned-up shirt, and a matching jacket. If Amberly didn't know better, she would have thought him a proper gentleman. Donning her oversized sunglasses, she looped her arm in Dev's, relishing the way his thin yet able muscles rippled as they walked along the dock.

Nothing had changed since she was last here. Hotels with golden columns royally faced the shore. Their delicately manicured lawns were buffed and trimmed to their finest emerald green. White limousines crowded the street ahead as the suits and dresses rolled leather suitcases to the various gates. The side streets were crowded with small grocers and fruit stands that boasted the freshest picks of the island, surrounded by chattering, well-dressed, and physically fit beachgoers.

The Ocean Royale loomed ahead. Its sprawling green acreage was furnished with a golf course and a wave-shaped pool, currently occupied with several guests basking in the sun. Amberly watched another group of guests walk down a meandering green path with tennis rackets and water bottles in hand as she led Dev towards the entrance.

An attendant opened the door for them, revealing the white marble hall beyond.

"Thank you!" Amberly called loudly in her practiced American drawl.

They passed the hallway to *Istura*, The White Sand Island's renowned Michelin star restaurant. It was closed, but the dark hallway was just as she remembered it; sea glass covered every inch of the corridor in cascading waves of blue outlined in white. Amberly quickened her pace. She kept her eyes down and watched her heels quickly pass over the golden carpet until she came upon the signs outside of each room.

A Conversation with the Author — Poems of Iselle, the bestselling debut from Sunavae Island's Margeaux Abel.

Istura reminded her of the day Jaquarde started her as a dishwasher after getting kicked out of middle school for the second time. School was such a waste anyway.

Birds of the White Sands — How Tourists Can Protect Them.

His toothy grin flashed across her memory, as did the way he'd sidle next to her in the restaurant's kitchen. Amberly absentmindedly touched her wrist, recalling the way he'd enclosed his large hands over her malnourished flesh.

Sunavae Golf Club Meeting.

She could still feel that tongue, bloated and stained, as it licked her body and whispered empty promises of what it would be to live on the islands in his luxurious wake.

She blinked her eyes to any further memories and eased her brisk walking to a careful strut, seeing the next golden easel ahead propping up a large sign. His signature cuisine wafted into the hallway. Fear crept up her spine.

Gann, Inc. International Client Conference. Welcome!

Two ornate golden doors were propped open. The chatter of dozens upon dozens of voices clamoring over each other came from the spacious ballroom ahead. Accents from all over the world launched repeatedly into new conversations, and she quickly noticed everyone wore a nametag. She acquired a blank one from the front table, Dev doing the same behind her. With a snicker, she scribbled *Nathalie* before walking purposely inside.

Champagne spilled out of glasses, and local islanders in white suits carefully offered hor d'oeuvres and appetizers on silver platters. "Go mingle, but stay close to me," she muttered to Dev. Amberly took a champagne flute and sipped daintily. She watched the women in the room hold their purses under their arms with deliberate ease and carefully tucked her own under her arm as well. She tensed her shoulders slightly to fit the crowd and shortened her steps. She narrowed her eyes at the scene before her, feeling the wealth of hundreds of businesspeople. The falsetto laughter of masked politeness rang around the room. Large canvas signs were situated in every corner, reading *Gann, Inc.* in large letters and boasting client testimonials from businesses across the world.

"Gann never disappoints," a tall man said in a thick African accent to his equally tall companion, their thick leather briefcases held lightly in their hands. "Did you see the charcuterie display?"

"Not yet, but the madeleines are *magnifique*," his companion replied as Amberly carefully moved further ahead. Burners were carefully set under steaming silver platters, where young men and women in starched white chef wear served portions of decadence. Thinly sliced meat and local caviar were delicately placed onto thin crackers. Her vision touched every face, searching for her old boss and former mentor.

"Hey." A tall young man nearest her walked closer. For the slightest instant, she saw recognition behind his square-rimmed glasses, his stoic hands gently grasping a champagne flute. She looked at his nametag, trying to remember if she'd met him before.

Jackson Rabonaf, Senior Web Designer, Gann Inc.

"Can I help you?" she questioned politely, cocking her head with a smile.

"No," he said, but his eyes continued to rove over her face. "You just looked like my co-worker. She's been missing, and I" — he adjusted his glasses — "sorry to stare, Nathalie."

Amberly bristled slightly and wondered if it was her posture that gave it away.

"I've always wanted a sister," she joked. "Good luck finding her."

A shorter man on a cell phone and a stout woman with her hair in a bun approached them.

"Come over here, Jackson, Mr. Curan wants to hear about the new template designs," the woman said bossily.

Jackson gave Amberly a longing glance before he was ushered away, exposing a long buffet table.

Jaquarde was right in front of her in his starched white chef's suit. Her throat felt like it was going to close with fear.

He'd hardly changed. His bulk and weight easily made him the largest person in the room, but the smile he wore was as charming as ever. Swallowing, Amberly moved forward slowly. Her hands wanted to shake, but she controlled them. She balled them into fists and imagined the way she would later grasp them around Jaquarde's fat neck. She knew she shouldn't get too close, but she was compelled to move closer to the steaming entrees. A gray-haired man spoke feverishly toward Jaquarde, his silver nametag reading *Richard Gann, CEO.*

Amberly gulped her champagne forcefully as the crowd moved past her. The man called Richard Gann was agitated. Jaquarde put what appeared to be a comforting hand on the man's shoulder, but she knew better — Jaquarde was making a threat. Gann's hands fumbled absentmindedly with the pockets in his three-piece suit while Jaquarde laughed loudly. His smile, though disarming, didn't reach his eyes.

Amberly walked over to a corner near a canvas sign that held company information and additional testimonials. Slipping an itinerary into her hand, she covered her face slightly, and she casually stepped closer to eavesdrop.

"I don't tolerate late goods," Jaquarde said, malice leaking from every word. Amberly felt her stomach turn cold. He only used that tone when someone's life was about to end. "You know that."

"It's not my fault." Gann's voice was hushed. "I canceled the reservation. Your men were supposed to grab her on the dock."

"I can take that, ma'am." A waiter reached a gloved white hand and took Amberly's glass. The waiter walked away as Dev walked in front of the buffet table. Richard Gann scuttled away anxiously. Jaquarde eyed the crowd, his eyes about to reach her face. Amberly felt her heartbeat jump into her throat.

"Watch out!" Dev moved in front of Jaquarde and tripped, theatrically but very convincingly, spilling his dark wine over Jaquarde's white uniform.

"Imbecile!" Jaquarde thundered at Dev. He grabbed Dev's shoulder and shoved him aside. A waiter passed him a towel that he used to sloppily mop at his chest. His eyebrows knit together for a brief spell until he raised his head. Amberly held her breath and stared, as did the rest of the crowd around them. Jaquarde relaxed his features completely.

"I'm so sorry, sir, there was a slight turn in the carpet," Dev said, handing him another towel.

"Not at all, nothing to worry about." Jaquarde's wide smile was dazzling before he laughed and spread his arms to the crowd watching, graciously accepting Dev's towel. "That was a terrible year for wine anyway!"

The crowd around them laughed. Dev apologized again as Amberly turned away and let herself be swallowed by an incoming group anxious for more caviar.

The brochure in her hand was covered with sweat. The ink from it stained her hands. She walked as casually as she could through the crowds and waited until Dev joined her in the marbled hallways.

She ushered him out of the hotel. Vomit formed in the back of her throat, but she swallowed it quickly.

"Well done," she said to Dev. "You will be rewarded for this. But we have to move fast."

"Yes, Captain."

She glanced down at the smudged itinerary in her hand. Jaquarde couldn't miss the scheduled catered luncheons or dinners. Forcing her heartbeat to slow, she took a deep breath.

"Emere will be alone soon enough," she whispered to herself, stepping back outside into the warm, relieving air of the sea.

There wasn't a soul in sight within Sunavae's hidden coves, but Amberly drew her curtains anyway. Auburn hair fell down her sweaty back as she tossed her wig into the corner. Perspiration continued long after she'd reached the safety of her boat, but she needed to focus. She ran her hands over her bare breasts and waltzed by Dev.

"Your little wine performance will not be forgotten. I always reward good behavior to ensure that it continues." Amberly turned on her heel and observed Dev's lanky frame, his eyes only darting to meet hers once she faced him again.

"Yet you're still so nervous," she said softly, placing her hands on her hips. "You weren't on our little mission just now." She reached for his lips and slowly traced them.

"No," he replied, tossing a steak of blond hair out of his eyes. "I'm better in those situations."

"Then let me help you. I want you to undress for me. Slowly. I'll tell you what to take off and when to take it off. Then you will fuck me. Understood?"

"Yes, Captain," Dev agreed.

"Good," she breathed, biting her bottom lip before licking it. "We have a busy afternoon, Dev. Only touch me where I ask. No lips. Disobey me, and you'll get another scar."

"Yes, Captain," Dev repeated, his face slowly turning a delicate shade of crimson. Amberly smirked to herself, hungry to watch Dev's nervous body writhe beneath her own.

"Let's begin," she said, and unsheathed her knife. Reaching the tip at his throat, she stared up into his eyes.

"Pants first. Slowly."

CHAPTER THIRTEEN

Claire's eyes fluttered open. She stared at her hands, neatly folded together in front of her face. Her nails were dirty, and the once perfectly applied pale pink polish was chipped and cracked. Her thirst quickly drowned out the ache that seemed to permeate every part of her body when she shifted in the sand.

An unfamiliar red hue of a t-shirt just barely covered her naked body. It gave her warmth, a welcome reprieve from the recent memory of bone-chilling cold. She looked around.

Kyle was at the water's edge, deftly tying palm fronds in intricate, sturdy knots on what appeared to be a long stick. The sun directly behind him made him look like a deity. He moved with purpose, in tune with his body and the task he was focused on. There was a stoic manner about him reminiscent of Jackson, but even in her wildest fantasies, she could never imagine Jackson sitting on a beach shirtless, now brushing what appeared to be blood from his knuckles and shaking drops of seawater from his hair. Jackson would be engrossed in thick bound books of literature, his glasses resting atop his neatly shampooed hair.

Claire sat up slowly. Sand danced down her chin and she brushed it off quickly, realizing something felt unusual in her right cheek. There was a slight puffiness, but also a strange void, so she waited for the touch of her fingers. It never came.

Claire rose and stumbled awkwardly on her stiff legs. She forgot about the strange short shirt she wore and forced her steps over to Kyle as fast as she could, her heart beating wildly, her hands never leaving her face as she stepped in the hot, glittering white sand.

Kyle saw her approaching and stood. His brown eyes searched her face.

"M-my face —" she stuttered, but he pulled her hands down. There was fresh blood on them. With a jolt, she realized it was hers.

"Stay here," he cautioned gently, squinting at her in the sunlight. He turned and kneeled in the surf, washing his hands in the clear water. He opened a nearby cooler, scooping up what appeared to be water with half of a coconut shell. "Drink this right now."

She took a sip, slowly at first, feeling the brown husk of the coconut tickle the left side of her face, but still feeling nothing on the right. He seemed satisfied when she finished and handed her something small, charred, and black. Claire bit into it, the crusty outside giving way to smooth, flaked pieces inside. It was fish — tangy, almost sweet.

"Do you remember what happened?" Kyle asked.

"A snake bit me," she replied with a mouthful of fish.

"The bite caused the swelling." He reached over to touch her cheek, wiping more blood from her chin. "How much can you feel here?"

Claire found herself waiting long after his arm stopped moving towards her face.

"Nothing," she replied. "It's numb."

"And your vision and hearing? Everything else okay?"

"Yes. I see Paul and Henry down the beach there and can hear the fire."

"Good. You were lucky." Kyle's voice sounded affirmative, but she struggled to believe it. He sat back down in front of her, pointing at the fish in her hands. "Keep eating that. It'll help you heal."

"But what do I do? Is this permanent?" Claire felt tears

sting her eyes.

Kyle turned and began picking up fish skins, throwing them in an additional cooler she hadn't noticed earlier. He turned to look at her.

"Yes," he replied.

Claire stopped chewing and stared at Kyle. Her hand found her face again. She touched it imploringly, willing herself to prove him wrong. When that moment didn't come, a tear did instead. But she didn't feel that either as it left her eyelid. Her bloody hands went limp while a feeling of dread began to form ominously in the pit of her stomach.

"I can't believe this," Claire whispered, but Kyle looked away, picking up the last fish and slapping it somewhat unceremoniously onto the nearby log. He opened it with his knife to reveal the flesh and bone beneath. Blood flowed from the incisions, creating red tributaries along the contours of the wood. Claire watched it pool on the white sand below, the image blurred with her fresh tears. She looked around, taking in the tropical scene around her. "What happened to the boat?"

"The boat's gone," Kyle continued. "We'll have to cross the island to get rescued."

Claire sat back in the sand, the weight of his words sinking in. A bloody hand reached over to her shoulder again.

"You're going to be okay, Claire," he said. "We'll make it. All of us."

Surprised at his consistent, kind tone, she frowned. He certainly hadn't been this considerate on the boat while throwing out accusations and suspicious glances.

"Look at that. The sleeping beauty awakens again!"

Paul appeared, with Henry on his heels. Both of their arms were laden with bananas, some of Henry's already slipping from his arms and flopping into the sand. Claire quickly wiped her tears away.

"You've slept so much on this trip I'm beginning to wonder if you are trying to avoid us," Paul said with a crooked smile.

"Good haul." Kyle rose to meet them and took some of the bananas out of Henry's arms appreciatively. "This is almost too much."

"It's nothing," Paul said dismissively, dumping his bananas in a small heap before settling himself next to Claire. She found herself drawing her shirt around her waist self-consciously, but Paul winked at her. "Closing those eyes for a bit has done you a world of good. That used to be my shirt, you know," he said, peering at her face closely. She saw a bruised cut under his hairline.

"What happened to you?" she asked, staring at the cut. "It's all . . . jagged, and . . ."

"Oh, this?" Paul gingerly swiped back a mass of his reddish hair to reveal the ugly, large, and crooked incision, with haphazard blue stitches closing up his skin. "Henry did a bang-up job sewing me back together. Good thing I have a lawn care job for him at the inn this summer, since his seamstress career has no future."

Henry laughed and looked mockingly offended.

"I tripped on some tree roots and spent the night getting soaked in that rainstorm. No matter, though, you can wipe that worry off your face. Scars will further attract the ladies to my dangerous lifestyle."

"Not anymore, since you're getting married," Henry interjected. "I'm the one who needs a scar to attract ladies."

Claire caught Kyle smiling slightly at the young boy. "We need to keep someone intact here, Henry," he said. "Scars aren't all they seem to be."

"You can have all the bragging rights when we get off the island for being unscathed." Paul rubbed some sand out of his eye before turning back to Claire. "Nobody's been out as long as you, though. Should have heard what you muttered in your sleep all day."

"What did I say?" Claire asked, blushing slightly, but only felt the sensation on one side of her face. She bit her lip, the memories of her fever sending a chill down her spine.

"I'll never tell." Paul gave her a small smile.

"You do look better, Claire," Henry piped up. He looked quite at home, sitting cross-legged in the sand. "You looked a lot worse when we found you, but after we got you and Paul in the sun, we knew you guys would be fine."

"I'm going to rinse my knife, then it's time." Kyle nodded at Paul, who nodded back, then walked to the surf. Claire watched him kneel at the water's edge and dip his bloody knife in the curling waves.

Claire turned to see Paul and Henry exchanging a glance. Their strange understanding and sudden silence caused her heart to skip a beat.

"Time for what?" she asked nervously.

"We have to fix your face," Henry said. "Kyle is—"

"Going to help," Paul interrupted earnestly. He took her hand. "And we're going to stay here with you."

Claire stared at her hand in his. "Paul, what—"

"I'm going to do this as fast as possible, Claire, and you shouldn't feel most of this." Kyle returned and knelt by his fire, placing the knife over the flames. Seawater dripped from the blade and hissed when falling on the burning sticks.

Henry appeared by her other side and took her other hand.

"Kyle? What are you doing?" Claire asked Kyle.

Kyle looked at her. His face was troubled, but he looked determined. "We have to take care of your wound."

Claire's eyes darted to Paul's, then Henry's. She squeezed both of their hands.

"No!" she shrieked. "By burning it? What about trapping a possible infection? Can't it just heal? I already have enough damage!"

Kyle turned towards her, his knife poised at her and glowing slightly with the heat. He didn't meet her eyes.

"The poison is gone. Burning it shut quickly will be easier to care for," he said, his calm voice wavering slightly. "I don't want you losing more blood. It might take a few days, or more, before we're rescued. I don't want you losing any more blood, even though you're right, this comes with risk, too."

"What doesn't really? We'll be right here with you, Claire." Paul squeezed her hand.

Claire watched the knife move closer to her face. Kyle knelt directly in front of her, moving bits of hair out of her way. She could smell the hot steel. It made her stomach clench. She pleaded with her eyes, her breath coming out in shallow gasps. Henry's hand was on her back first, then Paul's strong one, preventing her from scooting any further back in the sand.

If she ducked under Paul's arm, she might have a chance at a few more seconds to think about it. But Kyle's logic resonated with her, and the look in his eyes told her the truth. It was the only way.

Kyle hovered near her face, watching her closely. The end of his blade was poised parallel to her face. She blinked back her fear. With a tiny nod to him, she grasped Paul's hand the hardest. He squeezed back.

Kyle took her entire jaw and the cheek she could feel in his hand, his grip completely unrelenting. She tried to focus on the sound of the waves or the gentle sway of the palm trees, but the smell of the hot blade made that impossible. She squeezed her eyes shut and heard the hiss of her flesh burning.

CHAPTER FOURTEEN

The boat drifted to the rocky shoreline, where they secured it in a rocky inlet. Water splashed over her boots. Amberly gritted her teeth as she crouched behind the rocks. She saw the narrow road ahead, inconspicuous to anyone but those who'd spent years using it as a secret entrance to Jaquarde's hideout.

"Remember . . ." Amberly kept her voice low. "Keep close, and watch for any sudden movement in these trees. I'll only need fifteen minutes. The path to the ocean is directly behind the cottage."

"Looking forward to it, Captain." Dev's tall frame was much more confident. She smiled at it as he wiped his sweaty brow and tucked some of his blond hair behind his ear, his eyes narrowed in anticipation. She quite liked the force in his weedy body. The pleasure she got from it was enough to keep thoughts of Jaquarde away.

"Enjoy the dry land. Once we have Emere, you may not see it for a while."

Dev nodded curtly.

They walked in silence between stretches of trees and wild, untrimmed shrubs. The footpath betrayed little usage. This caused Amberly to wonder if Jaquarde had found a new hideout, but she pushed the thought out of her mind as they emerged onto a tiny road that had none of the grandeur of Sunavae's main streets. The slightest movement caught her eye ahead.

"Hide," Amberly commanded, waiting for Dev's footsteps

to disappear before striding ahead. A smirk played in the corner of her mouth. The cottage had crudely stayed together through amateur home improvement, but it was just as she remembered it. Tucked behind large shrubs, with the secret path behind it that led directly to the ocean—perfect for the many times Jaquarde and those who worked for him needed a quick escape. She recalled using it several times herself, and she knew Svante would be waiting for them there when the time was ready. She marched smartly to the door, her heart pounding with an exhilaration she'd not felt in some time.

"I know you are there, Rafael," she called in a singsong voice. "There's no need for old friends to hide from each other."

"A cunt like you doesn't have any friends." Rafael strode out from behind the cottage. The shark tattoo on his neck was marred with deep cuts. Amberly laughed.

"Tell me, Rafael, what did you screw up this time?" she called, pointing at it. "Not sucking Jaquarde's dick the right way?"

"That was your job, not mine," Rafael replied, throwing his neck to the side to crack it.

"You're still reckless," a sly voice said behind her.

Amberly glanced behind her at the shorter man, his gun pointed at her head.

"I warned you that a knife was a poor substitute for a partner, Amberly. But you never listen. Your ears must still be stuffed with your ego."

"That's where you're wrong, Lorick." Amberly whistled sharply. At her signal, Dev charged out from behind the trees and ran to Rafael.

Using the distraction to her advantage, Amberly whipped around and charged at Lorick. She narrowly missed his first shot while twisting his arm. As soon as she heard the gun hit the ground, she unsheathed her knife and forced it into his abdomen. Blood spurted from the wound and stained his white shirt. She leaned in, practically laughing, twisting her knife in quick jabs. She withdrew as Rafael lumbered towards her, Dev standing aside. One quick glance told her that Lorick would soon be dead.

"Why so silent?" Amberly bellowed at Rafael as he circled around her. Her eyes scanned his body, but he didn't reach for his gun yet.

Rafael grabbed for her arm, but Amberly was too quick for him. She always was. He was clumsy, off-balance, and had never learned how best to use his strength. With the back of her hand, she slapped him across his smug, dark features before taking his own arm and twisting it against him. She grabbed his gun and pointed it at him.

"That was too fast," she breathed as he backed away, hands in the air. "I would have preferred more of a challenge. Why didn't you just shoot me?"

Dev strolled to her side.

"You'll never see Iselle, whore," Rafael spat. "We don't kill like you. Killing me won't bring you any redemption. You're already so dead and so lost. I pity you."

Amberly aimed carefully at Rafael's chest. "Iselle might bring me redemption if I give her a present," she murmured to herself, firing three times. Rafael flew backwards into unkempt grass. Amberly thrust the gun at Dev.

"Hide the bodies. Be quick."

"Yes, Captain." Dev hurried away.

Amberly approached the door. The hinge creaked out of its screws when she thrust it open. She sheathed her knife. Her breath heaved in and out, but she ignored it and pushed herself forward. A damp, musty smell laced with whiskey greeted her. The setting sun barely shone in through a solitary dusty window adjacent to a small door that hinted at a tiny bathroom next to a narrow set of crooked stairs. Bricks of cocaine and guns lay openly on a table. But it was the tubes of paint lying on the floor near several canvases that made Amberly's stomach flip uncomfortably.

Emere's familiar technique of graceful strokes and fluid figures was evident, but the artist herself remained elusive as Amberly crept forward.

The largest canvas was propped up against the dirty wall. It featured a portrait of Iselle. Her long white hair turned into clouds, and her dark skin formed the local loncue trees. Leaning down, Amberly stared into her wise brown eyes.

"Where is she, Iselle?" Amberly said to the painting, hearing her voice echo strangely in the dank room. A crash was heard from above, followed by shuffling, nervous footsteps. Amberly's lips curled into a devilish grin as she waited.

Timid bare feet descended the stairs, slowly revealing the once stunningly beautiful woman she once trusted with everything. Haunted dark brown eyes stared back at her, growing wider as they took in her auburn hair. Jaquarde's most prized possession was clad only in shorts and a loose-fitting shirt. The generous curves Amberly once adored on her dark skin were gone, replaced with a deathly pallor. Gone, too, was the life that used to brim from Emere's now sunken eyes. Her beautiful hair was similarly unkempt and barely fell to her hunched shoulders, perhaps burdened with the responsibility of her betrayal.

Emere paused and reached towards the wall, bracing it for support. Amberly absentmindedly felt the knife strapped to her upper thigh as she looked into Emere's wide eyes, her fingers momentarily faltering. She blinked, her heart pounding with fresh anger at the stranger standing before her.

"Come down here," Amberly whispered.

Emere shook her head. "Leave," Emere whispered back. Her voice broke. "Please."

"Little Amberly came back to play."

A deep male voice permeated into Amberly's ears silkily, quiet but full of menace. She froze.

An additional pair of footsteps descended the stairs. Jaquarde pushed Emere out of the way. His dark eyebrows, almost growing into one straight line, obscured the tops of his deep brown eyes and gave him a permanent frowning look. Even when he smiled, it never cleared the suspicion in his brow, a look that had haunted her nightmares for years. Jaquarde forced his way forward, his large frame thundering down the last few steps and shaking the dust off of them with his weight and haste.

He looked different than when she'd seen him that morning—less polished, with slightly messy hair and a mustard-colored shirt that matched the dank room he entered. Spreading his arms to their fullest extension, he revealed his dazzling white smile and acted as if she was the only person he wanted to see. She stiffened with fear, seeing the shotgun at his side. He approached Amberly's stiff figure.

"You thought I wouldn't see you in the hotel, didn't you? Me, who taught you how to make the best disguises work?" Jaquarde's lips whispered, inhaling her hair. Amberly couldn't move as he stroked her cheek, his hands clearly eagerly moving onto her chest. He breathed his favorite whiskey into her face, the same smell that hung in the apartment. His large, questing hands and meaty arms encompassed her.

"I always hoped that those notices would draw you back, especially if Emere was the one who'd drawn them. You never could forgive betrayal, just like me." Jaquarde's hands moved back to her head and started running large fingers through her hair, harshly pulling the ends and causing Amberly's head to jerk towards his movements. "Did you know I'm the one who put up the million-dollar reward? A small price to lure you back here. Besides" —he twisted his features to that of mock seriousness and adopted a deeper, more distinguished voice—"it's my pleasure to serve the White Sands Islands by ridding us of dangerous criminals."

Amberly felt her teeth clench in an effort to not shake visibly. Her body wanted to move, spring out of his grasp and kill him, but she knew she'd be dead if she dared try now. Her eyes watched Jaquarde's fat tongue move over his perfectly white teeth. He licked his lips longer than necessary as he eyed her.

"I assume my men are dead?"

Amberly narrowed her eyes. "Yes." Her voice rang cold. The reassuring sound of it caused her body to relax a little.

A moment of silence passed before Jaquarde laughed delightedly. It filled the empty room before he looked to Amberly, still chuckling.

"Lorick and Rafael were never my best men, but you were always my best woman. I've wanted them dead for a while now. So hard to get good help these days . . . and nobody was as good as picking up . . . or picking off people as you, my darling." Jaquarde stood behind her, grazing her ear with his lips as he spoke. He pulled her knife out from her leg and traced the tip along Amberly's throat.

"This means nothing to me, and you know it," Amberly stated icily, watching her knife.

"Nothing? Disarming men with your beauty, ready to steal, kill or fuck whomever I order . . . that must mean something. Part of me missed you, and part of me hoped I'd be the first one to stand over your corpse and show all my girls, yet again, what happens when one disobeys me by running away." He placed his hands on her waist, guiding her closer until she was pressed against him. "Now and again, they need to be taught some obedience, as you may remember."

"I remember risking my life while you got all the rewards," Amberly spat out. "So I left and learned to work for myself. It was fun when I stopped taking orders from you and fucking idiots."

Jaquarde's hands squeezed her knife handle. Amberly braced herself, but he simply stood there, watching her, until he dropped the knife from her throat.

"I told you to never cross me," he said, moving away from her and towards the middle of the room. He settled himself into a yellow, threadbare armchair, his body spilling into all possible crevices. "You got plenty of rewards. I fed you, clothed you . . . when I wanted you clothed, anyway." He sighed appreciatively at his memories. "But really, Amberly, it hurts when family disobeys, and all my girls, especially you, are my family. But that's behind us now, isn't it?"

Gesturing towards the stairs, he beckoned Emere to come towards him. Amberly watched Jaquarde's dirty hands run over Emere's bare legs as she sidled into his lap, her head looking anxiously at Amberly. Jaquarde licked his lips as he lifted Emere's shirt, grasping her breasts and groaning appreciatively before shooing her away. "Get us all some drinks," he commanded.

Emere stood quickly and shot Amberly the briefest of looks on her way to the kitchen, her searing gaze boring into Amberly's as if communicating a message of plea. Amberly ignored it just as easily as she ignored the bruise under Emere's shoulder as she disappeared from sight.

"She'll never leave me now. I get her all the connections to have her art plastered all over these goddamn islands, and one day she'll like men. I've been teaching her that, but she sure needs a lot of learning."

Emere returned with glasses of a dark amber liquid. Amberly refused her glass and situated herself evenly on the stool to face Jaquarde with as much courage as she could muster. Jaquarde grabbed his glass and drained it in one gulp. He took Amberly's untouched drink. Emere sat on the bottom of the steps, her focus never leaving Amberly. Amberly ignored this and cleared her throat.

"I spent years earning the money for that boat. It was mine."

Jaquarde's second drink disappeared as quickly as the first one. He leaned into her. "Yes, years you spent preparing to escape from me with Emere. Well, nobody leaves my employ. Luckily, Emere knew that. She told me everything, begged me to spare you. Promised to do anything if I let you go. And she is a woman of her word." He sneered. "So, you see, I had no choice but to take your ship. How could I let my favorite girl leave? Still, I was surprised by how quickly you found another boat and how ruthlessly you executed those poor brothers."

"I couldn't let one of your new recruits take it from me. If I couldn't have it, no one would."

"New recruit? Hardly. He was my most talented chef," Jaquarde paused at the memory. "He knew I was up to something else. The only person I could never fool. When he'd found out enough, he said he was going to start a business with his brothers and needed a new charter boat. It was only a matter of time before he talked. So I decided to give him a little gift—a perfect deal, a discounted boat he needed." His eyebrows furrowed dangerously as his anger grew. "Like I said, nobody leaves my employ."

Jaquarde sighed. "So, yes, I took your boat. Selling it to my chef as a peace offering was a neat little solution. You went off the handle with your revenge, killed him, I got to keep Emere, donated your reward money to keep the government in my pocket, and had Emere draw that cute little portrait of you . . . from the survivor's eyewitness account. That was certainly not planned, but we flex, dear Amberly. I just never thought I'd have to clean up one of your messes."

The man she'd had on deck flitted to her mind from one year ago. She recalled Svante's words about a survivor and watching the last brother sink below the ocean surface one year ago.

"Yes, you slipped up," Jaquarde continued coyly, watching as she drifted in and out of memories. "Hell, I got contacts in nearby countries that report seeing your pretty face plastered in restaurants, on the streets . . . especially since one of *my* employees died by your hands. You gotta understand what a big deal it was. A ruthless nutcase murdered an entire family, right off the coast of the White Sand Isles number one tourist destination? A girl, too, no less?" Jaquarde momentarily paused, emitting a belch and laughing at her face.

Amberly held her breath, willing herself not to vomit at the smell as Jaquarde continued.

"You going to turn me in?" Amberly managed through gritted teeth.

Jaquarde regarded her through his furrowed eyebrows and snorted. "I fell into a new deal just after I sold your boat."

"With the survivor?" Amberly interjected, her voice low. "Where is he?"

Jaquarde leaned back. Emere coughed slightly in the corner, but both Jaquarde and Amberly ignored her. "No, not him. But from what the papers said, you made quite the impression on that young man. That notice, well, it did exactly what I hoped for, ever since you were a child. You're here, back for Emere, yes. Soon, there will be another here . . . the woman who's just like you." Jaquarde let out a truly evil grin at seeing Amberly's seething face. "And wait until you see what I'm going to do with her."

"There is nobody like me," Amberly said quietly.

"But there is," he said dangerously, toasting her with his empty glass. He walked purposely to a small table. "I'm very close to the government now. Don't forget I also have businessmen from all over the world in my pocket."

Jaquarde began gathering papers in his hand. "You

remember why it's so important to have a good reputation. Getting into people's stomachs is only the first step into getting into their business, and having my girls get into their pants practically seals the deal.

"Since I knew that Emere's notice would send you right back here, it gives me options. I *could* turn you in for real. I'll look like a right hero. But I have missed you, Amberly. So, if you beg, I might decide to keep you, as I did with Emere." The sight of him licking his fat lips again made her want to vomit. "And if you refuse, there's always . . . your twin."

The floorboards creaked as he stepped forward and placed the papers in her lap. There was a photo of a woman giving a tentative smile in a professional headshot. Her hair was the same shade as Amberly's, except cut short. Amberly stared at the delicate bridge of the nose, the long lashes, even the shape of her shoulders before the picture cut off. She felt her breath come in shallower bursts, her anger at Jaquarde increasing as he placed his hands on her shoulders, standing behind her.

"Who is this?" Amberly stood and flung herself around to face him, her shaking very hard to control now. "Another one of your tricks?"

"She's you, Amberly. Or rather what you could have been. I've waited for years to get her back. If you behave, I'll let you listen in when my contact calls. It's a funny story. The idiot, Gann, thought he found you at first, but one of my American colleagues tipped him off, told him the truth. One thing led to another, then Gann contacted me." He paused, letting out a mirthless laugh. "He's selling this girl to me. I convinced him to do it. I offered him one million if he just brought her down here."

"We both know you'd never give that money up for anyone."

"Of course not!" he said. "I'm playing along for now, so he'll bring her to me. Once he does, I'll kill him. Just a dumb suit who sank his own business with bad investments. You remember the type? He's desperate. Me, hell. I just want the girl back. Been looking for her for a long time. I can't wait to take her under my wing, let her get to know me like you did."

Jaquarde reached into his pocket and drew out a cheap cell phone. "I should be getting that call any minute now." He placed the phone back in his pocket while showing all his teeth in a grotesque smile. "Businessmen. You remember how arrogant they are."

Amberly stepped forward. "You should have told me."

"And ruin the years of anger you felt thinking you were alone, an orphan in this cruel world? It was your best motivator for getting work done. You like it, though, don't you? The anger? Revenge?" He unzipped his pants slowly. "Come on, Amberly. I see you shaking. You know you can't survive without me. Just admit you want to come back. If you put those perfect lips around my cock like you used to, I might just forgive you."

Amberly's muscles sprang to life. With one swift move, she grabbed her knife from Jaquarde and dropped to her knees in front of him, swiping fiercely through his pants.

Jaquarde howled, but she knew it wasn't enough. Gathering momentum to strike again, she sputtered when she felt her arm stop in midair and the knife drop from her purpling, useless fingers. Emere stood from the corner, then froze.

His movements were quick for being such a large man. They always were. He kept squeezing until it felt like he would rip her arm off, even after she hit the floor. She choked on her breath as his weight pressed into her, his lips to her ears.

"Emere never loved you. You should know that before you die."

His large hands found her other struggling arm. Leaning into her, he hummed to himself as if she were a rag doll he was simply arranging as he pinned both arms above her head. She saw her vision blur and felt her lungs collapse; her sides ached with pain. Heaving herself to meet his gaze, she managed to wriggle one hand out of his grip.

"You're going to die today," she said, swinging her arm towards his head, feeling his nose break instantly. Blood spurted out, but Jaquarde laughed in her face, his maniacal eyes wide with delight.

"Do better!" He wiped his face, freeing her other arm. "Fight!"

Amberly twisted her upper body enough to take a deeply needed breath. She put her hands around Jaquarde's fat neck and squeezed as hard as she could.

"Not good enough." Instantly his own hands were upon her much thinner throat. She felt her face slowly turn from red to puce. Her ears got hot as she struggled to maintain open eyes. She heard Jaquarde's phone ring. Her hands helplessly scrabbled his meaty arms, and her tongue bulged out of her mouth pointlessly.

"You won't feel a thing," Jaquarde said. "'Cause I'm going to fuck your unresisting body once you're dead."

Emere appeared behind Jaquarde. Amberly felt all her hate vanish. The light was back in Emere's eyes, gaunt as they were, and she cherished the sight until her breath escaped her without returning. Amberly's hands fell to her sides. Jaquarde pressed his thumbs further into her throat as everything began to fade to blackness.

CHAPTER FIFTEEN

"I want to try," Claire insisted. "It'll help distract me. Besides, I didn't do anything all afternoon but sleep after you treated my wound."

"You needed the rest," Kyle replied. "I don't want you at risk for an infection, and staying put with those leaves on your face helped." The charred red scorch marks on her cheek shimmered as the fading sun hit it. She'd been braver than he expected, the way she sat as still as possible, letting him burn her wound closed; she didn't even cry. Already the swelling had subsided. That was a relief.

"But I need food, too, and I want to help with that," Claire argued. "You taught everyone else."

Kyle couldn't help but smile at her with a foreign sense of pride. He beckoned her over.

"To filet this," Kyle said, carefully cutting along the edge of the fish's backbone towards the tail, "we'll split the fish in two. Sometimes this variety has fat stored here, but we're going to keep it instead of cutting it out." He peered into the incision he had made. Claire watched closely. "That fish there" — he gestured to the longer one — "is perfect for steak cuts."

"I think I know what you're going to do next." Claire pointed towards the backbone, where meat still clung. "Cut right here? I was watching you do it earlier."

"Exactly. Cut that meat free, carefully."

He handed over his knife, his fingers momentarily lingering over hers as she took the blade.

"Shorter cuts," Kyle instructed. "And slowly, to get more precision."

"Okay." Her face was fresh with determination. Her hands shook slightly.

"Slower." Kyle put his hand over hers and guided it gently upward while she held the fish on the rock.

"This just takes a little more practice," he said. "Even I don't always get it right the first time. Sharp shears are better for this . . . the bones are stronger here near the head."

Claire struggled with the spine until, eventually, he heard his knife hit the rock.

"You're a natural," he said, and she handed his knife back. "But, that's the last one."

"Thanks, Kyle," Claire said. She stood and inspected her bloody hands. "I'm going to rinse off, then."

Kyle joined Paul, who was stoking the fire. Additional wreckage they'd retrieved lay scattered along the shore. The sun settled in an indigo brilliance on the water, casting pink tones high in the sky. He picked up the fish filets and carried them to the fire.

"You should serve this at your inn. I bet the locals would love a taste of your travels," Kyle said.

"I'd like that," Paul replied. "I'd also love to get that recipe for the sauce you used on your boat."

"Ahh, that took me months to perfect. There are three main sauces of the White Sand Isles. That was the ginger root sauce, which is typically served with fish. Doesn't hurt to have on the boat either, in case anyone gets seasick."

"And the other two?"

"Mint, and the third is what we call the essence of earth and sea."

"What's in that?"

"A mix of many things," Kyle said. "It's the island specialty. Spicy and hot. You have to try it before you leave."

"Fair enough," Paul agreed. "But I would prefer you make it for my guests. Honestly, Kyle, I would hire you if you're looking for a new life after this."

"I've survived worse than a shipwreck," Kyle joked. The other man shook his head, an expression of seriousness crossing his face.

"I don't know what you have left here, Kyle. It's not an act of charity. I've been blown away by all you've done. You work hard, and you'd help my business. I'd pay you fairly. There's a place on the property for staff, if you want to live there. We live there, too. You'd have plenty of space. There are open fields, not unlike the open sea. Endless green in the summer, endless white in the winter. It's beautiful."

Kyle stared at him, waiting for one of the sentences in his mind to make sense enough to say aloud. How could he explain to Paul that he was as part of the islands as they were him?

"Paul," he began slowly. "Thank you, mate, really."

"You're going to say no." Paul looked into the horizon for a moment.

Kyle sighed.

"I can't leave. This is my home, and it always will be. Life will go on even after we get rescued."

"It will, but even so —"

Kyle shook his head. "I just know this is where I'm supposed to be."

"Can't argue with a true man of Iselle, can I?" Paul said.

Kyle put his hand out, and Paul shook it. "Thank you," Kyle said genuinely. Both men looked up to see Henry appear on the beach, jogging towards them.

Paul smiled at his brother. "Perhaps it's just as well. I can see how one prefers constant sun to one of our winters."

"I'll gladly help from afar to make your dishes as authentic to our cuisine as they can be."

"You can coax Henry into trying something spicy for a change. Kid's got such a sensitive stomach."

"I heard that," Henry called out. He ran forward and stood next to Paul and Kyle, panting slightly.

"Good." Paul put his arm around Henry. "Just trying to help you, little brother. I can't convince Kyle to come to Scotland so he can finally see snow. Remember how our snowmen get around, Henry?"

"Oho, don't," Henry groaned.

"By-*icicle*!" Paul ruffled Henry's hair.

Kyle snorted back a half groan, half laugh before carefully placing the fish in the fire.

Claire returned with clean hands, several bananas, and coconuts. Her face was creased in concentration as she sank into the sand beside him, digging her nails into the white flesh of the cracked fruit.

Henry lifted his nose to the air and inhaled. "Smells amazing!"

Kyle dipped the speared meat above the licking flames. Nearby sand reflected the fire's glow like a golden dust.

"Today was supposed to be your wedding day, wasn't it?" he heard her ask Paul quietly.

"Ten AM, the future Mr. and Mrs.," he replied, digging out the last of the fruit.

"I'm sorry," Claire said earnestly. "Your fiancé must be so worried."

"I imagine so, but . . ." Paul trailed off, while Claire looked on in sympathy.

"Here." Paul offered Claire his sharpened stick. "Better start before Henry and I eat them all."

"Thanks." Claire took a fish fillet and skewered it on the stick.

"I'm surprised we haven't seen animals yet." Paul gingerly touched the bump on his head, examining the stitches with his fingers. "Do we have to worry about anything getting into the food at night?"

"Hard to say," Kyle responded. "There are howler monkeys, bats, several species of birds that fly in and out of these islands. They shouldn't bother us, but the monkeys might make their presence known on this side of the island."

"How?" Henry looked to the nearest trees. "Will they attack us?"

Kyle shook his head. "They howl but stay high in the canopy of the trees. Don't be afraid, though. They howl morning and night. It's just what they do."

"It's weird not hearing cars or anything here." Henry set his stick into the fire.

"The world is so quiet here you can almost believe you're the only one in it," Kyle replied, almost to himself. He didn't miss the busy streets of Nusa Via, cluttered with wealthy tourists and hurried businesspeople. They occupied the islands with him but forgot how Iselle wanted them to live. Here, everything moved naturally.

Kyle enjoyed the sound of waves lapping gently to the shore, intermixed with hungry chewing. There was something comforting about the silence from the others — an unspoken understanding that the air didn't need to be constantly polluted between them with words of worry or any commentary on their predicament.

But it was time to move. Kyle looked to the unlit torch he had prepared earlier. He slowly dipped it into the flames. It sprang to life with ferocity and sparks. "If you're all done eating, let's kill the fire and pack up."

It didn't take long before they were ready, having spent much of the afternoon preparing. The woods were thick with darkness now. Surprised at the rapid decrease in light and the new shadows cast, Kyle felt like he was entering into a different island than a year ago. New trees had grown, and old had fallen. Perhaps it was also the light chatter of Paul and Henry behind him, or Claire's gentle laugh as Paul good-naturedly continued teasing Henry about sewing his head wound shut.

Turning back, he looked at them briefly, making sure all was well. Henry carried the cooler of filleted fish, while Paul and Kyle had similar-sized packs on their backs full of clothes and supplies. Claire claimed a spot at the rear of their procession; the bag of food, clothes, leaves, and sticks that had dried all day was hoisted firmly onto her shoulders and added several pounds to her frame.

An hour passed, at least, according to his body's reaction. Sweat from the humid interior of the island pooled on his back and drenched his forehead. His legs pushed further, the strain of his muscles clearing his head. He stopped to readjust the small ax slung through his belt. A flock of bats flew overhead, followed by something more sinister.

"Did you hear that, Paul?" Henry asked.

"Shh!" Kyle froze. The deep-throated growl was faint at first but within seconds seemed closer and louder.

"What's that?" Claire exclaimed, the growl joined by another, deep in the trees above them. The sounds were exactly as Kyle remembered — sudden guttural barks and calls that reverberated through the leaves and carried enough volume to be heard from several kilometers away. He thought he heard Henry say something, but the sounds were deafening, and he hunkered down with the rest of the group, observing their shocked faces. Claire hugged her knees to her chest and had her hands somewhat over her ears.

"Howler monkeys!" Kyle yelled. "They won't hurt us, just stay here, don't make any sudden movements!"

Nobody seemed convinced, and he didn't blame them. Henry looked more scared than when they'd been looking for Paul, and Paul had a look of shock on his face that matched his younger brother's. The monkeys barked and howled like feral dogs. Coupled with the rustling of leaves and unseen branches waving above them, he understood their reactions. The monkeys repeated the noises over and over until eventually they tapered off, the sound of moving branches subsiding.

"That was crazy," Henry muttered.

"I've never heard anything like that," Paul whispered.

"They were close. I swear I heard one swing right above us over there." Claire pointed in the dark.

Kyle looked ahead at the jagged rocks. "This is a good place to stop."

He heard Claire deposit the items on her back with a small sigh of relief.

"It's so humid in here." Henry touched the thin trunk of the tree closest to him. His hands ran up the slippery bark before he shook it gently, and drops of water fell upon the group.

"Yes," Kyle said. "With that, and the recent rain, I don't want us climbing slippery rocks at night."

The tiny clearing was soon home to multiple leaf beds. The group finished assembling them in silence, clearly on edge, but the monkeys made no more sounds. Kyle knew they were there, watching, likely swinging from the branches and moving above the group. He settled his torch on the opposite side of their clearing.

Claire rubbed her sore shoulders before peering at Kyle's bag. "Why did you just put your shoes in here?" she asked.

"They're wet, and scorpions and other bugs might try to make a nest in there if I leave them out," Kyle replied. "Trust me, all of you put your own shoes in there if you want to take them off for the night. I recommend it, so your feet can dry."

"I can already feel it getting cooler." Paul tossed his shoes to Claire, who stuck them in the bag. "But I believe you. Remember that spider colony we had to get out of the attic at the inn last summer, Henry? One became two, two became twenty, twenty became fifty . . ."

"I don't want to think about that now," Henry said, hastening to remove his own footwear.

"All right, I'll stop. No more surprises today would be nice." Paul flopped down on his leaves. "No, no, I don't need that, thanks," he said, waving away the towel Henry was trying to hand him.

"Not even for your head?"

"Too tired, little brother." Paul closed his eyes, running his hand over his stitched forehead once more. "But thanks."

Henry formed his leaves into a comfortable shape first, then proceeded to lie down, close his eyes, and not make another sound save for his calm breathing. Paul lay unmoving next to his brother, while Claire arranged for a place to sleep away from the boys.

"I've never slept outside before," Claire confessed. She sat up, looking towards the sky.

"You sure have," Paul joked beside her, his voice muffled and clogged with incoming sleep. "Spent quite some time curled up on the beach."

"Yes, but this is different," Claire insisted, still staring at the sky.

Kyle could see the firelight from the torch flickering in her eyes. He took out a few dead leaves from her pack and started a small fire.

"A little extra warmth won't hurt us as we go to sleep," Kyle said, answering her questioning look. Claire picked up a nearby stick and poked at the burning log, allowing the fire to brighten.

"I don't know if it's the fresh air or the snake bite, but I feel like I can think more clearly since coming here." Claire's voice was so quiet he hardly heard her above the crackling fire.

Kyle shrugged, although he knew she probably couldn't

see that in the dark as he rolled his own towel out. He propped the torch near the fire. "It's easier to think outside or on the water. It's a gift from Iselle."

Claire nodded but didn't say anything more, only continued to stoke the fire. Kyle sat up on his towel and ran a hand through his hair, brushing the unruly curls out of the way before holding his hand out to Claire.

"I can take that stick," he said. "Get some rest, Claire."

She gave it to him, glancing at the exposed part of his scar. He said nothing, though he was surprised that he didn't mind her lingering attention. Kyle watched Claire's face return to the small fire. He let several moments pass but knew the words were meant to be said long before he uttered them. He drew a breath, but still couldn't meet her eyes, so he stared at her knees.

"I'm sorry about your wound," he said quietly. "And for the way I acted on the boat. You really did just want to get to your conference."

Claire snorted to herself quietly, but she didn't seem upset. In fact, he thought he saw a tiny smile appear at the corner of her mouth, but it faded as quickly as it came. Relief coursed through him at the gesture.

"It's okay," she said quietly.

He watched her curiously as her eyes darted downwards. "No, it isn't."

"I don't really care about getting to the conference anymore," she whispered. "I hate my job. My boss is a jerk, my coworkers abandoned me, and my clients will never get to see the new templates I spent a month and a half designing because I'm only thought of as incompetent even though I'm right."

Kyle prodded the logs, causing several sparks to fly into the air. "Then quit. Your life isn't worth wasting if you aren't happy."

Claire looked at him incredulously

He put his hand up to stop her. "Don't tell me it's not that easy. It is. You aren't happy."

Claire stared at him. "I wasn't going to say that exactly. But something's just never felt right about my company, or where I am in life. I wanted to make a better life for myself, but . . . that isn't what happened. I've been consumed, I guess, by . . . other's expectations."

"There are sayings here about the power of Iselle's storms. People, visitors like you, get a real quick awakening to her presence, and many have life-altering realizations."

Claire absentmindedly stared at her fingernails. A curious expression stole her gentle features with a frown. "Do you always find comfort when you talk about Iselle?"

"I do, yes. Iselle is peace and rebirth here," Kyle replied. "Not just the goddess of storms."

"Then do you believe Iselle is the reason I almost died in that storm?" Claire asked.

He stared at her intently. "No," Kyle said, unaffected. "Iselle is the reason you survived."

"Interesting," Claire mused.

"It's our culture here. Being near death has a way of reconnecting you with life and what matters, no matter who you are," Kyle said, tossing a few extra dead leaves into the fire. "Iselle is life and love. Death is just part of life. And you didn't die."

Claire watched the leaves burn for a moment before looking at him. "What really happened to you when you met that pirate Amberly?"

Kyle threw a fresh piece of driftwood into the fire. He'd only told Paul and Henry pieces, yet there was something about Claire that made him feel he could share anything, even if it was the same painful story he revisited in his mind every day.

"My brothers and I were just taking our new boat out for fun. We planned to start our own business as a charter service, and it was our last day before we had customers. A celebration, really. Do a little fishing, toast to our new business." Kyle paused for a moment. He could almost hear his brothers laughing in his head as they got ready. He swallowed, embracing their merry faces in his mind. "A storm moved in really quickly. We would have made it back safely, no problem, but saw her yacht and thought it was in trouble." Kyle's voice grew lower. He felt his eyebrows knit together angrily. "Amberly jumped aboard and killed my brothers, and one of her men tried to kill me."

He couldn't bring himself to look at Claire's horrified expression. Kyle continued in a stony voice. "The man failed to kill me. She'd already jumped back on her own yacht, and I followed. So she sent me to the bottom of the ocean to make sure I really died. I barely made it to a rocky cliff underneath with an air pocket. My brothers and I used to dive for them when we were kids. The caves are small, but you can catch your breath and hide for a while. We used to make it a game." Kyle paused.

"I sawed out of my bonds on a rock. Took over an hour." Kyle shook his head. "Then I swam to Ildetache, and after a few weeks on the island, I was found by a passing group of birding researchers."

Claire didn't speak for several minutes.

Kyle watched the flickering fire pass over her face, wondering if her curiosity was dampened.

"And here I've been complaining about my job," Claire finally said in a low voice. "I'm so sorry, Kyle. I can see why you hate me. I can't imagine what it's like to look into the face of the person who killed your family."

He waited for Claire to continue, but she looked lost and sad, not knowing what else to say. Her fingers traced little patterns in the sand.

Kyle shook his head as he grappled'with a response. How could he explain that any anger at her had evaporated once he saw her helpless figure behind the waterfall?

"I'm not angry at you, Claire. Not anymore."

She leaned further forward, the graceful curve of her shoulders playing host to the light of the flickering fire before turning her burned face in full view. Kyle closed his eyes as his next words finally formed in his head. "After I found you in the cave, I realized you're nothing like her." He opened his eyes and saw Claire looking at him. "You're kind and good, Claire. Even a little foolish for running off in the woods like that."

Claire remained silent for several moments. Then seeming to steel herself, she pointed at his scar.

"Did she do that? Amberly?"

Kyle nodded. "Part of me still wants to find her. I have to know why she killed my brothers and sank our boat. Ever since that night, nothing makes sense. People don't just treat each other that way . . . there has to be a reason."

"Were your brothers boat captains like you?" Claire asked. "Did they know her?"

"No." Kyle saw their faces in his head again and smiled to himself. "Jake, my younger brother, worked as an assistant chef at a really popular restaurant. He was ready for a change, and Nick, the youngest of us all, helped manage the Sunset Cruises' main office off of Feulia Island. I was always a captain. Teaming up just made sense."

"Cool."

"Yeah. Nick was the most technology oriented. He was going to design our website."

"Oh?" Claire pressed.

"It's not that good," Kyle confessed. "I have no patience or interest in that stuff. I only maintained what he made. I know it's important, but it took months before I could even look at the site after what happened."

"That tends to be where my company would come in. An exceptional website to draw in exceptional business."

"Paul told me that, too, when you were sleeping on the beach. He said I should hire you."

"Ha," Claire replied, but she was smiling. "I love talking to people about what they want and need but . . . Gann Inc. charges so much money for a consultation for someone like Paul, or even you. People with small businesses don't have that kind of money, and they're so passionate about their work. Kind of like you. I can hear it in your voice."

Kyle shrugged. "I suppose I am."

"That's the best part, to hear that love," Claire mused. "But we're . . . unaffordable. Gann knows it, too, but he thinks it's a great way to seem more prestigious. What it does, in reality, is scare people off. I still don't understand where the money is going. We sure don't get raises and always seem to be in the red."

"You going to charge me for this fireside chat?" Kyle couldn't suppress his grin.

Claire smiled back, and Kyle watched her look down at the soft white sand falling from her fingertips. "If we get off this island, I can take a look at what you have," she offered. "For free as well, so don't worry about that. I doubt I have a job anymore, and I feel like I owe you something, for your boat, my face . . ."

He nodded, grateful, and at a loss for a response. Having an expert improve his website would only improve his quality of life.

"So Paul and Henry don't know all of this?"

"Not all of it," he replied. "They've seen my scar and asked about it. They didn't see a notice, though, and frankly, I'm surprised you still did. The White Sands government has had its hands full with the additional tourism that keeps coming in. New hotels are being built, and restaurants, too. That woman isn't the only person around here up to crime sprees, either."

"It's been over a year. Do you really think there's hope left?"

"Yes," he stated matter-of-factly. "I could never stop looking for her, on some level anyway, while still moving on and starting my own business."

The fire crackled and its light diminished, so Kyle rearranged the log and caused a fresh wave of sparks. Claire curled up into a small ball under a yellow towel.

"Thanks for talking with me. Goodnight, Kyle," she said. He watched her stir until she was comfortable. The burned edge of her face was just in the flickering light's reach. It was such a relief to no longer see the pirate women even faintly lingering on her features.

"Goodnight, Claire," he replied softly.

CHAPTER SIXTEEN

"**I** 'll race you!"
Emere tossed her head back and smiled widely, disappearing behind the beachfront palms. Amberly grinned at her musical laugh
echoing over the waves. It was beautiful and made her forget how
exhausted she felt. Emere's bare feet raced across the dock as she sped
up her pace. Amberly rounded a corner and emerged from behind
the palms, hearing a splash as she came upon the empty dock. She
shook her head. Emere never waited to take off her clothes before
jumping in.

"It's warm today?" Amberly leaned over Emere's head as she was
bobbing in the sparkling clear waters. Her skin seemed to glisten in
the sun.

"The best." Emere watched impatiently as Amberly sat on the
edge of the dock and put her feet in the water. "Jaquarde has one of
the best private beaches here. You can't argue with that."

"Okay, let me at least take my shorts off."

"Don't bother."

Emere hoisted herself up on the dock and took Amberly's hands
away. Gentle fingers traced a line lovingly along each of Amberly's
fingers before she kissed them and set them aside. Amberly closed
her eyes to the warm sun as Emere's fingers found her shorts. They
were unfastened and slipped off of her legs. She allowed her body to
relax a bit – it had been a terribly long day, but Jaquarde was happy
with her progress. Emere slowly lifted Amberly's shirt off. The kiss
of sunshine touched her belly as she leaned back and lay on the dock.
Emere lay next to her, sliding the straps of Amberly's bikini top off
until her bare breasts were exposed to the sun.

"So beautiful," Emere whispered, gently kissing Amberly's soft neck. *Amberly felt herself growing wet with pleasure, and her breathing shook slightly with the rush of emotions and sensations Emere caused her to feel.*

"I'm so dirty, Emere. Let me at least wash off," Amberly pleaded, but Emere just laughed lightly, the same musical notes, but this time they sang of love.

"I don't care, Amberly," Emere said, and slid a hand under Amberly's panties to caress her, deeply probing her fingers as far as they could reach. "I don't think your pussy does either," Emere said, and as if to prove her point, she slid her hands up and down the slick folds that were rapidly swelling. "But if you want, I'll stop."

Amberly shook her head and arced her back slightly. Emere laughed lightly before settling her mouth over one of Amberly's nipples. She suckled and licked the deep pink tips until they hardened. Nipping and biting them gently with her teeth, Emere pulled her fingers out of Amberly and licked them.

"I know what happened," Emere murmured, running her tongue along her fingers, savoring the taste with her eyes closed. "I know what Jaquarde made you do. None of it matters now, Amberly. Not when you're here, and we're together."

Amberly blinked and opened her eyes to the sun, still breathing heavily. The most beautiful face she had ever seen moved in front of her, and Emere winked with a smile.

"Let it all go," Emere whispered. "Just be here, with me." She traced Amberly's oval face before meeting Amberly's lips with her own. Amberly put her hands around Emere's neck, drawing her in. She put her hands under Emere's wet t-shirt, but the other woman pulled Amberly's hands away before they could remove the fabric.

"Let go," Emere repeated. "Just lose yourself, Amberly."

Amberly looked into the beautiful brown eyes and nodded. Emere moved to Amberly's other breast, sucking hard on the nipple and gently tugging at the tip, allowing a moment of pain before caressing it away with her tongue, then starting all over again.

Amberly's heartbeat pounded so loudly in her ears she could barely hear the waves lapping on the dock. Her midsection throbbed with need and calmed when soft fingers ran past her belly button, fondling the soft curly hairs below. Amberly relaxed as Emere's thumb and forefinger knew exactly where to go. Amberly closed her eyes and allowed herself to moan as Emere made delicate motions with her fingers, but still intentionally out of reach of Amberly's clitoris.

"Emere, please," Amberly whispered, her voice cracking.

"Please what?" Emere murmured, her tongue flicking Amberly's nipple playfully. "You finally ready to let the day go? Leave the past in the past?"

"Yes, I promise, please," Amberly moaned. She couldn't get up if she wanted to. Her body ached with need, rendering her limbs helpless.

"Lift your legs up for me." Emere continued to speak in her soft melodic tones. Amberly obliged, but her legs were shaking. Whether that was with pleasure or stress, she hoped Emere wouldn't notice as she was placing her feet on the dock.

Emere stroked her legs gently until she reached the soft lacy fabric. She pulled Amberly's panties off.

"Just relax," she whispered. "Open your legs to me, Amberly." Emere ran a hand down Amberly's inner thigh. A purple bruise was forming there. Amberly quaked slightly, even at Emere's gentle touch, and knew Emere would notice it immediately.

"I'm sorry," Amberly whispered, embarrassed. "I'm so sore." A slight tear ran down her cheek. She tried to wipe it away, but Emere stopped her.

"Don't be sorry," Emere murmured. "You know how much I love you, no matter what, or who, touches you."

Amberly felt another tear forming and squeezed Emere into a hug, and held the other woman when she tried to move away seductively.

"I love you, too, Emere," she whispered.

Emere squeezed back, then Amberly let go. Emere moved her body gracefully downward, her face never leaving Amberly's gaze, not when she removed Amberly's bikini top fully, or when she allowed Amberly to lie in the setting sun, open and vulnerable, completely naked. Emere tenderly stroked the bruise on Amberly's inner thigh, her face creasing with concern and love. She opened Amberly's legs further and sank downward, kissing the bruise gently before tenderly exposing Amberly's clitoris with her fingers, kissing it first, then settling in and licking it with her expert tongue.

Amberly writhed on the dock, letting her arms flop helplessly to the side. Her body, drenched in pleasure, shook slightly as Emere brought her to the edge of an orgasm, then drew back to lighter, tiny licks, probing her fingers deep into her vagina, pulsating.

Pleasure cascaded over Amberly. Whether it was ten seconds or ten minutes, Amberly didn't know. Emere once again found the bruise and kissed it gently. Amberly gasped as Emere returned to her clitoris, blowing gently on it before finally taking it fully into her mouth, bringing Amberly to orgasm. Amberly could barely keep up with her need to breathe. Fluid dripped out of her vagina, but Emere slowed her tongue on the swollen flesh, gently lapping it up as it came out, drinking it deeply, and Amberly felt her inhale lovingly. Amberly opened her eyes, noticing the sun was setting. Emere's legs were cheerfully crossed in the air. Her toes were pointed, and her head worshipfully bent into Amberly.

Amberly raised her hand to stroke the top of Emere's head, but the other woman stayed carefully put. She grasped Amberly's leg with her free arm, holding her legs apart until she was sure Amberly was finished dripping. Emere's fingers never left Amberly's body until she stopped quaking. With a final kiss on her engorged clitoris, Emere's tongue made final patterns up her body before once more settling on Amberly's lips.

Amberly kissed her back, truly exhausted. She gave the other woman a passionate squeeze before allowing herself to be completely lost in the warm embrace of Emere's arms.

" . . . and, we don't have much time," the gruff voice said far away. Amberly wanted to respond, but she couldn't. Her lips wouldn't form the words. She opened her eyes with a start, feeling a crushing pain in her side.

Smoke tendrils billowed above her. Heat waves ran across

her exposed skin. Maybe it was the fiery volcanic hell under the islands Iselle selected for the unfortunate.

"Is this death?" she whispered to herself. A new cloud of smoke passed above. She managed to turn her head. Blood-soaked floorboards hissed with fire beside her. Her body was equally covered with blood. It felt sticky, and the smell made her nostrils flare. She choked back the urge to vomit.

"It will be if we don't move." Dev loomed over her. "Let's get you up, Captain. Here." Dev thrust her knife forward. Amberly stared at the blade, blood dripping from the edge as she tried to heave herself up on her knees. When that failed, Dev grabbed her arms and pulled. Her head spun uncomfortably, but she ignored it. The knife quivered in her grip, and it took all of her concentration to keep her fingers around it. She followed the trail of blood until she saw the source.

Jaquarde. His body was sprawled near her, and Emere was lying beside him.

Knife wounds were torn across Jaquarde's side, jagged and executed with little precision or skill. His shirt was torn into bloodstained scraps. Jaquarde's face was mutilated, his eyes slit, his jaw protruding through stringy bits of flesh. Years of hatred fueled every wound, and she knew he hadn't been killed quickly.

She tried to make sense of it and blanched when she remembered scattered images in between the darkness. The frail hand carrying her knife out of the corner of her eye. Emere had been shaking so violently, Amberly had half expected the knife would clatter uselessly to the floor. Jaquarde's eyes went wide as the knife went into his neck. She'd felt his blood spray over her lips. Then there was nothing.

"Found the girl crying over you, Captain. Knocked her out cold before she could do any harm," Dev boasted. "Still alive, though. You want to kill her? Or let her burn with him?"

"No." Amberly shakily wiped her knife off and strapped it back to her leg, not taking her eyes off Emere's still face. "We take Emere with us. I have to find . . . something, he must have something . . ."

Dev picked Emere up effortlessly and draped her over his shoulder. Amberly bent down to check Jaquarde's pockets, frantically pulling out his wallet and cellphone as smoke clouded her nostrils. Coughing slightly, she hobbled limply to the papers on the floor. Scooping them quickly into her arms, she attempted to follow Dev to the door, but pain shot down her leg. Amberly felt herself sinking long before she buckled to the floor. She blinked at the smoke and attempted to stand again, coughing.

"Get up, Captain." He wasn't the same Dev she'd brought on board. The nervous look in his eyes, the hesitation — all of it was gone. "You gotta move faster. Fire's gonna eat this shit hole faster than you think."

Dev dragged Amberly unsteadily to her feet. They passed the portrait of Iselle and the bodies of Lorick and Rafael as fire burst through the room, melting the kitchen with an inferno of heat and spreading quickly.

"Purify them, Iselle," Amberly whispered down on them. She followed Dev with difficulty down to the small clearing. Night was falling fast. Every inhale brought her discomfort, as if her lungs didn't want to expand fully. Her steps came awkwardly, not the same brisk pace she knew so well but punctuated by jabs of acute pain in her side. She knew that her ribs were broken. They rounded a bend in the trees down the small path to the ocean, until the sight of Jaquarde's hideout was out of view. Amberly heard flames licking the old house.

"So? What happened?" Dev turned to her, Emere limply swinging with his movements. He batted her arm out of the way impatiently as if it was nothing but a pesky fly.

Amberly cleared her throat, but her voice was still hoarse. "After I killed him, the girl was on the floor, screaming," Amberly lied. "I think she was trying to wake *him* up after what I did, but my exertions exhausted me . . ."

"Then I came in," Dev added.

Amberly started at Emere's tear-stricken unconscious face and eyed the rusty stains streaked over her hands. She never thought Emere capable of taking a life, especially Jaquarde's. Her bare legs sported dried rivulets of Jaquarde's blood, creating a myriad of paths that had clearly pooled by her feet.

"Yes." Amberly wheezed with extreme difficulty in a low voice. "She was inconsolable . . . after I killed Jaquarde . . ." Her voice trailed off, choking on the pain in her side. Taking a jagged breath, she clutched her ribs with one hand, the other maintaining a firm grip on the papers. Smoke curled in the night sky. She sent a silent prayer to Iselle that something in these papers would lead her to the woman Jaquarde claimed was her sister.

"We'll talk later. Let's go," she commanded, ignoring the pain in her voice. She froze as something shook from inside the papers. Dev continued walking ahead of her, Emere still limply hanging over his shoulder. She set the papers on the ground with a pounding heart, each beat reminding her it would have stopped, forever, had Emere not saved her. A small black phone vibrated amidst the papers.

Amberly stared at the screen. It revealed only a number — no name. She tried to catch her breath and answered. An impatient man cleared his throat loudly.

"It's Gann." A man said in a commanding voice. "I've located Claire."

CHAPTER SEVENTEEN

Claire was one and the same with the ground. She listened to the rustling of the leaves. The birds above sang peacefully. The soil felt pleasant under her fingers, and she gently gripped a handful of it. The bird nearest to her flew away and joined others above in a large palm, singing cheerily.

Within a few moments, Paul shook himself awake, looking bleary-eyed.

"Morning," he managed with effort, yawning widely before turning to shake Henry awake. The younger boy resurfaced under his beach towel, tousled hair surrounding his sleepy face.

"Here, Henry." Claire edged her way over to the cooler of rainwater, which was much shallower than the day before. Henry accepted one of the discarded coconut halves, rubbing the sleep out of his eyes.

"You look awful," he said. His forehead was creased with sleep lines as he surveyed her face.

"Yeah?" Claire replied, fishing a banana out of one of the nearby bags and biting into it. "You should see your hair, full of dirt and sand."

Henry grinned, running a hand through the absurd angles of his hair.

"Nothing for me, pink bikini?" Paul put his hand out.

Claire was about to reply when Kyle reappeared, his shirt splashed with water.

"Breadfruit for breakfast," he announced. "Eat up the leftover fish, too." The large pieces of fruit in his hand reminded

Claire of footballs with short hair, although the fruit was green. The group ate hungrily and in silence, eager to resume their journey.

Within minutes they were ready to resume their trek through the jungle. Under Kyle's direction, they switched packs to distribute the weight of their supplies evenly and stopped at every opportunity to collect fresh rainwater held in leaves and large fronds. Claire couldn't help but marvel at Kyle's ability to identify where the largest palms would be growing and where the leaves would lie on the island floor.

The birds kept the group company with sweet songs while Kyle pointed out which plants to look for that could be useful later, and how to observe the growth and placement of the trees and vegetation to help them make their way inward when following the stream was too difficult to walk along.

"Wouldn't your compass cover that?" Claire asked.

"Yes." Kyle patted his side pocket. "But it's also helpful to look and listen. Even the birds singing here are guides. They make their nests near the water, and sing slightly different songs if they hear danger."

As if on cue, a panicked chirping rose from deeper in the forest.

"Like snakes?" Claire interjected. The chirping ceased, and she felt a chill down her spine. Instinctively she stared at the thick brown trunks of the trees around them, as if waiting for a green snake to appear.

"Like snakes," Kyle agreed.

Regardless, Claire felt more at ease the more she moved. Several times she caught herself absentmindedly touching the dead skin on her face. Sweat pooled on her lower back where her pack came in contact with her skin, and the knotted ties of her pink bikini were soaked. The air was hot, and moisture seeped from her pores. Claire wiped away the sweat that fell from her face as they stopped for a short break.

"This is cheaper than my gym membership, but good lord, is it humid in here." Paul dried his face off with his shirt. Henry opened the cooler of water.

Claire inspected her arms and shoulders, which were turning red.

"I'm not used to being out in the sun this much." Claire grimaced. "It's quite different in Minnesota right now."

"Too bad none of that sunscreen survived, eh?" Paul said between drinking water.

"Take my shirt," Kyle offered, stripping it off quickly and handing it to Claire. It was warm when she accepted it, damp with his sweat. Her eyes lingered on the dark curly hairs scattered across his chest. The scar along his neck reached further down than she expected, and she watched it glisten down his collarbone in the light. She looked away, embarrassed at how eager her eyes were.

"It doesn't feel like we've been in that much sun," Henry piped up, pulling a piece of cooked fish from the cooler.

"Even just an hour here will do enough damage to the fair-skinned, such as yourselves," Kyle said.

"Is this the last of our fish?" Henry asked, stomach still gurgling.

"For now." Kyle handed Claire the last filet.

Claire took the fish, charred and black, from Kyle's hand and bit into it. "Is it parrotfish?"

Paul looked quizzically at the other man. "Wait, not the pooping fish?"

Kyle smiled. Claire felt the fish jump in her stomach as his face lit up with a genuinely happy expression.

"The very same," he replied. "Let's get moving again. We'll rest at the waterfall for the rest of the day and night, get some more fish, maybe even some plants. Henry, you take the lead. Keep close to the stream. It should be getting wider soon."

"All right." Henry leapt forward, and Claire shared his

enthusiasm. Relaxing soon sounded good.

"Will you teach me to fish then?" she asked as Kyle motioned for her to continue with Paul.

Kyle bent down to inspect some plants low to the ground. "Yes," he replied, before looking up at her. "I can do that."

Claire smiled to herself as she turned to catch up with Paul and Henry. Kyle lagged behind, still inspecting the plant before carefully severing some stems with his knife.

"We'd be dead without him, wouldn't we," Paul said, gesturing towards Kyle. "While you were unconscious, he was overcome with guilt about his boat not making it out of that storm, but hid it well. He's being strong for us."

"I definitely would be dead," Claire replied. "The poison would have rendered me useless at this point. I don't even want to think about that. And Kyle was steered right into that storm, but he didn't put us in that kind of danger on purpose."

"Oh, not at all. I told him that, too. It was all a perfect combination of an accident, really. Slow down, Henry." The older man cautioned his brother before shaking his head. "I swear that kid's going to break a leg on one of these roots."

They walked in silence for several steps, moving fronds out of the way and listening to the serenity of the jungle around them. Claire watched with adoration and a twinge of jealously at Paul's protecting gaze towards Henry.

"Paul, I'm really sorry about crashing your trip."

"That's quite all right, Claire. It's like I kept telling Kyle before you woke up. No use placing blame now. It's sure been an adventure we won't forget anytime soon."

Claire stifled a laugh. "True."

Kyle appeared several steps behind them. Henry moved further from the stream and away from the rocks that jutted out of the greenery.

"What's your fiancé's name again?" Claire asked Paul as

he held a prickly branch away from her face.

Paul paused. A somber look crossed his face, almost as if uttering it would cause some bad omen. "Justine," he said slowly, letting the syllables relax on his tongue.

"That's beautiful," Claire said softly.

Paul surveyed his hands and picked a thorn from his knuckles. A droplet of blood formed, and he brushed it away absentmindedly. "We met when she visited my inn, three years ago this winter. Her plane was delayed in a snowstorm, so she wound up on my doorstep."

"Very nice." Claire shifted her footing to ease down the sloped hill.

"But what about you?" Paul asked. "Did you leave a boy pining for you in the States? Your work friends must be worried sick about your disappearance, at the very least."

"I don't know," she said thoughtfully. "I'm sure they notified the local police, but I don't know what else they would do." She suddenly had a vision of Jackson doing her presentation, and to her surprise, found herself chuckling over it.

"But no boy?" Paul prodded her in the ribs gently. "I can't imagine that. Beauty, brains, and a pink bikini?"

"No, no boy," Claire said quietly. Jackson's face flitted out of her mind. It felt as vacuous as the unfeeling void on her face. Surprised, she tried hard to imagine him worried but couldn't. When Aiden materialized in the vacuum Jackson created, she felt her hands tightly grip the cooler she was carrying. Her face turned red at the turn of her thoughts. Shame filled her as she realized Jackson would never be able to take her to the heights of sensation Aiden was capable of.

A branch hit Claire's face. Even though she didn't feel most of it, it shook her out of her thoughts. She'd been straying off the path slightly. Paul was still glancing up at her.

"My face will scare boys away now, Paul."

"Not all of them, I'm sure," Paul said jovially, but she

caught his eye, and he gave her a slight wink.

Staring after him quizzically, she watched as he moved up to join Henry. Surely he hadn't noticed her staring at Kyle's smile earlier?

It was impossible anyway. Kyle was the captain, their survival expert, not to mention she looked too much like his brothers' killer—despite their conversation the night before. Claire became aware of her heart pounding at the thought of Kyle in a more sexual nature, but immediately, her shame returned and dulled it.

Several footsteps later, Kyle fell in step with Claire. Her heartbeat threatened to rise again, and she sincerely hoped the color in her cheeks had disappeared.

She waited for him to speak, not wanting Paul to be right. When he didn't, she stared at the sunlight slipping between the leaves, warming the ground they walked on.

"I can hear the water ahead!" Claire said, immediately forgetting her idea to stay silent. Her excitement mounted at the prospect of more rest.

"The waterfalls here are impressive."

Kyle's voice had a sense of purpose, and she found herself growing fond of his calm relaxation. Claire noticed him picking a thorn out of his finger as they passed through the trees, just as Paul had, and her stomach flipped again. She inspected her own arms as a distraction, and to her surprise, saw tiny pinpricks of thorns embedded there.

"Don't worry, they'll come out easily," Kyle assured her. "Tell me what was so important about your conference."

Surprised, Claire stared at him. "It was just a presentation," she responded slowly. "I don't even care about it anymore."

Kyle raised his eyebrows at her before pushing his sweaty curly hair back from his face. "Sure didn't seem that way when you were so desperate for a ride on my boat."

"Well, I mean it now," Claire said earnestly. "I can't care

anymore. It all seems too far away."

"Well, Sunavae isn't that far away anymore."

Claire shook her head. "It won't matter. It's too late for me. Besides, I thought about what you said. I think that bite gave me a second chance." She swatted a tree branch out of her way, watching it snap back into place as she moved past it. "Nothing like this has ever happened to me. The wild, being in a tropical place, surviving this adventure so far."

Whether it was from her outburst of truth or the constant walking, Claire suddenly felt exhausted, and could tell Paul was tiring up ahead from the way his bare shoulders seemed to curve towards his chest. The moisture in the air increased in intensity as the sounds of rushing water grew stronger. Claire picked at Kyle's shirt, pulling it away from her sweaty body to allow air to pass over her skin.

"It looks good on you." Kyle picked up his pace and moved past her.

"What, your shirt?"

Kyle turned back at her and smiled, gesturing ahead of himself. "No. This adventure."

Following where he pointed, Claire felt her breath catch in her throat. There were long cascading tiers of rocks and water as they rounded the last bend. The further forward she stepped, the more she felt her feet sinking in moist soil between mossy rocks. Even in her dreams, she couldn't have imagined the serene canopy of palm trees or the soft spray of the water in the air. The current wasn't very strong, and white bubbles of all sizes were spraying in the air before falling.

The sand along the bank looked like diamonds at the right angle when bathed under a sunbeam. Never had she seen anything quite so pure and divine.

"Maybe there's something to this Iselle after all," Claire whispered to herself.

"Henry, not too close to the edge," Paul yelled ahead of

them and beckoned his brother to step backwards as he set his cooler down.

"Don't worry, it's not even slippery over here. See?" Henry jumped about just to prove his point, when his foot caught on a nearby rock, sending his whole body off-balance.

"*Henry!*" Paul ran forward, but Henry was already tumbling with gravity towards the edge of the bank. The heavy pack on his back propelled him faster and inhibited his efforts to stop his own movement. Claire brought her hands to her mouth in shock, watching Henry disappear over the edge. Paul grasped his brother's forearm before he, too, fell from view. She bolted forward with Kyle, forgetting about her fatigued muscles.

Claire looked over the edge of the cliff. Mossy plants grew sporadically over the glistening rocks. They were sprayed constantly with water. She felt cool mist on the half of her face she could feel, but Paul and Henry were both laughing hysterically, grabbing the gear that had gone overboard with them in the current while Paul swore loudly to his younger brother and grabbed him in a headlock. They managed to climb up to a nearby ledge, setting their soaked backpacks down.

"So much for dry clothes!" Paul yelled.

Kyle's hand gently took her own. She was startled at the gesture, but more surprised at the current she felt pass between them.

"Let's go on three," Kyle said, smiling at her. Her stomach flipped again as she stared into his deep brown eyes. Claire smiled back and took a deep breath, looking down into the water as he began counting. "One . . . two . . ." Claire braced herself on the edge and gripped his hand, " . . . three!"

They sprang from the ledge and soared into the mist weightlessly. Paul and Henry whooped encouragingly below them. The palms ahead were momentarily closer as Claire gasped and held her breath. The refreshing white bubbles of the waterfall jostled over her body as they slid with the waterfall into the lagoon below.

Claire squinted her eyes in the fading light, lines of concentration furrowing on her brow. Kyle stood beside her, his movements gentle. The water barely moved around them.

"Again," he said, readjusting her grip on the fishing net they'd rigged up with a t-shirt.

Claire gritted her teeth as a fish swam close, then darted away as Henry splashed past.

"Catch us at least a dozen more than I caught, Claire! I'm really hungry tonight."

"What else is new?" Paul hollered from the other side of the bank.

"You do know I haven't caught one yet?" Claire yelled back. Kyle sighed as the fish swam completely out of sight.

"You're just getting warmed up. Good luck!" Henry waved so vigorously he almost fell over again.

Paul gave them a knowing look before following his brother up the stream. Kyle had shown them where to set up camp for the night. The thought of settling down sounded amazing, but Claire couldn't leave, even though her every limb commanded it. At least, not until she'd caught a fish.

"Keep holding still," Kyle whispered, once they were alone again. Claire stood frozen, her stance exactly the way he instructed. Several fish came back. One slowly inspected the net. Claire's curiosity got the better of her and the wooden pole Kyle made slipped slightly from her hands.

Kyle placed his hands over her knuckles and tightened her grip. She saw from the way his sinewed shoulders tensed he was ready to spring to action at a moment's notice, but he slowly let go once her grip was tighter. She envied his concentration and grace. His closeness cast a warm glow over her. "I meant what I said before. You'll only have a second before they swim away."

"I know." All traces of light-heartedness disappeared from Claire as she stood still again, adjusting her shoulders, her brow furrowed in concentration, focused with eagerness at wanting to learn. The strings on her bikini bottoms flowed with the current and ticked her legs. A yellow-finned fish swam toward her.

"Now," he whispered, as it darted towards the edge of the net. "Scoop it up fast, with purpose."

Claire needed no more instruction and brought the net down as quick as she could. It caught the fish near her feet.

"Excellent!" Kyle's exclaimed. Claire could hardly believe it. She lifted the net and stared at the fish, wriggling helplessly, and then looked at Kyle's face. He beamed at her, flashing a proud smile.

"I can't believe I did that! I finally caught one!"

Kyle took the wooden stick from her. "Easy does it, right?"

"You make it look easy. Henry did, too."

"Just takes lots of practice, Claire. That's enough for tonight. We must have at least twenty by now."

"It's almost as if you see it happen before it happens and know when and how to strike," Claire said breathlessly, still shocked she had actually done it.

"All part of the process."

"I've never killed anything before, other than bugs in my office."

"I can tell." Kyle leapt up the ledge and placed the fish next to the others on the rock face. "Like I said, it takes practice." He paused and closed his eyes. "Be thankful. The fruit of the water is a gift."

Claire hoisted herself up after Kyle and sat next to him on the rock. She rinsed her hands in the water, watching Kyle's expression as he worked.

"Are you still reminded of her when you look at me?" she asked quietly. Kyle's face was inches from her own. Surprise showed momentarily on his features before they softened.

"No," he said quietly, after several moment's pause. "You have kindness in your eyes."

As if in slow motion, she leaned closer to Kyle. One of her hands found his neck and gently traced the scar running down it, imagining what it would take to do something so violent to another person. The thought disturbed her as she felt the smooth skin and scar tissue, envisioning the weeks it must have taken him to heal.

Kyle froze and watched her arm move.

Claire's gaze left the scar and turned towards his eyes, and they burned with an intensity that she'd not seen before.

"Kyle—" She stammered before drawing a breath, and quickly put her arm at her side. Fear gripped her as she remembered the last time she was this close to a man, seeing a similar look of intensity in Aiden's eyes. It used to mean only minutes before she was on his desk kissing him. The emptiness that followed their encounters haunted her now— but this felt different. Whatever it was, this was real, and though she could clearly see that Kyle felt the same, it didn't erase her fear.

"Thank you for saving my life," she whispered.

Kyle stared into her eyes without blinking, the intensity replaced with bemused surprise that etched into his dark features. "Did you have to get so close to tell me that?" he responded gently, in an equally quiet tone.

Claire shrugged awkwardly, thinking of nothing suitable to say. Her heart pounded, and her past slipped further away the more she stared into the kind brown eyes before her.

"You're welcome, then," he responded. For the briefest second, she saw him incline his head closer to hers, his gaze searching her face and lingering on her lips. She leaned into him tentatively until she could see the droplets of water hanging off of his eyelashes. Her lips met his to the pounding of her heart. She felt their delicate softness, and he returned her kiss. Kyle traced the cheek she could feel until Paul's boisterous laughter echoed through the trees.

Claire broke away from his lips, but Kyle didn't let go of her face. He pushed back the wet hair from her cheek with a knowing grin. She returned it, slowly, feeling desire form in the pit of her body, deep and purposeful. Tenderness and understanding bore through his eyes and into hers. Nobody had ever looked at her this way before. It was as if he asked, and she accepted — the bond between them was sealed. The beautiful moment hung suspended above and around them. She wondered what it would be like to stay on the island forever with him, completely wiping out the tendrils of all her time and efforts elsewhere, embracing that moment as long as she lived.

CHAPTER EIGHTEEN

Amberly carefully adjusted her long, blonde wig before inspecting her nails. A tiny spot of blood had been overlooked. Scrubbing it clean, she sucked in a shaky breath and held her posture straight. A knock sounded at her cabin door. She grasped the handle and opened the door, clutching the edge of her black dress. Her eyes focused on Svante's figure, dressed up in a black suit and tie.

"You need to rest more, Captain." Svante's voice swam into her ears slowly. "Broken ribs don't heal quickly, and you've had one hell of a day."

Amberly turned to face him. After inhaling a shallow breath, she managed to stand. She slapped his outstretched hand away.

"We have no time," she muttered crossly. "We'll be back here soon enough, and this plan will work. Dev will be at the helm and on the lookout for anyone approaching. Jaquarde's cell phone has been destroyed?"

"Yes, Captain."

"Then we must leave," Amberly commanded, and exited her cabin. Within ten minutes, they skirted through the small crowd of tourists and businesspeople towards the nearest ferry terminal. Cell phones and conversations echoed inside. Amberly brushed past a middle-aged woman, her luxurious perfume smelling of blackcurrant and vanilla. It momentarily overpowered the soothing scent of the sea and made Amberly wrinkle her nose. She scanned the crowd for Gann, but she stopped once her eyes settled on a nearby notice board. She frowned at the familiar poster in front of her.

Emere's sketch stared back at her, mocking her. A sudden anger rose up inside her as the memory of Emere's betrayal returned, until she saw another notice pinned next to her own.

Tourist Missing. She recognized the same photo that Jaquarde had possessed. Blown up to a larger size, she could see the similarities, yet they were distorted by a different personality. A tentative smile, bright eyes, and the uncomfortable way the woman's shoulders tightened jumped out at Amberly the most. Svante causally tore them both down and stuffed them into his pocket.

Amberly turned on her heel and recognized Gann at once.

He was seated alone on one of the many wooden benches, still looking sweaty and anxious. His grey hair glinted under the terminal lights.

"Richard Gann?" she said loudly. Turning, he surveyed her in great surprise, and after several moments, he let out a nervous laugh. Amberly extended her hand, and he took it.

"My *God*," he drawled. His American accent was as atrocious as she imagined — drawn-out words with an obnoxious emphasis on vowels. Furtively he glanced around at expectant passengers, chatting pleasantly with each other, commenting on the setting sun or pointing out distant islands. "Jaquarde told me you were dead! He's coming . . . isn't he?"

Smiling sinisterly, she clasped his hand tightly and used it to draw herself next to him on the bench. Inspecting his shock was her favorite part of his reaction, for the rest of him was pathetic. He smelled of fine cologne, had a perfectly shaven face, slicked back silver hair, and a spineless body covered in an expensive suit — typical of the entitlements of his kind. Her fingers itched on the hidden hilt of her knife.

"Jaquarde preferred to send me as a surprise," Amberly stated, her face impassive. "I was never dead, just waiting for the perfect time to return. I'm the best one to find my sister, don't you agree? I'm sure you've seen the notices out for me. I can handle a scared city girl."

"Yes." Gann placed his fidgeting hands in his pockets. "He did tell me that the twin was an assassin. Though I don't quite believe it yet. If you're anything like Claire, I imagine you squealing at a bug."

Amberly maintained her composure with difficulty. The desire to place her long fingers around the clean shaved throat and choke him until he turned purple and confessed all else he knew was so overpowering that she had to clear her throat loudly and briefly glance around. A businesswoman rifled through papers in a black leather portfolio on the bench nearest them. A call came over the speakers for ferries going back to various ports of Nusa Via within five minutes. When it finished, she slid further next to Gann. "So. You found her?"

"More or less. One of my employees already notified the local authorities that she was missing. I couldn't stop them."

"What did you do wrong?"

"Nothing," Gann snapped. "I don't need any more heat on this. It was your colleagues that missed her. I canceled her reservation on the charter boat and discontinued her credit cards, too, just in case she tried to get a ride somewhere. Jaquarde said there are less police on Nusa Via, even with the tourists. He told me it was better to kidnap her there. It's not my fault she managed to get on some charter boat with cash."

"A charter boat? How can you be sure?" Amberly leaned in, her face inches from Gann's.

"I had one of my employees check the records at the port, and only one ship is unaccounted for during that timeframe. The *Emmy Fioni*. The boat seems to have vanished, and was scheduled to come to Sunavae. It never arrived." Gann checked his watch and started to get up.

Amberly pushed him back into his seat. "We aren't done, Richard. I want to know why a man like you would risk kidnapping his own employee? Tell me, really, what has Jaquarde promised you?"

Sweat pooled on Gann's forehead. He tried to get up again, but Amberly held him in place. Her firm grip caused him to twitch uneasily.

"Fine. Jaquarde's followed Claire for years, trying to figure out a way to get her back to the White Sand Islands. It must have been one of his men that sent me your wanted notice, then his men hacked my personal records. He found out I'd stolen over a million dollars from my company and started blackmailing me, threatening to expose me if I didn't have my conference here and bring her with. It would have been the end of Gann, Inc., and I'd go to jail . . . I had no choice . . ." Gann trailed off, briefly rubbing his temples with his fingers.

"I'll bet Jaquarde didn't tell you he was the one who donated all that money for the reward, and that he was planning to kill you." Amberly forcefully turned his face towards her and let her lips part in a wide grin. "It may also interest you to know that Jaquarde is dead. Do you expect me to turn in my sister now?"

Gann looked towards the corner of the room. His new-found perspiration only seemed to worsen his twitching. "I don't think you can do much," he managed, an edge to his voice.

"How unfortunate for you." Amberly gritted her teeth before continuing, "As you will learn, I'm not nice when I'm angry and wounded. Especially when I find out that I have someone else to call my own, better than that pig of a man who used me my whole life."

"I don't care about your petty problems," Gann whispered, his tone dripping with condescension. "I've already contacted the authorities. They're here in this room. I thought I'd be taking down Jaquarde, but this is even better. I'll look like a hero for catching such an infamous criminal. If Jaquarde is dead, then I'll definitely get that money, and I can put everything back into Gann, Inc., and no one will ever even know. My hands will be washed clean, I'll get so much good press for this, and all will mourn for my missing employee, lost at sea."

Amberly leaned forward, having heard enough. She draped her leg across Gann's lap seductively to keep him in place. Wrapping her arm around his neck, she pressed her hand into his windpipe, hidden under her hand. Her other hand signaled Svante with a stroke on Gann's face. As she imagined, Gann squirmed under her, but Svante quickly meandered to his other side and restrained him casually.

The passerby's paid them no heed. "You're doing well." Amberly tossed her hair to cover up her knife. "That tight grip you've got on my arm makes our little show all the more convincing. I don't care if you called the police." She kissed his cheek gently and breathed in his ear. "If you call out for help or try to escape, I will slit your throat."

Gann coughed erratically, then promptly passed out. The second and last call for those on the ferry to Nusa Via for the night rang over the loudspeaker, prompting the rest of the lounge to slowly empty.

Amberly scanned the room and saw a man amidst the tourists clad in dark jeans and a black shirt, muttering to himself and walking towards them briskly. His eyes bore into hers, and she spotted the concealed gun at his side.

"Move," Amberly said. They hastened towards the door, Gann balanced precariously between them. His shoes skidded across the floor. Svante kept his stance upright and dignified while carrying the majority of the weight. Tourists stared openly at Gann's drooped head and slouched shoulders.

Gann's man was closing the distance between them.

"Run," she snapped at Svante. His strong arms lifted Gann over his shoulder. They cleared the door with haste. A crowd had gathered to watch the sunset on the boulevard above, and Amberly felt their heads turn as they ran past. A flurry of concerned whispers swept through the tourists like wildfire, but they didn't know who she was. That much she was certain of. There was no recognition in their eyes, nor the pointing that would have happened last year if she'd dared show her face in port after murdering those brothers. A flash of the official White Sands light green uniform blurred through her left eye.

"You, miss! Stop! Turn around now!" the officer shouted. Her hand was on the hilt of her knife in seconds. She saw her yacht in sight before she whipped around, brandishing her knife. It divided the light green uniform easily, tearing flesh with it. The man looked at his bloody chest and started yelling for backup.

"Do not stop!" Amberly hollered at Svante. Tourists sprang out of her way as she half hobbled, half ran along the crowded docks.

Gann's arms bounced awkwardly against Svante's back as he ran. The police wove their way into the crowd, running after them. The wooden planks of the dock shook under her feet. She ignored the pain in her side and controlled a need to desperately gasp for air. *The Duchess* was just around the corner. The nearest officer was less than two steps behind, a gun in her hand. Amberly ran faster, paying dearly for each step.

Amberly pushed into a group of passing tourists, ensuring the most elderly fell into the water. The bow of the Duchess was in full view now. Faintly she heard the engine of her yacht roar to life and the scream of tourists behind her, and knew the officer would have no choice but to save the lives of the people in the water. Amberly drew in a gasp for air.

Svante had already dumped Gann and was coming back for her. With little effort, he picked her up and walked her across the gangway before kicking it out of the way.

"They see *The Duchess*," she spat angrily, grappling with

proper speech from the discomfort of her broken ribs. "Go Dev, now!" she shouted. She nearly fell to the floor as the Duchess lurched forward. It took all her effort to keep from passing out from the pain. Gann was on the floor in a heap, his fine grey suit crumpling elegantly around him. Amberly exhaled and let the pain cross her face as Svante cut the ropes securing them to the harbor.

Amberly climbed painfully into the helm, Svante at her heels.

"See to Gann," she managed to say. Ignoring the *slow* buoys on the water, she backed away from the dock with a roar of the engine and steered out of the narrow channel. The ocean sped under them at full throttle, dousing the docks and causing passing smaller craft to bounce in the heavy current. Without turning to look at him, Amberly extended her hand toward Svante.

"Give me the notices," she commanded. Paper unfolded behind her until Svante placed them in her hands. With one hand on the wheel, she held the two notices in the air, steering past a sailboat.

"Last seen on Nusa Via," Amberly read in a low voice as she glanced at the black and white photocopy of her sister. The paper crinkled in her grip, and she slapped it against the surface of her console. Snapping her attention back to the horizon, she pulled her wig off with her free hand. Cascading waves of her auburn hair fell down her back as Sunavae become a distant shore behind them, the azure coast nothing but a strip of land dotted with hotels and seemingly endless docks.

"There are seven islands between Nusa Via and Sunavae," Amberly muttered to herself. "My sister could be on any one of them, if she's alive."

"You want to start looking tonight, Captain?" Svante asked.

Amberly gripped her wheel and breathed heavily. "No. Night's falling, and darkness will give us time and cover from the police. Tonight, we'll take cover in the coves off Ildetache. Tomorrow, we search. At daybreak."

CHAPTER NINETEEN

Claire heard the waterfall splashing on distant rocks before she opened her eyes. Faint stars were scattered across the sky like satin dust. Stretching, she discovered that she'd rolled off of her palm fronds and into the sand, the towel once under her head abandoned a foot away. The small fire from the night before had not even the slightest trace of smoke unfurling from its ashes.

The peace she felt, the tranquility upon waking, even the gentle lapping of the waves on the rocks would be things she would miss when they left . . . if they ever left.

With a pang, she realized her returning flight back home was supposed to be this afternoon. She twirled particles of sand beneath her fingers absentmindedly. Her gaze rested on the dirt under her chipped nails, once meticulously manicured, and suddenly reminding her of the life she left behind. Simply considering the possibility of going back to her grey cubicle made her twist uncomfortably in the sand, especially when she recalled the way she often waited for Jackson to walk by.

Why had she never asked him out? He wasn't Mr. Hartman, nor was he bound to be married. If she squeezed her eyes tightly enough, she could recall his square-rimmed glasses, the scent of his aftershave, the stoic mannerisms. A pang of abhorrence erupted in the pit of her stomach, not unlike when Paul had teased her the day before. It had always been exciting to imagine engaging in some secret office romance with him. Now it all seemed so empty, like everything else back home. Before long, his image was lost, and without thinking, she ran a hand along her cheek she couldn't feel.

She looked at the three boys, completely lost to sleep. Kyle's chest rose and fell, his knife at his side and inches away from his hand. The seriousness in his eyes the night before burned her mind. Her stomach flipped right on cue, and she just expected it now. Never before had anybody studied her with such a deep fervor like he had, nor had she felt such a combination of tranquility and yearning when looking back.

The stars faded completely during the progression of her thoughts. The color of the sky and the slight shadow of the trees suggested the sun would be up soon. She moved closer to Kyle and stared at the way his arm lay draped over his stomach, the other behind his head. His faded blue shirt was streaked with sweat from the night, and his hair was submerged in the sand behind him in sleep-induced angles.

Her breath caught in her throat as she studied his face, realizing the feelings she wanted to explore with him. What would it feel like to touch him? To hold him, to hear his heartbeat on his sleeping chest? She felt the memory of his lips on hers, this time accompanied by a twinge of desire in the pit of her midsection. A flush crept on her cheeks until a loud snore from Paul snapped her back to reality. Careful not to disturb more than the grains of sand she stood on, her feet edged their way out of their small camp.

Claire combed through the leafy vegetation until she was several yards from the spot where they had gone swimming the day before. The waterfall was gentler now, cascading groggily down the cliffs. There wasn't a whisper of an animal, or even the lyrical chirping of the small birds. She marveled at how fulfilled she felt, simply standing in the quiet. Sticks and small palm fronds tickled her feet as she stepped onto the dark rocks, not yet warmed by the sun.

Claire peeled her shirt off and let it fall by her feet. The rock felt cold as she sat, even through the bottom of her swimsuit. She ran a hand over her face while dipping her feet in the water until her ankles were submerged. It was cool, but not unpleasant. Three orange and black striped fish swayed near her feet, their fins fluttering in the current. She eased herself to standing in the water and let her feet sink slightly into the sand. The fish scattered in different directions, and she followed them.

The water felt exhilarating, but her suit clung awkwardly as she tried to run after them. Claire looked around sheepishly, then peeled off her bikini top and bottoms and tossed them onto the shore.

The water on her skin was even better than she imagined. Claire moved slowly and smiled with curiosity at the fish's path until she was almost waist-deep in water. The current from the nearby falls swirled around her. She shivered slightly but marveled at the alertness the water gave her senses. Bubbles swept past her, and she lost sight of the fish completely, as well as her ability to see her own feet. She let her knees give way and submerged her head and arms into the water.

Her heartbeat quickened as water touched every part of her. Never before had she felt so refreshed, as if the current itself was washing away the thoughts that she knew had been holding her back. Forcing herself to stay under a few seconds longer, she touched the soft sand with her fingers and knees before resurfacing. Taking a breath, she flipped herself over, and floated lazily on her back. The greenery around her was the perfect frame for the blue sky. The rising sun chased the jungle's shadows away. Claire allowed the current to gently take her several yards away until she noticed a figure among the trees. Water splashed into her eyes and mouth as she sputtered to get up.

Kyle stood near the rock she'd left moments ago, one hand

leaning casually against a tree and the other loose at his side. Instinctively Claire looked where she'd left her clothes. She remained underwater as her knees found the sandy bottom again, which she used to slowly creep forward. He regarded her with a bemused smile and a slight wave, kneeling. The curiosity from their moment alone the day before had returned to his eyes.

"I couldn't sleep anymore," she confessed truthfully, stopping several feet before him. "I haven't been able to stop thinking about last night."

"Me neither," he said, stripping off his shirt with ease.

Claire's heart beat faster as he tossed his shorts onto the rock beside her suit. With a growing blush, she stared at his body in the brief moment she had to do so before Kyle jumped in the water. A sudden fit of recklessness seized her, strongly familiar, yet profoundly different. She wanted to touch him, to kiss him, to have him fill her — but echoes of dark memories made her pause.

Claire dunked her head under the water to clear it. This was not the same as before. She was not the same. She resurfaced and watched as Kyle's bronze body streaked towards her underwater. Her heart fluttered in preparatory beats.

Kyle drew closer and resurfaced, wiping water out of his eyes. He, too, stayed on his knees and watched Claire with a focus and affection she knew was in her own eyes.

Claire opened her mouth to speak, but no words came out. Her breathing was noticably deeper. She clenched her fists with nerves and the fear of the genuine emotion growing in her heart.

Kyle drew closer to her and enveloped her against his body.

A warmth came over Claire.

"Whatever you want to do," he replied quietly, meeting her longing gaze.

"Are Paul and Henry still sleeping?" Claire whispered, squeezing his hand.

"Yes." Kyle traced his other hand on her side with a warm tenderness. She breathed a small sigh of relief.

She splayed her hands across his chest, the slender fingers curling around damp hairs. She knew how hard he was underneath the water, but he was calm and composed. A sacred understating passed between them as they stared at each other, equally vulnerable. When Claire's fingers traced the soft scar where Amberly's incision had healed, Kyle caught her wrist.

Her breath came quickly as she gave an impish smile that felt so unlike her. Her aching body flared to life below the surface with an insistent longing. She wanted him. A slight breeze played over the water, barely audible above her heart pulsating in her ears.

"Whatever I want?" she asked.

He nodded, watching her carefully.

"I don't think I've ever been surer of anything." The truth of her words rang in the air like a confession. There was freedom in the safety of his strong arms. Claire pulled back and stared at him, tracing his cheek. Her breath came out slowly and calmly. Kyle waited patiently, watching her think.

"We have no protection," she whispered.

"I'll pull out, I promise," he whispered back.

She nodded. The thought of Kyle, with no barrier between them, was intoxicating. Without her consent, the thought of Aiden briefly putting a condom on appeared in her mind as clearly as if someone had put a film in front of her face. She closed her eyes and frowned. It wasn't until this moment that the thought of Aiden and her past finally felt like a different lifetime, a different Claire. With a sudden sense of relief, she realized that she'd let go of him a long time ago. She welcomed the thought and breathed into it. How could she forget his disrespect, lies, the cold use of her body, and his abuse of power? There was simply nothing there that was healthy. It wasn't real.

But this time was different. This time would be real. Claire sighed, and the frenzied thoughts quieted. Slowly she looked deeply into Kyle's eyes, knowing that as soon as she did, there would be a point of no return.

Closing the heated distance between them, she kissed his lips, tugging at the pillowy softness. She traced the strong out-line of his jaw, the growing whiskers tickling her fingertips. One of his hands left her back and began following her leg, which she draped around his waist eagerly. He ran his hand along her inner thigh until he reached her aching core, tracing her most sensitive skin.

She gripped Kyle's shoulders. His touch was more than she could have imagined it to be. Sand and tiny rocks dug into her knees as she pushed further into him. Claire dropped her head back and breathed deeply. The last thing she saw before closing her eyes was the golden sunrays drenching the green canopy above them.

Her hips thrusted forward, trusting him. He met her with equal strength and surged deep within until he filled her. One hand took her waist with longing before sliding down her lower back. His other hand rested behind her neck, fingers gently entwined into her hair and held her. She rocked against his careful movements slowly, until the pure ecstasy of his en-trance passed and she was able to meet him with a ferocity of her own.

The waterfall hit the rocks near them, but Claire barely heard it. Water glided effortlessly around her, as uninhibited as she felt. She marveled at every touch she gave and re-ceived. The feeling was almost more than she could handle. The force of their movement caused her chest to rise out of the lagoon, completely exposed. Kyle's hand glided over her breasts. She moaned with pleasure. She felt more alive and beautiful than she ever had in her entire life, almost as if she were in a dream. Water flowed down her hips as she rose higher, enjoying each of his fingers searing across her skin. His mouth was at her nipple, and she gasped so loudly he looked up at her.

"This feels amazing," she managed to heave, forcing her head to meet the gaze of his kind brown eyes. He nodded and smiled, watching her enjoy herself with pure devotion, and it warmed her soul.

"You're amazing," he murmured emphatically. His mouth crushed into hers. She met his force equally, winding her hands into his hair. Tendrils of pleasure forced their way between her legs.

She cried out slightly, feeling her body erupt with euphoria. She pressed her face into his chest, inhaling him, listening to his heart beat wildly as he continued to enjoy her. Claire grasped his shoulder tightly before sneaking her other hand under her leg until she felt the tender space between Kyle's legs, stimulating the soft skin with her slender fingers. Kyle moaned at her touch and grasped her butt firmly into himself, over and over, while her fingers gently quested and pressed his delicate skin.

Kyle pulled out and finished with a blissful release in the water. Claire closed her eyes as Kyle's warm hands encircled her back and held her. He was gasping as much as she was. Their chests, pressed against each other, rose and fell in unison. Time and space no longer felt real to Claire. Not when she felt like this, in the deepest peace.

Chapter Twenty

Amberly gulped the last of her whiskey straight. She slammed the bottle down and looked through her windshield, setting the wipers to remove the early morning sea spray. "Update me."

Dev cleared his throat slightly. "As requested, the businessman is in a separate room. The whore is alive but still unconscious. When ready, I'll throw the businessman down in the hold between Emere and your other guest."

"It's exactly how they deserve to spend their last moments," Amberly replied. "We'll keep searching for my sister when I'm done with Emere. Dismissed."

"Yes, Captain." Dev slipped out of the wheelhouse. Amberly waited until his footsteps subsided, then followed.

A wave threw sea spray near her feet as she hobbled along the deck. She collapsed slightly into the railing and held her injured side, grimacing as the water rejoined the ocean just below. The view of Ildetache's coast was evident even from her vantage point. A fresh wave of pain shot through her as she stood. She wished she could walk on the beach like she used to, white sand sticking between her toes. Would she ever again move with ease? The memory of Jaquarde's weight crushing her helplessly taunted her. The lack of sleep and persistent pain did her no favors either. But her path was clear — that much was certain. She flung one of the lower cabin doors open with renewed determination.

The room was dim with the curtains drawn. Svante was already inside, waiting. His presence pleased her and proved a welcome distraction from the persistent throbbing in her side until she heard the pleading noises.

Emere was finally awake and bound at her ankles and wrists. As Amberly had instructed, Tom's body was propped up against the wall next to Emere. His body was bloated, and his face was blackened with unhealed injuries. She hadn't seen him since she'd brought him onboard. Sticks from the forest still clung to his dirty head. The smell was unearthly and reeked of death. His clothes had absorbed much of his blood, but barely fit his swollen body.

"Please, Amberly," Emere sobbed.

Amberly didn't meet Emere's gaze nor acknowledge the woman's fidgeting body. She unsheathed her knife and carefully ran her tongue over the blade's edge, savoring the cold taste of steel while staring casually down at the proceedings.

Svante moved behind Amberly. She heard his long inhale and with a deep breath of her own, smelled his fresh cigarette. Amberly knelt down next to Emere and finally faced her.

The body she once knew every inch of was as unfamiliar as her new feelings of bitter emptiness.

"Why did you betray me?" Amberly whispered, pointing her knife at the palm of Emere's hand.

"He wanted you to come back." Emere's voice was rushed and frightened, her accent betraying her roots in the southernmost chain of the White Sand Isles. The musical undertone caused Amberly's heart to skip a beat, but the distraction only angered her.

"He already told me that." Amberly forced the knife into the woman's palm, causing Emere's eyes to tear up with pain. Amberly slowed the progress of her knife and inhaled deeply at the scent of fresh blood.

"Please, you know how powerful he always was." Emere cried and choked on her words.

Amberly's hand moved so quickly it was a blur, even to

her. The slap caused Emere's face to crash into Tom's out of sheer force. Emere whimpered as her lip began to swell.

"I'll bet that hurt, don't you think, Tom?" Amberly gestured at the body propped up next to Emere. "Let me introduce you, Emere. This one tried to save me. He didn't realize that drunk rapists are nothing but a warm-up act after Jaquarde's jobs."

"I didn't want to betray you," Emere cried.

Amberly grabbed the woman's hand and cut deeper this time, gouging under the skin to fresh screams. Blood pooled out of Emere's hand and onto the floor. A memory floated to her exhausted mind unwittingly, the time when she accidently spilled red paint onto one of Emere's canvases years ago in their tiny apartment.

"I didn't mean to do that." Amberly hastened to stop the paint, but it was too late. By the time she grabbed the bottle and righted it, Emere's canvas was half covered in a rusty glow.

"I hated that sketch anyway." Emere edged her body over to sit next to Amberly on the floor. She tossed her sleek hair back. "You still haven't answered my question, you know. How did it go last night when you found that snitch? Was Jaquarde pleased that you killed him?"

Amberly wiped the paint off her hands. "He's happy as long as he doesn't have to do it. I'm happy because I don't have to do him."

The blood ran warm over Amberly's hands. She placed the knife above Emere's dominant hand and held it right over the center. Amberly's hand shook, but the memories won as she stared into Emere's eyes once more.

"I'm glad you can stay for a few days." Emere rested her head on one of Amberly's shoulders, taking one of her hands into her own. "I thought of you when Jaquarde was here last night. It helps me stay sane. He comes more often now."

Amberly leaned into Emere's head and gently traced the fresh bruise on her arm. "It's only a matter of time before he gets suspicious."

Svante stomped loudly on his cigarette, bringing Amberly's focus back to her knife.

"Why?" she breathed menacingly.

Emere shuddered. Her voice struggled to form words without cracking. "Jaquarde was so angry when you didn't come back. Then the whole island knew the story of the man who came to the hotel with the police, the one you tried to kill with his brothers. He was trying to find out more about who sold his brother the boat. He was willing to do almost anything for justice."

Amberly's hand gripped her knife. She heard Svante growl angrily in his throat behind her.

"So who prompted the wanted notice then?" Amberly leaned into Emere. "Jaquarde? You? Or the surviving brother?"

Emere hiccupped slightly. "Jaquarde pushed for the notice when the surviving brother came to the police. He wanted to help, as usual, keep his contacts where he needed them. Kyle was the surviving brother's name. He was found on Ildetache, but I swear it's all I know about him."

"All you know?" Amberly laughed humorlessly. "With your assistance, my face was plastered across every port from here to the Americas. I can't even get a drink without a disguise, much less pull off a job. Did you really think I'd forgive you for that?"

"I'm telling you, Jaquarde put me up to it, not Kyle." Emere's expression worsened with each word she spoke. "He was going to kill me, and almost did when he . . . guessed our plans to leave." Emere's voice was so low that Amberly could barely hear her.

"Traitor," Amberly said. "You destroyed our one chance at

happiness."

The other woman seemed to shrink into the wall, and Amberly felt her body shake with anger as Emere continued. "I swear, Jaquarde already knew our plans. It was probably one of the Istura girls trying to do good by Jaquarde. He said if I told him everything, he'd let you live. If I didn't, he'd kill us both. I had to tell him what your plans were. I was never as strong as you, defying him."

Amberly felt her stomach clench. Her ribs followed suit, but she tightened her abdomen quickly to keep the pain from spreading to her face. She stared momentarily at the purple bruise swelling on Emere's lip.

"Please say goodbye before you leave." Emere tucked a long strand of Amberly's hair behind her ears.

Amberly gathered Emere in a tight embrace, inhaling her flowery scent. "Remember that move I taught you when he tries to hit you again. If he's drunk, it should knock him out faster. Do not hesitate, and do not throw yourself into it like you did when we were practicing, or you'll lose your balance. Keep a strong stance."

"I'll do my best." Emere wrung her hands nervously. "He's coming back tonight, again. He's obsessed with me."

"Just remember the deal for my boat when he comes back," Amberly implored. "I can't believe Jaquarde still thinks that I'm going to use it for his business."

"I'm scared." Emere's eyes suddenly filled with tears. "After Lily and Mereoni tried to leave . . ."

"Stop." Amberly gripped the other woman's strong shoulders and stared with such intensity that Emere immediately quieted. "Stop thinking of their failure. If anything, we learned what not to do, and we can honor their deaths by doing it right. We have to leave this life. The more lives I take, the more like him I become. If I don't leave now, I'll never be able to stop." She leaned in and gave Emere a hug and didn't let go for several minutes.

"I will be back for you. I promise."

Emere's eyes drowned with emotions. Fresh tears trickled unabashedly down the woman's exhausted, broken face. Amberly stared at them. She couldn't forgive anymore. She traced the knife down Emere's cheek, pausing to pick up a single tear with the tip of her blade. Amberly licked it slowly off of her knife before picking up Emere's bloody hands, the dark skin now gouged deeply with knife wounds as blood dripped silently from them.

"I believe you when you say Jaquarde put you up to it," Amberly said quietly. "If Jaquarde already knew we were planning to escape on that boat, why sell it to stop me?"

Emere breathed deeply, steadying herself from pain. "He took your boat and sold it to one of his former employees to make you mad. He wanted you to go after it. The guy knew something, and Jaquarde wanted him gone. It was a job, but also revenge for your disobedience and plans to run. He also knew Svante was still alive, through some contact." Emere's eyes glistened with a new wave of unshed tears. "Then you left, and never came back."

"Svante always held his tongue and kept his head down, out of trouble," Amberly whispered. She ran the tip of her knife over Emere's index finger. "Maybe after I hit the bone, I'll find the strong, beautiful woman who was also always on my side." She paused for several moments, and waited while running her knife further along Emere's nail, tracing patterns, before settling on her palm.

Emere let out a bloodcurdling scream. Fresh, warm blood stained her jean-shorts and trickled towards the floor before she vomited.

Amberly pursed her lips.

"That will only make the smell worse."

Emere shook violently and seemed to be steeling herself to not vomit again. Amberly moved to sit in between Emere and

183

Tom.

"We really aren't that different, you and I," Amberly murmured, resting her head onto Emere's shoulder, feeling the other women tense at the contact. She picked up Emere's nearest hand again, flicking useless tendons out of the way and tracing what was left of the palm she'd gutted with her knife and observed the bile dripping from it. "We were both drawn to Jaquarde from the beginning. We trusted him. He had a way of making us feel safe."

Emere said nothing, her eyes focused ahead.

"Just kill her, Amberly!" Svante roared, moving towards the captain but halted as Amberly pointed her bloody knife towards him. Never before had she seen such passion behind his eyes, or such a protective stance as she let the moment suspend between them. An understanding smile curled on Amberly's lips.

"I'm glad I chose you, Svante," she said. "I always knew how smart you were, but I didn't think you were capable of such jealously."

Svante flushed slightly as he stared into Amberly's face. "If you can't bring yourself to do it, then I'll finish her." Svante took out his gun and pressed the barrel to the side of Emere's temple.

"She's mine, Svante," Amberly said, standing. Svante eyed the tip of her knife warily, blood dripping from the blade to the floor. He lowered the gun.

Emere's breath came out in shallow spurts as Amberly leaned back down into the other woman's face, sheathed her knife, and whispered into Emere's ear.

"Until next time."

Amberly shook her head to clear the venomous attitude coursing through her, but it showed no signs of retreating as she sat back in her captain's chair. Turning on the engine, she shifted her boat out of the sunbeams and back into the shadows. Ildetache's deadly caves sheltered them perfectly. Dev was busy below, bringing a shaking Richard Gann into the room with Emere and Tom while Svante listened to the radio with her intently, waiting amongst static for law enforcement to give an update on the chase.

Svante turned up the radio slightly, but only din voices cracked. "The frequency is out of range, Captain. Luckily still no choppers down here."

"Just as well." Amberly adjusted the wheel slowly through the black rock. Small whitecaps folded into the azure waters as she slowed her yacht and shut the engine off.

"Ildetache." Svante bowed his head and closed his eyes. "Personally blessed by Iselle."

"Iselle will have answers for us." Amberly bowed her head quickly, not taking her focus off the horizon. "We'll stay towards this cove, have the bow facing the sea, in case we need to exit." Amberly pointed with difficulty, but the whiskey's effects still helped her from fully feeling her pain. "It'll be enough cover, and I'll see anyone approaching."

"Shall I drop anchor and prepare the raft, Captain?" Svante asked.

Amberly stood and walked out of the captain's quarters, Svante at her heels. She inhaled the fresh spray of the ocean and peered over the side of the railing, nodding.

"Yes, drop anchor." She pointed her finger at his chest, her drink dulling the edge of her voice. "Go to shore with Dev, just to ensure no one's around."

Amberly walked back into the helm and eased herself back into the captain's chair. She picked up the folder full of Jaquarde's papers. Carefully, she turned over the topmost one with her long fingers. She stared at the photo of her sister. Her lips had a tint of gloss reflecting the camera flash, something she hadn't noticed before.

"Who are you, Claire?" she murmured. "And what have you done with your life?"

Amberly heard a splash and knew the rowboat had hit the waves. Looking up for the briefest of moments, she saw no signs of any boats on their way, and the sailboats they'd passed earlier had all gone back to Sunavae. She turned back to the paper.

Gann, Inc. is proud to welcome Claire Vaughn to its team of talented web designers. Claire recently finished her undergraduate work in computer science, programming, and graphic design at Delacroix University. Claire is responsible for our middle-tier clients and is bringing the latest innovations in the industry to Gann, Inc. In her spare time, she enjoys reading and one day plans to travel the world.

Amberly carefully drew a breath and became aware of her quickening heartbeat and inability to focus. Her mind buzzed with the life she imagined her sister had, one of opportunities and support, the freedom to choose who to love, and who to work for. Svante's strong figure appeared on the rocky beach beyond the coves ahead. She stared at him absentmindedly before setting Claire's biography down.

The next items were fuzzy, pixelated photos of two people that were, according to the notes scribbled on the back in Jaquarde's scrawled writing, Claire's last foster family before she became independent at eighteen. Amberly squinted at the last few sentences.

Claire Vaughn attacked a fellow student over an altercation regarding an affair with a teacher. Resulted in suspension. Pending adoption was canceled.

She had barely finished before the photos fell from her hands unwillingly. This time the pain shook her entire frame, causing her to sit further back into her chair and close her eyes.

It was perfect. If the notes were correct, she was exactly the type Jaquarde wanted, in addition to being her sister. Alone in the world. Capable, and strong. *Maybe stronger than me,* Amberly thought as she pulled out a miniature bottle of whiskey. She eased the contents of the entire bottle to the back of her throat in two swift gulps and willed the golden elixir down.

Her sister had managed to make a new life for herself. A jealously quite different than she'd ever felt coursed through her.

"I will find you, Claire," she whispered to the empty bottle. The logo of the local whiskey distillery had smudged in her sweaty fingers' grip, but she could still make out the deadly green snake that wound its way around the wrapper. The diamond scales seemed to jump out at her as future plans formed and scattered in her mind.

"No point in planning yet," she said to herself. With difficulty, she got out of her chair and met Dev and Svante at the stern. Her senses felt sharper. She stood upright and gripped the railing of her yacht. Peering down, she watched as Dev helped Svante climbed the small ladder to join her on the deck.

"Someone was here!" Svante called, hoisting himself over the railing. He pulled a black rock out of his bag and threw it at Amberly. She caught it and ran her fingers over it until it crumbled to dust in her hand, leaving charcoal streaks.

"Ash," she said through gritted teeth. Her gaze wandered aimlessly into the palm trees beyond the deck railing. "Could be tourists, or the Feulia whiskey smugglers."

"I don't think so, Captain," Dev said confidently. Amberly raised her eyebrows and fingered the hilt of her knife. Svante gripped the handle of a waterlogged black bag. It looked identical to the many she'd seen businessmen and women carrying on Sunavae, despite being streaked with sand and ripped in several places. Water dripped out of it as her fingers opened the clasp. It was empty.

"These have human marks." Svante reached into his bag and handed a coconut to Amberly. Teeth and nails had scraped the fruit bare. "Clearly, they have an ax of some sort, the way the discarded ones were opened. That's not all. I think they went into the island. No sign of them. These coconuts are a day or two old. And we found this."

Amberly opened her mouth but her words died in her throat as Dev handed her a white waterproof tag with writing that was unable to smudge against the saltwater. Brushing sand off of it, she stared at the graceful handwriting incredulously.

Claire Vaughn
Gann, Incorporated
8358 Huron Avenue,
St. Paul, MN 51504

CHAPTER TWENTY-ONE

Kyle took a bite of mahi mahi fish. The stuffed flesh teemed with flavors of earth tones and flaked perfectly with every bite. The group was equally savoring their meal. It was the heartiest they'd eaten since arriving.

Next to him, Claire bit into a piece of fruit hungrily and adjusted her pink bikini top. Kyle stared at the clumsy bow on the back of her swimsuit, remembering how he'd helped tie it for her. Sunlight glinted through her short auburn hair. Her cheeks were still glowing from his touch that morning. Claire caught him staring and gave him a quick smile, which he returned.

"Delicious." Paul brushed his hands together. "Five stars, Captain."

Kyle nodded in thanks. "I had help," he said, and winked at Claire. She blushed slightly.

"I'm going to jump back in the lagoon before we go, is that okay?" Henry asked.

"I'll come with you." Paul stood and stretched. "What should we do with the fish skins here?"

"Toss them over in the trees beyond that clearing." Kyle pointed across the lagoon. "You'll have to cross by water. There are loncue trees that way with some snakes, so be careful."

Claire stiffened in mid-bite. Kyle placed a hand on her shoulder, one of familiarity, and felt her muscles ease.

"Noted," Paul said cheerfully. He picked up as many skins and discarded innards as he could. "Come on, Henry, you don't expect me to do this all by myself, do you?"

"I'll put them in a palm frond." Henry hastened to find one nearest and scooped up what he could. Paul started to walk towards the water's edge.

"Wait up!" Henry called to Paul, precariously balancing his frond.

Kyle turned back to Claire as their voices disappeared. When he looked at her now, he saw a beautiful woman with the grit of Iselle herself. She was far from the frightened tourist of only a few days ago. He wanted to tell her that, but the words stuck in his throat.

"It's a beautiful day, isn't it," he said lamely. He almost groaned, but was cut short by Claire's knowing laugh.

"Very beautiful." She placed a hand on his knee and rubbed it affectionately. "I can't stop thinking about this morning,"

"Neither can I." Kyle relaxed and looked her in the eyes. "It was . . . amazing. I can't believe we did it right there in the lagoon."

"I also can't believe we didn't get caught. Maybe a miracle from your Iselle?"

"I'd like to think so," Kyle replied. He'd hoped to see one of her radiant smiles, but she was looking down at her hands, those beautiful hands that gave him so much pleasure that morning. Now, however, they twisted in the sand absent-mindedly.

"You okay?" he inquired quizzically.

She nodded, but didn't look up.

"I need to tell you something, now that we're alone," she began slowly. "It's about my past. You may not like me afterwards, but I need to tell you."

"Okay." Kyle rubbed her arm reassuringly. "You can tell me anything, Claire, I'm sure it won't change how I feel about you."

Claire took a deep breath. "I didn't think it was possible for me to feel the way I do right now." She paused. Her hands shook, almost violently. Kyle eased himself next to her and took her trembling hands into his encouragingly.

"Go on," Kyle said.

"The Claire you know was an orphan, spent her whole life bouncing around foster families. I was going to be adopted, finally in high school. I was happy because I still wanted a family to call my own, even though I was almost eighteen. Things seemed okay, well, as okay as they could be for a teenage girl. Then I met him." Claire sighed. "Aiden Hartman, my Life Science teacher. He was six-foot-two with a chiseled jaw, stereotypical tweed coat, and very engaged. I was lovesick for him."

Claire paused, as if the words themselves caused her pain. Kyle tensed slightly, not sure what to make of her tense expression, but he didn't interrupt.

"I really thought he loved me. We had sex . . . the night of my eighteenth birthday. It was amazing, or so I thought. He said he would leave his fiancé and that he realized how much better life was with me. I was drunk with the attention he gave me, and when he finally touched me . . ." Claire shut her eyes tight and lowered her voice. "I thought he liked who I was as a person. But he only wanted to wait for sex, I guess.

"I started to hate who I was with him." Her voice was barely a whisper. "And I loved it."

Kyle saw tears glimmer in her eyes and with a gentle swipe he wiped one away.

"Everyone found out in high school that we talked all the time. They called me a slut, whore, every awful name you could think of. I was still a virgin then. It made me want to hurt them and then . . . one day I did. Senior year. Pulled a girl's hair out and punched her in class, in front of everyone. My grades plummeted, I nearly got expelled, I lost all my friends, and my adoptive family backed out. But he never left my side. He supported me, told me the girl deserved it, whatever. I believed him, ignoring the red flags because my birthday was finally approaching. I was really under his stupid spell. He pulled out all the stops on my birthday. Bought me dinner, drinks, and got a motel room so we could be alone."

Claire faltered, and took a steadying breath.

"He promised to call me after my birthday, after that night with me . . . that we'd be together again. It was supposed to be the beginning of our time together."

Claire paused, toying with sand between her fingers.

"He left a week later. I called him, emailed him, but . . . nothing." Claire took a deep breath. "I never heard from him again. He ghosted me and broke every promise, and I finally realized the whole thing was a lie. He was grooming me. He used me, when I was vulnerable."

Her voice lowered to a whisper. "It got so bad I wanted to kill myself. I thought about it a lot. My first semester of college should have been happy, but all I could see was his face. It was everywhere. Then, I just . . . I don't know, made up my mind I guess." Claire's voice returned to its normal pitch, her eyes lost to memory. "I didn't trust myself around men. I resolved to study hard and turn things around. I didn't want to waste the government's money I got for scholarships.

"Instead of thinking of him, I threw myself into school. It was the only thing that made sense, because it gave me a way to support myself independently. I shot to the top of every computer science class I took and was the first one in my cohort to have a tech firm offer me a job right out of college. Gann, Inc . . ."

Claire smiled wistfully as the words rushed out. "I wanted to be successful and self-sufficient. I wanted to be more positive about myself and my body. So I haven't had sex since then. I haven't even dated, Kyle. I didn't want to risk the old me coming back, even if that meant being lonely. I thought I preferred to be alone with my resolve, but — "

"Claire," Kyle interrupted. He drew her into his arms and held her strongly. He felt the weight of her proclamation in her shoulders, but far from shocking him, he felt even closer to her.

She sighed and continued. "I felt you needed to know that about me. I like you, more than I thought I would like someone again. And I realized finally when we were together, I'd been letting go of Aiden all these years. Every step I took to get where I am, I built a new heart. I grew tougher so I could never let myself be corrupted like that again. I have no regrets, the mind loop I was lost in about him was a huge lesson learned. So, I — " Claire took a shaky breath. "I just wanted to tell you. His memory will never touch me again. And I hope you'll still be interested in me, after this island, if there *is* an afterwards. I know I would like that."

"I would love it, Claire. And I'm glad you told me," he said as she pulled away to look at him. "I was wondering why your hands were shaking so badly."

"I didn't want to break the spell from this morning."

"Nothing could do that," he replied firmly. "I want to know anything you want to share from your life, Claire." He took one of her hands. "I'm glad you chose to be with me this morning."

"You aren't completely repulsed?" she asked, the tears in her eyes replaced with relief.

"Courage to admit that aloud doesn't deserve repulsion," he said slowly, not a hint of reproach in his voice. "We all have a past, Claire. I can't imagine what you went through, but I do know what it feels like to hate yourself. When I was stranded on this island, I didn't feel anything but hate and sadness for days. Every night, I would think how I should have died with my brothers, that I'd have been better off if the woman had just cut my throat deeper and been done with it. The grief consumed me and when I couldn't take it anymore, I blocked it all out. I barely ate when I needed, or slept when I was tired. I existed. I wasn't even trying to survive by the end. I half hoped I'd just die in my sleep, or get bitten by a snake myself. They told me I looked hollowed out when I was finally rescued. I was told I was lucky, being the only survivor of the woman, ever, but I didn't feel lucky. I didn't feel any-thing. The only thing that pulled me out of it was the hope that I could find my brothers' killer and bring Amberly to jus-tice. But . . ." He paused. "I've been stuck in a mind loop, too, replaying the same event over and over, hoping for a different ending. And you finally helped me see there's more to life than that."

Claire leaned into his chest. Her hair tickled his chin. He wrapped his arms around her.

"Thank you for listening," Claire whispered. "I can't be-lieve everything that's happened since we've been here. I want to hear more about you and keep getting to know you in every possible way, but, do you really think we'll reach the other side tonight?"

"Yes. With any luck we'll have the signal fire up by night-fall. After that, who knows how long it'll be before a ship sees us."

Claire gently brushed away a long-legged brown bug that crawled towards his leg. "Where will you go when we get off the island?"

"I'll stay in an inn somewhere if I need to, or with another fisherman until I get another boat. Or, maybe I'll start looking for the woman again. Meeting you, getting shipwrecked, I al-most feel like Iselle is doing this to remind me I need to finally move on from this. Maybe we can do it together, Claire."

"You saved my life, so if I can help you locate this woman, I will. I need to know who she really is, too. Those men chasing me, it must have been her they were after. Besides, I don't want to leave you. I feel like together we might be able to find peace," Claire replied.

"Yes." Kyle kissed the top of her head. She leaned up to look at him. He got the dazzling smile he was hoping for, before meeting her lips once again.

CHAPTER TWENTY-TWO

Claire wiped her forehead free of sweat from the late after-noon sun. The stream trickled ahead and guided them around jungle thickets. It proved tricky to navigate once they crossed over several large boulders, but Kyle pressed on. Sometimes Claire heard him mumbling to himself and point-ing carefully forward.

"I reckon we have enough dry branches and palm fronds to start our own basket weaving and woodcarving conglom-erate," Paul joked, as Henry piled logs into his arms.

"All the better for the signal fire, Paul. Some of these need to dry out more, but we can find a sheltered area for that. We need as much to burn as possible. I've got to get you back to your fiancé again," Kyle replied, adjusting one of the coolers rather awkwardly due to the steep terrain.

"I hope Justine's staying strong through this. I also hope she and our parents didn't already have our funerals."

"Think of how her face will light up when she sees you again," Claire joined in. "It'll truly be magical, like you're re-turning back from the dead or something."

"That's quite a thought, isn't it." Paul's voice seemed to lift a little. "If it does, I hope she'll be okay with me changing my name to Jesus."

"I think you should stick with Paul." Claire let out a small smile, then her voice became serious. "Your entire family must be beside themselves."

"Mum especially," Henry piped up. "She was worried enough when we told her we were coming down here for a

196

vacation."

"They'll be thanking every god known to mankind that you're alive." Kyle lifted a dead branch and inspected it. "Don't take it for granted, Paul."

Henry suddenly stopped.

"I hear water! A beach!"

Claire strained her ears and also heard faint waves. Without thinking, their packs and coolers were abandoned in favor of faster speed They moved as briskly as possible, not minding the sticks under their feet, nor the loncue leaves slapping their faces. When the ground evened out, they ran until they broke through the thicket of trees and a new world greeted them; one of blue waves and crystalline sand mixed with shouts of joy. Claire gasped and hugged Henry, who was nearest, then Kyle, and finally Paul before the group moved into the ocean, enveloped by waves.

"Almost home," Paul said to Henry, getting his little brother in an affectionate stronghold before tossing him unceremoniously into the water. Claire and Kyle laughed as Henry resurfaced and tackled his older brother.

Claire slowly made her way back to the lighter surf, collapsing in the sand. She watched her legs stretch in the water cresting on the beach's edge. Abundant light from the setting sun illuminated the white sand around her. There were numerous rocky black jetties beyond, being showered by the ocean waves. Claire spotted an island in the distance. Its emerald shape was barely visible.

"That's Feulia Island." Kyle appeared at her side, water dripping down his chest. "Huge whiskey distillery there. It's further away than it looks, but someone should notice our fire when we light it. Together we should be able to get a regular inferno going in no time."

"Well, since we probably won't be found tonight..." Claire eyed a set of narrow caves set into the nearby cliff. One of the caverns nearest would easily fit all of them in the soft sand, and the generous rocky ceiling sloped far above would be perfect for smoke to escape. She pointed to it. "We should set up camp under that rock. I can move our supplies."

Kyle stared from where she pointed to the sun sinking lower into the sky, before running a hand behind his neck and leaving it there. "Yes. We should be prepared to stay there. I don't like those dark clouds in the distance."

"Should we start our fire soon, then? I can move our supplies."

"Yes," Kyle began, as Paul and Henry were making their way back up the beach. "Wait, Claire."

She turned, giving him a quizzical look. Kyle swallowed. "When we leave, I want to take you out for dinner. Of course, I'd have preferred to cook something for you on my boat, but somewhere else will have to do."

She turned to him, her smile wide. "I would love that."

"Me, too." He smiled back. "It's a date, then."

Claire reached for his hand, their fingertips brushing, just as Paul and Henry came ashore.

"What's the difference between listening to you mow the lawn and play the bagpipes?" Paul asked.

"Nothing, because you think I'm tone deaf?" Henry tossed his head back and forth, shaking water out of his red hair.

"Nice try, little brother. The difference is that you can actually tune the lawn mower."

Claire and Kyle both stifled a laugh as Henry picked up a piece of driftwood and threw it at Paul, who caught it with ease.

"Time to move our supplies, Captain?" Paul pointed to the coolers and driftwood they had abandoned in their euphoria earlier.

"Claire's going to do that," Kyle said. "We'll set up in the cave for the night. It won't be our big signal fire, we'll do that when the rain stops. Every stick that's dry, we need to get in that cave."

Still smiling to herself, Claire left to pick up the bag and cooler she'd dropped earlier in the lush greenery. Large boulders of black rock were all over this side of the island, but Claire barely registered the change in terrain. She moved through the splintered branches of a dead loncue tree, unable to stop thinking about a date with Kyle. Her memories drifted to their time together under the waterfall and she blushed as she worked. The sun quickly sank when she hauled the gear to the mouth of the cave. In the distance Claire could hear rumbling thunder.

Paul ran forward to meet Claire as she emerged with the last, and heaviest, of the coolers.

"I've got this, Claire." Paul took the cooler from her hurriedly and practically threw it in a corner of the cave. It crushed the leaves and branches beneath it.

"You okay?" Claire looked at him questioningly.

"Never better," he replied, giving her one of his winks. "Just ready to leave."

"I can imagine," Claire said sympathetically.

"You're all full of dirt, Claire," Paul observed, brushing her sleeve gently. "I bet the Captain would be more than willing to help you wash off. Should we give you two some alone time in the cave?"

"What do you mean?" Claire replied, trying to keep her face straight.

"Oh, come now, you two haven't been exactly subtle. You've barely taken your eyes off each other from the start and I practically had to cover Henry's ears this morning."

Claire opened her mouth to respond in surprise, but Paul had moved several steps away with a knowing twinkle in his eye. He winked at her.

"A storm's moving closer," Kyle called. Claire shook off

the lingering glow in her cheeks and looked in the direction he was watching. A distant band of dark clouds moved towards them.

"I wouldn't mind swimming a bit longer. The clouds are so far away," Henry protested.

"They'll be here faster than you think," Kyle warned. "At least with these caves we'll stay a bit drier, and if we keep our fire here at the entrance of the cave" — he pointed to the mouth of the cavernous shelter — "the smoke will curl up and out, and should be fairly sheltered from any wind or rain."

"We're on it." Paul gestured to Henry. The younger boy slumped his shoulders somewhat but started helping Paul regardless. "Need a light, Captain? Or should we preserve the supply?"

"I'm going for the old-fashioned way," Kyle replied. "But thanks, and if this doesn't work, absolutely."

Paul and Henry dragged the remaining logs into the large pile. Kyle sat at the edge, corkscrewing tinder together to catch a spark. Claire stacked several large sticks against the tetrahedron pile. Kyle let out a murmur of success and inserted a smoking palm frond at the base of the stacked wood.

The pile hissed and steamed. Smoke signals were sent to the sky. The storm clouds closed in and extinguished all lingering daylight. Kyle poked at the bottommost logs with a long stick, stoking them as they lit. Paul clapped him on the back appreciatively as sparks flew upwards, rising to the top of the cave before disappearing. Even Henry's face lit up, all thoughts of playing in the ocean forgotten.

A fondness for all of them made an unexpected lump form in Claire's throat. The island felt like a strange home to her, more so than some of her other homes. There was a bond between them that she'd never felt before with other people. The way they worked as a team, Paul's relentless jokes and positivity, Henry trying to keep up with his brother, and Kyle . . .

Kyle who knew all the answers, knew the island, and knew her.

Paul tossed one last piece of wood into the fire. It sent a fresh wave of sparks upwards.

"We have some food left over, not a lot, but it'll get us through the night," Kyle continued. "Let's all try to stay dry."

"What's that noise?" Henry sidled up next to Kyle, staring off in the distance.

"Probably incoming rain," Kyle replied. Claire looked back out at the dark ocean and felt herself being pulled towards the hypnotic sound. Kyle was right—droplets danced across the surface of the ocean in a chorus of peaceful serenity. The warmth of the fire, combined with the sound, sent goose-bumps over her body.

"No, I hear something else," Henry said firmly, and the entire group stood still. Claire stared into the distance. The rain grew louder. Waves crashed into the beach with increasing wind. Kyle stood still beside her. Suddenly a faint *whirrr* rang out in the dark, and then she saw it. A pinprick of light had appeared in the distance directly ahead of them. She met Kyle's brown eyes with ferocity.

"It's a boat!" Paul yelled, and both he and Henry took off to the shore, waving their arms and shouting with jubilation. The tiny hum of a motor echoed across the water.

Chapter Twenty-Three

"I'm surprised anyone's out in this weather!" Kyle took her hand firmly and ran towards Paul and Henry. Claire felt a jolt in her body as she tried to keep up with Kyle's quick movements.

"I can't believe this," Claire said, hearing her dubious voice as if it was far away. Henry couldn't be contained, and even attempted a cartwheel.

"Christ Almighty, look at that. Hey!" Paul yelled and waved his arms. "Over here!!!"

The pinprick of light grew larger, and soon was close enough to shine all over them. The small craft was approaching fast, but the occupants gave no response to Paul's yelling. Claire felt her stomach grow cold and a distinct chill went up her spine that she knew wasn't from the incoming wind. They were mere yards from the beach now, mechanically steering the craft to shore. The searchlight continued to blind Claire and the others. A slow paralysis encapsulated her. She felt Kyle tense beside her.

"All of you, be quiet," Kyle barked loudly, breathing deeply and gripping Claire's hand so hard she knew her fingers were turning purple. "Something's wrong."

"Henry, come here," Paul's voice was steady, but Claire could tell he finally felt it, too. The group backed away closer to their signal fire and the warmth, instinctually, although it was too late to hide. Henry joined Paul and was restrained by the older man's grip on his shoulder. The searchlight finally shut off, and the signal fire danced across three shadowy figures in the raft. Kyle's fingers parted with Claire's abruptly. Several pairs of feet splashed in the shallow water until three figures began to materialize out of the shadows.

Long, auburn hair whipped about the face of the woman that approached. Her slim, black clad figure was an exact replica of Claire's slight frame. Unable to move, Claire watched as the woman walked across the sand with a staggered, yet purposeful step.

"It's her," she heard Kyle say in a strained voice.

Claire quickly turned to glance at him. He was staring coldly ahead with his hand on the hilt of his knife. She recognized the dark look in his eyes and forced herself to look away.

Her doppelganger's shoulders were arced slightly back as the two men dragged the raft onto the beach behind her. One was burly, muscled and tattooed, his skin the same dark color as Kyle's. A small pistol was strapped to his large chest. The other one was tall and thin, his short blond hair blowing as a product of the advancing storm. He wore the same expression as his male counterpart — menace.

"Hello, sister." The woman spoke calmly, stopping a foot in front of them, a set of familiar hazel eyes looking at the snakebite but showing no emotion. Her tongue drew out the syllables in a cadence not unlike Kyle's, but it lacked the soothing melody and instead came out with a deadly promise hinging on each letter.

"You killed my brothers and left me to die, Amberly." Kyle stepped closer to the woman.

Amberly's focus shifted to Kyle's face, and she searched him with a look of sinister recognition.

Claire held her breath and felt her eyes widening at the arch of Amberly's eyebrows, the gentle downward curve of her delicate nose — they even had the same shaped teeth. It was so disturbingly familiar that Claire felt her knees give way slightly as Amberly licked her lips, a smirk forming at the corners of her mouth.

"Yes," she whispered, the cadence of her voice softer and more alluring. "And I'll do it again if you take another step closer."

Claire looked at Kyle, who was gripping the handle of his knife with such a ferocity that veins were popping out of his arm. The look in his eyes scared Claire. Just behind him she saw both Paul and Henry had turned ashen white, the tension in their faces contorting them into a far cry from the jovial smiles she was used to. No sooner had she turned away than she felt a firm grip on her chin. Amberly turned her head so they were face-to-face once again.

"But I don't want to do that, Claire, so tell Kyle to relax a little."

Surprised to hear her name spoken aloud, Claire turned to Kyle, who lowered his knife back into its sheath.

"You know about me," Claire whispered, more to herself.

"And I intend to know more, sister." Amberly studied her carefully. Claire gasped, but in her heart she knew it was true.

"Sister," Claire repeated.

Amberly nodded gravely. "I need to take you with me. No witnesses. Too many people know my face." Turning towards Kyle, she raised her voice.

"All those flyers made sure of that, didn't they? I don't impress easily, but that did it, Kyle. How did you survive that night?"

Kyle lunged forward as thunder shook the earth. Amberly seemed to brandish her knife out of nowhere and sliced it down Kyle's bare chest. Claire felt herself gasp as Kyle roared out in pain. His anger was nothing like she'd ever seen before.

The other two men aimed at Kyle, but Amberly held up a hand.

"I can handle this myself. I owe you that much." She smiled

coldly and ran at Kyle. He deflected a blow from her, but she kicked him firmly in the chest, rearing up for another strike with her knife as he grabbed her leg and attempted to twist it in the air until she was off balance. With an incredible agility, she raised her arm up, knife in hand and was about to bring it to the hand Kyle was using to grip her leg. Paul and Henry attempted to dodge along the dark beach, but were stopped by the two men. Henry kicked the tall blond one in the leg and Claire saw the flash of a pistol. Claire felt herself propelled forward by adrenaline.

"Stop!" Claire screamed and stumbled forward. Both her sister and Kyle froze, and he let go of Amberly's leg reluctantly. The white sand below glinted with blood in the firelight. Paul and Henry had pistols pointed at their heads from the two men. The sound of rain was no longer soothing, but advanced threateningly, sprayed the ocean with thousands of droplets.

"I'll go with you," Claire stated firmly, "Amberly."

Amberly's shoulders relaxed slightly with Claire's words. She lowered her knife and slowly turned to face Claire.

"Please," Claire pleaded, edging closer to her twin. Her palms shook but she pressed on. "Just don't harm him, or any of them, and I'll go. Willingly."

The other woman looked at Claire, giving her a hard glance. "Agreed."

"What are you doing, Claire?" Kyle cried out and made to angrily march towards Claire, but she put a hand out to stop him. Amberly nodded at her men and gestured Claire to follow as she stalked back towards her boat with a limp. The men let go of Paul and Henry and closed in on Claire, but not before Kyle grabbed her arm.

"No!" Panic sounded foreign coming from him.

"This is the only way," Claire whispered. Sadness and fear etched between the anger in his eyes, and caused her own to tear.

"Don't go with them, Claire!" Henry yelled, attempting to tackle the blond one again. The man rounded on Henry and hit him across the face. Paul ran forward to defend his brother but was stopped by the tattooed man.

"Shoot the small one," Amberly commanded coldly.

The muscular man's gun was poised in less than a second.

Claire screamed as the gun went off. Her eyes teared as Paul rushed to Henry's side. Kyle let go of Claire's arm as if it were a hot poker. He stepped back from her, his head whipping to stare at Henry. Paul yelled for his brother. Claire felt herself get pushed towards the raft, tears dripped down her face. She saw Henry's unmoving legs, Paul bent over him, and Kyle, his face stricken with pain and desperation as he turned from Claire to Henry.

"Be thankful we spared the life coursing through you and that of your last red-haired companion. I'm only letting you live because Claire asked." Amberly looked at Kyle. "Come after us, and I'll ensure you're killed."

Claire felt Kyle stiffen and shake with anger. He stepped forward but Claire screamed as the gun was pointed at Kyle.

"No!" Claire pushed Kyle's stiff frame away, although she knew they were all at the pirate's mercy. Kyle seemed unable to speak; she saw a look of defeat in his eyes.

"Go, Kyle," Claire begged, desperate to deescalate the bloodlust in the tattooed man's eyes. "I'll be fine. Go! Please!"

Kyle gave her the briefest look. The defeat had disappeared from his eyes. There was anger, shock, and a now, a strange resolve there. Claire knew he had some plan, but he didn't betray anything further with his eyes. Without a word, he left her side to run for Henry.

Claire felt sick. The blond man turned on the raft's searchlight. The rough hands of the tattooed man pushed Claire and she toppled awkwardly into the raft, facing the dark ocean ahead. Amberly situated herself across from Claire. Within seconds, the raft was in the water, the tattooed man at the motor. They bobbed through the undulation of the incoming waves as fast as they could. Claire stared at her sister, who stared back.

"Why did you have to shoot him?" Claire yelled over the wind and the motor. "I said I'd come with you."

Amberly's eyes glittered. "There was no need for his heroics."

Claire gripped the seat she was on, shaking in fear. The raft reached the open ocean and went extremely fast.

She looked back at the shore, but was only afforded the briefest glances of the fire on the beach before the rain finally reached them. At their speed, it felt like sleet—sharp, cold, and soaked her clothes within seconds. Claire blinked at the cold-blooded eyes of the burly man behind her. Turning back ahead with a shiver, she saw the searchlight illuminate a long, slim yacht with multiple decks and a handsome wooden trim. Her mouth fell open as the raft finally slowed, and Amberly stood with a rope in her wet hands, leaning over Claire and dripping water from her long hair.

"Welcome home, sister."

CHAPTER TWENTY-FOUR

"Set him here, next to the fire." Kyle hastily moved a cooler out of the way for Henry. Paul struggled with the extra weight of his brother before carefully laying Henry down.

"Stay with us." Paul held Henry's limp head in his hands. Henry breathed fast and blinked rapidly with panic. The once light green fabric of his shirt was stained dark red. A sense of dread formed in the pit of Kyle's stomach. He ripped open Henry's shirt from the collar and saw the punctured, ripped skin.

"The bullet didn't hit any major organs, but it looks like it nicked an artery. We need to control the bleeding."

Paul took off his shirt and stuffed it against the boy's shoulder. Within seconds it had blossomed with blood.

"It's not getting better," Paul said in a slightly panicked voice, watching his brother moan slightly. "I'm pressing as hard as I can."

"It's not too bad," Henry said, but his voice cracked and his eyes fluttered to a close. Paul stood and pressed his weight into Henry's shoulder.

"Keep the pressure while I try to slow down the bleeding here." Kyle located the brachial artery under Henry's armpit and pressed with all four fingers. Within seconds the bleeding had slowed. "He isn't bleeding internally. Something else to be thankful for."

"How do you know?" Paul demanded.

"No swelling. We need make a tourniquet, or cauterize it."

"I can make a tourniquet." Paul's speech was slurred with

haste as Kyle stepped in to resume the compress. Paul moved faster than Kyle had ever seen him before, locating the emergency kit and rifling through the depleted contents with the ferocity of a mad man.

"Can you still hear me?" Kyle asked, but Henry didn't answer or open his eyes.

"I've got this." Paul reappeared and didn't look at Kyle, but a silent understanding passed between the two men. Kyle stepped away from the two brothers until he reached the edge of the fire.

Kyle ignored the sting of his own flesh wound, retracing his steps until he reached the blood-splattered sand. Rain coursed through his open eyes as he stared at the last place Claire had been.

Exterior and interior lights were blinking on the familiar yacht ahead. His blood began to boil. After a year of rebuilding his life, the woman had swept in once again, and taken someone he cared for.

Someone he loved.

He stared into the angry sky, cursing Iselle, watching her fingers of lightning strike the turbulent ocean waves.

His feet found the water, his legs felt the direction, and his focus never left the yacht. The seawater stung at his cut chest. The force of the waves pulled him back to shore several times, but he was determined to reach the calmer waters in between the looming black rocks. This time, he would finish what he wished he could have done one year ago.

Claire entered her sister's bedroom with apprehension. Thunder cracked through the sky as she took in the heaps of glittering jewelry, fine paintings, and a closet full of outfits for every season and occasion, complete with matching wigs. Claire swallowed uncomfortably while her sister busied herself with glasses and a dark brown liquid in a long bottle. Sneaking a look out the small window only brought a muddled view splattered with rain.

"Let's have a toast, shall we?" Her sister stood with difficulty, offering her a glass. It smelled strongly of alcohol and a harsh scent she couldn't identify. The boat lurched slightly and Claire tipped off balance for a moment, but her sister, despite the injury she was clearly trying to ignore, remained steadily rooted as she eyed the burned mass on Claire's face.

"Beautiful," Amberly murmured. "I value scars."

Claire clutched the drink in her fingers. "How long have you known about me?" she asked quietly.

Her sister gave a slight smile and downed her glass of liquid in one gulp and set it on the table. "Not long at all," she answered, her voice low. "My former boss knew about you for a lot longer. Sent men after you. But don't worry, I took care of them."

Claire regarded her carefully, digesting these words. "If I hadn't come on board with you —"

"I do *not* leave witnesses," the woman interrupted, watching her with an intensity that made Claire involuntarily shudder. "Consider your friends lucky that I want us to get off on the right foot, Claire. Your courage will be rewarded. Drink."

Claire gripped her drink harder before steeling herself and throwing her head back. She drank the liquid in two fierce gulps, the unexpected burning sensation causing her to emit several fierce coughs.

"And what else do you know about me?" Claire suppressed another cough and swallowed profusely. "How did you know my name?"

"My boss," Amberly whispered. "Jaquarde."

"Jaquarde?" Claire repeated.

"He raised me." There was a hard edge to Amberly's tone. "Not as a daughter, but as a whore, and eventually, his weapon. He runs these islands. He's the reason you're here."

Claire frowned. "Is that how you knew I was here?"

Amberly took a breath with difficulty before responding. "If you want more answers, I'll show you. But know that it won't be as pleasant as drinking here in my cabin."

"I want to know," Claire stated firmly.

Amberly took Claire's wrist and led her abruptly out of her room until they reached a small staircase leading to the lower deck. Rain beat the windows and thunder echoed inside the small stairway. Claire's heart pounded. She moved as quickly as possible to keep up and soon they reached the tall blond man, standing in front of a door.

"We're going in, Dev," Amberly said. The blond man moved aside.

"Open it," Amberly commanded, but Claire already had her hand on the doorknob.

The smell reached her first. Claire's hands flew to her mouth as she involuntarily gagged. Immediately she recognized Mr. Gann's crumpled figure and gasped. His bloody face rested against the shoulder of a dark-skinned woman covered with bandages around her hands, stained a deep red. Claire's drink was in her throat when her gaze moved to the frozen expression of the blue faced sandy haired young man.

Claire took shaky breaths. Her knees wobbled as she stepped back, her mind racing with horror and disgust at the three prisoners. Amberly leaned into her shaking figure. Claire recoiled as her sister pointed at the dead young man.

"No witnesses," she said malevolently. Claire turned for the door, terrified for her life. She'd barely taken a step when Amberly held her in an iron-clad grip and prevented any escape. Dev watched them from the doorway.

Claire took a steadying breath and felt her eyes harden in a way she'd never felt before. She looked directly back into the hazel eyes so similar to her own, yet they pierced her with a jetty gaze capable of unspeakable things.

"You're a monster."

"I am what I was raised to be, Claire," Amberly whispered, her breath hued with alcohol. "I have no mercy for selfish traitors. Do not fear, I would never hurt you. You're my blood. Instead of behaving like these cowards, you stood up and fought for what you wanted. To save the lives of others. Now, we can finish bringing justice to those who tore us apart."

"Justice?" Claire turned and saw her sister's gaze boring into her. "What do you mean?"

"Gann is here because he betrayed *you*," Amberly said quietly.

Dev walked forward briskly and kicked Mr. Gann's feet. "Let's find out if he'll talk to you."

Mr. Gann stirred at the movement, his head rolling from side to side until he blinked at the punishing lights above. His eyes widened in surprise as he saw Claire and took in the woman next to him, fright flitting across his aging face. The once intimidating man was gone. His fingers twisted in his bonds.

"Claire, is it really you? Your face is different . . . yes . . . it is you," he said. His eyes focused on her, and his tone became more authoritative. "You have to help me escape. They're all criminals!"

"What are you even doing here?" Claire kneeled shakily to the mahogany floor, the smell of the inhabitants worsening with her approach.

"Don't listen to what she told you," Mr. Gann whispered. Claire leaned down, holding her hand over her nose.

"Do you know her? Did you know about us being twins?"

"I'm innocent in all of this, Claire." Mr. Gann continued the attempt to speak in his brusque tone, but his voice was too fear-stricken to pull off any of its former glory. His slumped posture brought little of the powerful effect she was used to, and he groaned as he tried to put weight on his left arm. "She's completely crazy. She thought that I knew about you, and blames me, but it's a lie. You help me out of here, and I'll explain it all. We can turn these people in. We can bring justice to the dead in this room."

"I'm not dead yet," a small broken voice whispered, rich with the island accent. Startled, Claire turned to the woman beside Mr. Gann, and her eyes fluttered open, revealing a piercing brown gaze.

"Who are you?" Claire moved towards the woman, who regarded Claire with a beautiful sadness and wide eyes. Her thick dark hair stuck to her sweaty face.

"Someone who deserves this," she whispered. "You're real . . . you're identical . . . so beautiful . . ."

"That's enough." Amberly stepped forward and Claire stood, watching her sister shaking with anger. Her face had been drained of color.

The woman on the floor stared at Amberly with unblinking eyes. "Jaquarde always knew about Claire, but it wasn't until you left that he told me, Amberly."

"Claire, please, help me," Gann interjected. "She only kidnapped me because she wanted my money. I'm the one who told her what charter you were on. I wanted to find you, Claire!"

"Lies." Amberly interjected, and turned to Mr. Gann. "Tell her why she missed the first charter boat to your little conference."

Claire recalled the *Clarion* sitting on the dock, her name missing from the list of passengers, and Beverly arguing with the attendant until he refused to let her board. She locked gazes with Mr. Gann.

"That was you?" she heard herself whisper angrily.

"He canceled your reservation and your company card, so that you wouldn't find other transportation," Amberly continued from behind Claire. "Some men were supposed to find you and bring you to him, but they failed, because you're clever, and got on a different boat. That was the only part not planned. The only reason Gann's conference was here was because Jaquarde told him to bring it here. They just wanted to get you to the White Sands. Alive, but powerless."

Gann shifted his gaze between the pair of them uncomfortably. Claire felt her head start to spin.

"I got stranded on an island because of you," Claire snapped at Gann. "I almost died here. Look at my *face*. And for what? Why am I so important?"

"We were supposed to be raised together by Jaquarde, who was *our* boss." The woman next to Gann turned imploring eyes to Claire. "All of us, even you, were involved in his illegal adoption trade as the children of the men and women Jaquarde either killed or sold to settle debt. You must have gotten adopted early. It appeared real to the outside, but those of us that didn't get picked for adoption all knew what he did . . . and what he did to us, and with us. A year ago, Amberly and I tried to leave. She was his favorite, but he couldn't trust her. He always knew she had a twin, so he traced you to America, and has been looking for you ever since until he found you at Gann, Inc. this year. He made a deal with Gann to lure you here."

Claire knotted her fists in anger. She stared hollowly at the woman.

"What's your name?" Claire asked.

"Emere," the woman replied.

Claire was pushed aside, and in an instant, Amberly was at Emere's throat.

"*Now* your tongue has loosened."

Emere didn't flinch.

Amberly looked to Claire. "Your boss here got himself into some money troubles. It was perfect bait, and for turning you in, Gann was offered a sizable reward that would save his little company."

"This is absurd, Claire." Gann distastefully eyed a blood-stain on his shoulder. "Jaquarde was just an investor. I had no idea he was involved in anything like this. Help me, untie me so we can get out of here, and I'll absolutely give you a promotion for going through all of this. How about Jackson's job? Head of the web development team?"

"Enough," Amberly uttered coldly. With one blink of her long lashes, she pressed the cold steel knife into Claire's palm. Gann's anguish turned to panic.

"We're on the same team here, Claire!" Gann's voice rose as he struggled against his bonds.

"You were going to turn me in, weren't you?" Claire said, not bothering to keep the accusatory tone out of her voice.

"Of course not! Together we can bring her in! I've already called the police! They should be looking for us right now! *Claire!*" Gann snapped. "Listen to me!"

"He betrayed you, and his life is my gift to you. Finish him," Amberly said.

Claire staring incredulously at the knife in her hands. Amberly pushed her forward slightly.

"He's told me all I need to know, and he's useless. We can silence him, so it's easier for you. The screaming of a coward is disgusting anyway."

Amberly gestured at Dev. He walked forcefully to Mr. Gann, whose protests became louder and more panicked. Realizing what he was going to do, Claire closed her eyes tightly at the sound that ensured Mr. Gann was silenced.

"Finish him," Amberly repeated.

Claire realized her hand that held the knife was shaking, and she pressed it into her side only to realize her legs were shaking, too.

"I don't think I can," she said. "Even after what he did. I've never killed a man."

"I'll teach you," Amberly said emphatically. "How to do it quickly, or slowly . . . however you want to feel it."

"Can we be alone, please?" Claire asked Dev.

"Leave us, Dev," Amberly demanded. Dev gave a curt nod and left the room.

Claire's heart pounded and the thunder outside seemed to reverberate through her skull. Even Emere stared at her expectantly, waiting, or perhaps wondering, if Claire was capable of the same violence her sister was. Claire looked at the horrible angle at which her boss sat, his limbs crumpled beneath his unconscious, bleeding face. Her throat went dry; her fingers gripped the knife as her mind drifted back to the other lives the knife had taken. The sandy haired boy in front of her, Kyle's brothers . . .

The memory of his familiar brown eyes swam over her.

"After I found you in the cave, I realized you're nothing like her." *Kyle smiled at her. "You're kind and good, Claire."*

A sense of calm spread over her body and replaced her fear with courage. Her breath came at a normal pace and her limbs stopped shaking. Amberly watched her carefully, but the curiosity Claire once felt about her was extinguished.

Raising her hand, Claire gripped the knife and faced an unconscious Mr. Gann, angling the knife inward so it was parallel to her forearm. A slow grin spread across Amberly's face from the corner of her eye.

With all the strength she could muster, Claire threw her body's weight onto her sister until she heard Amberly's head hit the floor with a terrible crunch upon contact.

It was worse than the girl she'd punched in high school. She gave every ounce of her strength to each blow until her arm ached. Claire closed her eyes and took deep breaths, tears leaking out of the corner of her eyes at the sight in front of her and the violence she created. Blood seeped from Amberly's askew nose and leaked down into the folds of her bent neck.

With a shaking hand, Claire fearfully found her sister's wrist and checked for a pulse. Finding one brought little relief.

Claire crawled to Emere.

"Help me," she pleaded, kneeling to the floor. Claire cut the ropes that bound Emere's feet.

"I'm too weak to escape," Emere whispered back.

"I want to signal another boat to get us home." Claire helped the woman stand uneasily. Her eyes wandered to where Amberly lay but she could only bring herself to look for a second.

"She wasn't always like this," Emere whispered. "You have to know that."

"That doesn't make up for what she's done."

"Nothing ever does," Emere agreed. "But the other men are just as dangerous."

"I know." Claire gripped Amberly's knife in her hand. "We don't have much time."

The boat was eerily silent as Emere shakily led Claire down the narrow hall.

"Svante is the bigger one, with tattoos," Emere explained quietly. "I never knew Dev, so he must be new. Svante has been with Amberly a long time. She saved his life, and he would do anything to protect her." Emere's muscles struggled to move. Claire gripped her thin arms with support.

"Where are they?" Claire eased a door open and cautiously peered around the corner, but it only revealed an empty dining area, the smell of cooked fish hanging in the air.

"Probably in the captain's quarters, or keeping watch." Emere's leg gave out and she lost her balance. Claire caught her under the armpit.

"Sorry," Emere mumbled. "I've lost too much blood. You go."

"You have to try." Claire helped Emere stand fully. They approached another door to the outside deck area, but it was locked.

"You aren't going to make it out of here," Emere stated, staring at the door. "Even if we send a signal, we're no match for those men. It's so dark, and with the storm and the rocks I can't escape if I wanted to. I can't fight. I'm stiff . . . and weak . . ." Her voice trailed off, and her eyes filled with tears. "I'm sorry," she whispered again, wiping them away with her heavily bandaged hand. "I know it's only looks, but you remind me of her, you even sound like her when we were happy, a long time ago . . ."

"I'm not about to give up yet," Claire snapped, and grabbed Emere's arm. Emere nodded.

"I have no energy to argue. To the next staircase ahead, then." Emere pointed. They made slow progress down the small hallway around the exterior of the ship. Claire glanced out the tiny window. Rain continued beating the rocky jetties beyond. When they reached the small staircase, Emere stopped walking behind her.

Claire didn't need to ask what was wrong. She could smell the cigarette smoke coming from above. Peeking cautiously up the stairs, Claire could only assume it was the pilothouse.

"He will kill. Turn and run." Emere tried to pull Claire away, but Claire stepped on the staircase, taking each step carefully, in full view. The tattooed one watched her approach from the captain's chair as he blew another smoke ring.

"Svante?" Claire asked tentatively as she awkwardly took the last step into the room, hiding Amberly's knife behind her back.

Nodding, he narrowed his eyes as he watched Claire strangely. The small pistol that shot Henry was holstered at his waist, tucked underneath the meaty forearm decorated with intertwining skulls and leaves. White ocean spray splashed the glass around the room loudly. Nervously she stepped towards him, holding her breath when she heard

Emere slip away quietly.

"Where's Amberly?" Svante's accent was thick.

Claire brandished the knife and swiped at his chest. He ducked, and with little effort Svante grabbed the hand behind her and twisted her arm painfully.

"Please!" Claire protested, but Svante was upon her, his hand clutching her throat, the smell of cigarettes pungent as she coughed and sputtered on her own breath.

"Tell me what you did." Svante's words were quick, his fingers pulsing deeper. Claire felt her vision blur as her airways closed. Svante gripped her harder as she struggled.

"In the room—with the others—" she managed to choke out. "Unconscious."

CHAPTER TWENTY-FIVE

K yle jerked back from untying the grey-haired man. Seawater continued to drip freely from his clothes. The exertion of swimming and moving, as quietly as he dared, lingered on his muscles as he kneeled down.

"I was so close to turning her in . . ." the man sputtered and rubbed his raw wrists.

"What's your name?" Kyle asked.

"Richard. Richard Gann," the man replied. He began to stand, but his legs gave out, and he fell back into the wall.

"My name's Kyle. She kept you alive. Be thankful," Kyle placed a hand on Gann's shoulder to steady him.

"Alive . . . for now. She wants me dead. She'll turn Claire against me."

"Claire? You saw her?" Kyle placed both hands on Gann's shoulders until the other man looked him in the eye.

"Yes! I saw her. I'm her boss!"

"Her boss? But why would Amberly want you? Unless . . ."

"Leverage," Gann said. "Imagine how worried sick we all were when Claire didn't come to my conference! Nobody could find her for days. But I discovered that she took your charter, and Amberly kidnapped me."

"Amberly will want us all dead if she finds us here." Kyle felt his heart rate rise with anger.

"There must be a small passage out of here leading to the upper deck. Their footsteps always go in that direction."

"We don't have much time to find Claire and try to get to safety."

"Then let's go."

"Can you stand by yourself?"

"I think so."

Kyle placed his hands under Mr. Gann's arms. The older man wobbled to standing. Kyle let go and turned, only to face the blond pirate standing in the doorway, gun pointed at Kyle.

Kyle froze. The man easily stood over him by a foot.

"Stupid to come back, islander," the blond pirate said.

"Dev," Gann snarled. He ran forward but fell, his weak muscles convulsing out of his control. Dev strode over and kicked him squarely in the stomach.

"No!" Kyle threw a hand up to stop him, throwing himself out of the pistol's range. Kyle pulled at the man's fingers while Gann jerked his blond head back until the gun was released — it clattered to the floor. Kyle pushed the thin man backward. Dev swung his arm forward and struck Kyle in the jaw, sending him reeling back. Recovering, Kyle strained with effort and pushed Dev into the wall, kicking the man's knees out from under him. Dev howled in pain but came back with double the force and tackled Kyle until he hit the ground. Dev gripped Kyle's neck in his hands and laughed, crushing Kyle with his body weight. His eyes were narrowed, and Kyle knew he would go in for the kill. Already he could see darkness creep in from the corner of his eyes. His exhausted muscles moved as much as they could to leverage Dev off of him, but it was no use. The darkness was closing in, no matter how hard he fought.

I'm sorry, Claire.

Dev's smile widened.

"I'll make it quick," he promised. Kyle felt long thin fingers grip his neck more tightly until he choked on the last breath he had in his body.

A shot fired loudly. Blood spattered over Kyle. The thin fingers released his neck, and Dev toppled mostly off of him.

Kyle gasped for air, the darkness clearing. He blinked as Gann lurched forward, pushing Dev the rest of the way off of him. Kyle stared at the blond pirate for any signs of life, but Gann had shot him in the back of the shoulders, just below his neck. He knew Dev was dead.

Heaving, Kyle forced himself to turn away. Gann was visibly shaking with the effort of his quick movements.

"Criminals. All of them," Gann spat angrily and staggered slightly towards the doorway.

"Thank you." Kyle heard the words coming out of his mouth in his shock, but Gann was already leaving the room. Thunder sounded, and the boat rocked slightly.

"Wait!" Kyle called out, but Gann was out of sight. His footsteps moved out into the hallway. A woman's voice yelled in surprise.

Kyle stood unsteadily, rubbing his throat and taking deep breaths. He felt more alert when he reached the hallway, following the noise, until he came upon a woman cowered against the wall. He softened when he saw her frightened face.

"It can't be . . ." he whispered to himself as the familiar features matched the memory in his mind. "Emere Marama?"

Nodding, she regarded him with a pleading stare.

Kyle grabbed her arm to help her up, careful to avoid her bandages and soon realized nearly every inch of her body was cut or bruised. He knew Amberly was the only one capable of such cruelty.

"Come with me." Emere limped towards a different direction from which Gann had run. "I can hear them coming. They'll have heard the gunshot."

A bandaged hand gestured to a set of doors ahead, laden with an oval window. Footstep moved with haste overhead and shook the boat.

"Did she do this to you?" Thoughts of Claire's gentle

fingers lying in a pool of blood brought an alarming chill down his spine. "Have you seen Claire?"

"She's with Svante," Emere said in a soft voice. "There isn't any time to waste. We have to signal for help."

"Can you do that? I have to find them."

"Yes. Go."

Claire's heart pounded in her chest as Svante released his hand from her throat. Tiny lights danced across her vision. She squealed in pain as Svante's large hand grabbed her hair and pushed her in front of him, his grip on her wrist unrelenting. He shoved her painfully down the stairs. She fell forward clumsily against gravity and Svante's force. Emere was nowhere to be found, and Claire struggled to keep up. Dozens of hairs parted ways with her scalp, but Svante thrust her along even harder when her head hit a doorframe and interrupted his pacing. Claire gripped Amberly's knife tightly but didn't dare use it.

They burst through a different set of doors and down the stairs to the room Claire and Emere had so recently vacated. Claire squeezed her eyes closed as they watered in pain, and only when Svante kicked the door in powerfully with his foot did she dare open them.

Amberly was gone, as was Mr. Gann. The thin man had been shot dead and laid behind the door. Claire murmured in pain and disgust at the sight of it. The body of the blond-haired boy was the only thing that hadn't changed. Claire grappled at Svante's forearm in vain as he dragged her out of the room, her feet slipping in the copious amounts of water that led to the place Claire had last seen her sister.

Amberly heard the movements through the thin walls. She

paused to listen. Two sets of footsteps.

She reached forward to open the nearest door but was greeted only by pain shooting down her side. It reverberated throughout her ribcage and encompassed her face. Thanks to Claire, she couldn't even grimace. The footsteps thundered closer.

"Svante!" she hollered.

The footsteps paused, then turned, and soon the door opened to reveal Claire, restrained by Svante.

"Dev is dead," Svante announced tersely.

Amberly pressed her lips together, but she didn't look at Claire.

"Bring Claire to the deck, then find Gann and Emere."

Svante turned Claire around and burst through a set of doors leading to the mahogany deck. Amberly followed closely behind. Rain fell in waves upon them, illuminated by the exterior lights. Svante let go of Claire, throwing her to her knees.

It was a surprise to see Claire quickly recover as Svante took off. She ran to the deck railing until Amberly gripped her arm and stopped her.

The waves washed over her booted feet below. Amberly's nose burned, the damaged cartilage causing her eyes to water in pain, but it didn't stop a twinge of excitement. Her sister was powerful and driven. Amberly gritted her teeth together and ignored the sharp pain in her side as she leaned closely into Claire's face. There was a resigned acceptance there, a strength and purpose that was anything but superficial.

"You think you don't want this now, that you would be better off with your friends, but you would regret it for the rest of your life. We're bound by blood. Let me show you what it means to feel alive!" Amberly watched Claire stare absently at the black rock in the distance. Rainwater dripped freely down her face.

"This isn't the way I imagined things working out," Claire whispered back quietly, without looking at her.

Amberly laughed. "What's your other option? If you jump, you'll die on these rocks. But look at what I can offer you, Claire. You saw the notice posters and my special room downstairs. Or maybe you wish that we could've met over coffee in some oceanside cafe, then decide if you'd keep in touch?" Amberly paused. "We're alike, you and me. Look what you did to me. You don't even understand what you want to walk away from yet. Logic still guides you. You want to spend your life working for people like that weak man or making people like him work for you? Stay with me, and you'll wake up each day seeking the next adventure, feeling the wind on your face, directing your own future with as much fortune as we can make together."

"I think we have a different idea of what adventure really means," Claire whispered. "I prefer a different fate."

"I won't lose you." Amberly's lips grazed Claire's ear.

Claire's eyes filled with tears. "I was never yours to lose."

Amberly felt her insides freeze. Waves crashed into the rocks ahead, the island briefly illuminated in the distance by the lightning.

"Weakness," she spat. She turned her sister to face her and slapped her as hard as she could muster, as if that would rid Claire of the emotions in her eyes. "When we find Gann, you will kill him, Claire, or I won't stop you from jumping down to the cliffs below and be—"

The doors splintered open, the hinges fracturing the doorframe as wood parted from the walls. Glass from the oval windows rained on the mahogany deck as the person behind it geared up for a second try. Gann's silver hair glittered in a flash of lightning as he fell awkwardly to the rain-soaked deck, skidding on the shards of the door.

Svante ran out from behind him and watched Gann with

an acidic stare. Gann looked weak and suddenly unsure of himself when he saw Svante's pistol.

"That door was open, Gann!" Amberly bellowed over the rain.

"I don't care. All of you sick bastards deserve death." Mr. Gann panted as he withdrew Dev's pistol and fired a shot near Amberly. Svante drew his own gun and aimed at Gann, but Amberly put her hand up and signaled him to wait.

"Was it you who killed Dev with a shot like that?" Amberly called. "Maybe you were aiming for her? Here. Let me help!" She shoved her unsuspecting sister in front of her like a shield and wrapped one arm around Claire's waist as Gann shot again. Claire screamed as Amberly gripped her sister's hair, forcing her head up, and walked the pair of them closer until Gann had a perfect shot of them. Thunder crackled through the air.

"The first one is the hardest," she whispered into Claire's ear. "You haven't let go of my knife. You couldn't kill me. But you can kill him." She watched Gann point the barrel at them through tendrils of Claire's wet hair. Suddenly a figure dashed through the splintered door.

"Stop this, Gann!" a voice from the entryway yelled. Amberly's smile faded when she realized it belonged to Kyle. Her grip tightened possessively around Claire, who stiffened with shock. Kyle put his arms up in surrender and addressed Gann.

"Claire's not one of them. She doesn't know anything that can hurt you. Amberly, just let us take a raft and leave. I'll not call the authorities."

Amberly laughed. "Such lies, Kyle!"

Gann said nothing, but Amberly watched his finger move over the trigger. Her sister's arm quaked with adrenaline and fear.

"Please!" Kyle howled.

"Why can't you understand?" Gann's wild eyes darted between Kyle and Claire. "They're all criminals. They deserve this. You deserve this, too, don't you?"

The gun pointed away from Amberly and Claire, resting shakily on Kyle. Amberly felt her sister's posture shift. It was subtle, and if she hadn't been holding on so tightly, she might have missed it, but the rage was there. Claire would avenge and protect what she loved.

A slow smile of pride spread across Amberly's face as she let go of Claire's arms.

CHAPTER TWENTY-SIX

Claire stared at Gann. Soon, it was the only thing she saw. Fear felt far away. The path had been laid out for her, and nothing else mattered but stopping Gann. The rain wouldn't impede her, nor would the wet knife. Her legs propelled forward with no hesitation; every last bit of her anxiety melted away. Gann stared at her, but the sight of his shaking hand pointing the gun at her couldn't stop her now. A shot fired, and he missed her head by inches. Her ears rang, and someone yelled. Strength coursed through her body, and her arms thrust forward, one grasping the gun upwards while he fired another shot, the other plunging the knife into Mr. Gann's stomach with a sickening ease. A howl escaped from Gann's lips, but Claire barely noticed — adrenaline spread through her limbs. She'd done it, and she'd done it well, for the gun clattered to the deck as Gann stumbled backward.

"How could you?" Gann screamed. Claire locked gazes with him as he convulsed in pain, struggling to reach the gun.

Claire gripped Gann's wrist as hard as she could muster. Gann coughed in pain.

"It's too late," he managed to yell at her. "The police are after you! You'll lose! My death will be further evidence!"

"Evidence that you planned to use me for your own gain!" Claire screamed back. "It *is* too late, Gann. For you!"

"What will you do now, Claire?" he demanded. "You going to kill me with that knife?"

You are not a killer.

Claire heard Kyle's voice in her head, and the brief moment

of mercy made her lose her ground. Her strength was not going to defeat Gann, and her stance was weakening. The advantage of her surprise attack was over. The roar of the sea was just below them under the railing. Gann grabbed a fistful of Claire's hair and began pulling her to the railing, where she was unable to resist his strength as he fought to lift her over. She clung to the wet railing as hair parted from her scalp, and blood poured out of it. She yelled, fighting back, but Gann was stronger. Her feet lost her footing on the deck.

Suddenly she felt Amberly next to her. Her sister shoved Gann into the railing. He buckled, and, in that moment, Claire fell back to the deck and cut at the hands restraining her by her hair. Gann let go, howling in pain. A stinging saltwater wave crashed over them. Blood washed from Claire's scalp and face, clearing her vision. Amberly leveraged her body weight against Gann's until he was halfway over the railing. Claire grabbed at Gann's thinning hair and jerked his head upwards roughly. He was possessed with rage.

"I'll take you with me, bitch!" Claire heard him scream. He grabbed Claire's neck, but Claire pushed Gann above and away from her, and with Amberly, they gave one last heave.

Gann hit the water. Claire watched, feeling far away from herself, as if she was in a dream. Gann's flailing arm disappeared with an incoming wave.

Claire's body ached with exhaustion and shook with a dangerous energy she didn't like. Her heart pounded in her chest, and her breath came in shaky gasps. Her head throbbed and felt as if it weighed a thousand pounds. She sank to her knees for a moment, just to breathe. Another wave hit the side of the boat, splashing her in the face with cool seawater and stinging her scalp. She closed her eyes and felt it wash away some more of the blood from her scalp before turning to her audience.

The rain had ceased. Amberly picked up the gun Gann had

dropped, looking down at Claire with an expression of sinister delight.

"I couldn't have wanted more than that, despite your hesitations. The first kill is always the hardest."

Claire stood shakily and faced her sister.

"He was going to kill me."

Amberly stepped towards Claire. "I think you enjoyed that. We're more alike than you care to admit. You served justice for yourself. Now you have blood on your hands, too," she said with aggressive pride. Disturbed, Claire stared at the knife in her hand, the dim white glow of the deck lights reflecting in the blade. She wanted to throw it overboard, but her fingers wouldn't let go.

"What about him?" Svante raised his pistol towards Kyle.

"Ahh, yes." Amberly walked toward Kyle. "You've proven hard to kill."

"We could use someone like him with Dev dead," Svante added.

Amberly smirked. "And Claire seems to be quite infatuated with you. After what she just did for you, I'd be willing to keep both of you."

"After what you did to my family?" Kyle shouted incredulously.

Claire hastened forward, stepping over the splintered, broken door. She gripped her sister's knife tightly, still jarred by what she'd done with it.

"Leave him alone, Amberly."

Her sister gave her a curious look, then turned back to Kyle. Fingers danced on his chest before drifting downward along the wound she inflicted earlier on the beach.

Claire bristled as Amberly's gaze raked over Kyle hungrily. "I said leave him—"

Kyle caught Amberly's wrist and began to twist it. Amberly squealed in painful delight, but Svante was next to him in an instant. He fired a warning shot, then pressed the pistol into Kyle's throat. With a pained grimace, Kyle slowly let go.

Amberly laughed loudly. "*That* was fun." She straightened herself and leaned back into him. "I'm sure we could both keep you satisfied."

"I would prefer to join my brothers," Kyle spat, his neck craning from the pistol.

"Let me handle this one, Svante." Amberly's smile disappeared. Svante backed away, never taking his eyes off Amberly. Claire felt her insides harden as her sister dug her fingers into Kyle's scalp until they were eye-to-eye.

"Such a waste," Amberly murmured in a cold voice. "Be the good girl you are, Claire, and give me my knife? I promise to make it quick."

"You will not *touch* him," Claire snarled to her sister. Within an instant, she was at her sister's side, pressing the bloody knife into Amberly's throat.

"You were right." Claire drove the knife further into her sister's neck, pleased at her own power. "The first one was the hardest. Imagine how easy this will be for me now."

Amberly smiled devilishly, letting go of Kyle.

"How far can you go, Claire? Can you really kill your own sister?"

"This is never going to end unless you're gone," Claire whispered, feeling Svante's gun on the back of her neck.

"Easy, Svante," her sister said cautiously, but Claire didn't care. She stared down at the knife in her hand, looking at her flexed knuckles. Angrily, she pressed further. Droplets of blood continued dripping down the curve of her sister's delicate neck, identical to her own. Claire took a deep breath. Her muscles tensed as she was about to push the blade further until there was a stir to her right.

A bandaged hand lay over Claire's shaking one, pulling the knife away from Amberly's neck. Claire felt the gun removed from the back of her own neck. She turned abruptly and stared.

"Don't do this," Emere implored, trying to take the knife from Claire.

Claire shook Emere off of her. "After what she did to you? How can you say that?"

"I made her into this," Emere pleaded emphatically, "We were going to leave together, forget about what Jaquarde had done to us and this terrible life, but he suspected. He fed off of my fear. I told him everything and begged him for mercy. After that, he sold our boat to Kyle's brother. The boat we planned to run away with. Amberly ran away with Svante instead, whom Jaquarde requested she kill years ago . . . but she didn't."

Claire saw Kyle look away and clench his fists. Out of the corner of her eye, Svante tensed.

"You didn't make her do anything," Claire replied angrily. "She made her choices. She's responsible for them."

"Listen to me," Emere pleaded. "Jaquarde knew Amberly would go after her boat. That she'd be so angry she'd kill the brothers to send a message to him. He was counting on it. He even called the police before they set sail. He set everything in motion."

Emere faced Kyle, who eventually looked back at her through tear-filled eyes.

"Amberly killed your brothers because of Jaquarde, but I killed Jaquarde." Emere looked back at Amberly sadly, and out of the corner of her eye, Claire saw Svante's poise falter slightly. "It's over. Jaquarde's business will crumble. This isn't your fight, Claire. You were only caught in the middle."

"My brother worked for Jaquarde at the restaurant," Kyle stated abruptly, his voice hard. "Jaquarde was his boss, and sold Jake the boat. The boat was a parting gift. He cut Jake a great deal so he could start off on his own. How do I know

Jaquarde wasn't innocent like my brother was?"

"Jaquarde was far from innocent," Amberly spat. "Nothing bad in the White Sands ever happened without Jaquarde getting his greasy fat fingers in it, or causing it. That overpriced restaurant was a cover."

"Don't punish her for what Jaquarde made us do." Emere stared into Claire's eyes. "We were only trying to run away."

Claire looked down at the knife in her hands once again. A twisted and painful knot formed in her stomach. She stepped away and stood near Emere, who sighed with relief.

A soured look came upon her sister's face.

"Shoot Kyle, Svante," Amberly commanded.

The pistol aimed at Kyle's heart.

"No!" Claire shrieked and grabbed Svante's thick forearms, trying to twist the gun somewhere else. He grabbed her by the neck and pushed her to the floor. Gasping, Claire stood, running to Kyle as fast as she could across the slippery deck, desperate to put a shield between him and death, terrified she was going to be too late. The thought sickened her, and she heard a second shriek from somewhere in the back of her throat let loose, as if it would help her reach Kyle faster. Adrenaline propelled her forward. The desperation caused her soul to ache, and her heart felt fit to burst. She couldn't be late.

The shot rang out as she reached Kyle. Claire held her breath. Her pulse throbbed violently in her ears, sure to be the last thing she heard, and with an impending sense of dread, she turned to face the bullet.

The breath Claire had been holding expelled from her mouth when Amberly slammed into her chest and knocked her backward. Claire hit the deck; her head slammed into the rain-soaked mahogany. Bright lights popped into her vision. Heaving for air, she sat up and blinked. She looked down and touched her chest gingerly, but there was no wound. She turned to the figure at her side.

"Amberly . . ." Claire whispered.

Red blossomed uncontrollably out of her sister's abdomen. Amberly's face was frozen, yet she was alive. The sky was darkening, and the white glow of the deck lights barely outlined the feeble rise and fall of her chest. Her once-powerful stance was reduced to a crumpled heap of defeated limbs, stacked haphazardly as they'd fallen.

Svante dropped his gun. It clattered down the deck with an incoming swell of a wave until Emere picked it up. An unnatural, guttural sound came out of his mouth as he ran toward Claire and Amberly.

"Why would you . . ." Claire grasped her sister's shoulders first, then her arms, unsure of what to do, where to hold her, how to make the bleeding stop. Amberly looked at Claire fiercely and reached for her hand. Claire let her squeeze it, hard, as Svante knelt and pushed long hair out of Amberly's motionless face.

"I thought you wanted to kill me," Amberly whispered reproachfully.

"You knew I couldn't do it." Claire felt herself shake at her words. She wanted to say something more, but her tongue felt thick and clumsy in her mouth, and her throat was dry.

"You were the only good thing I had left." Her sister's eyes closed, yet her grip on Claire's hand was unrelenting.

"Go." Emere appeared next to Claire. Svante's gun was tucked into the seam of her shorts. "I sent an SOS on their radio before I came out here. Help will be here within the hour."

"But what about . . ." Claire trailed off. Thunder rumbled above them.

"You know what you have to do, Svante," Amberly commanded softly.

Claire looked between them.

The burly man gave her sister a hard stare and shook his

head. His fingers were desperately clamped over the wound on Amberly's abdomen. Lightning illuminated his stricken features.

"No, Captain," he said urgently.

"Yes," Amberly replied firmly.

"Go," Emere repeated, taking Amberly's wrist, and pulling her fingers from Claire's hand. "Take the raft and get out of here, now."

Claire stared at her sister's face, no longer looking at her, but imploring Svante with her eyes. She couldn't leave. Not until the scene before her made sense. Even her body wouldn't allow it when she tried to move, her breath caught in her throat erratically, and her legs felt numb.

"Come on, Claire," Kyle's voice whispered in her ear. Large, powerful hands lifted under her armpits until she was standing. Claire forced herself to look away from Amberly and saw Kyle's face swim into focus. His warm hands found either side of her face. His eyes met hers with determination and softness. Serenity coursed through her body, and she felt dreamlike.

"Come on," Kyle repeated, and Claire nodded, falling in step with him, half running, half walking along the edge of the dimly lit deck until they reached the stern of the boat. A fog was creeping along the water ahead of the storm, humid and dense.

"There." Kyle pointed at the raft used to bring Claire onboard.

With great effort, she walked toward it, but Claire was only half paying attention. The raft looked slippery, and the waves were eerily calm. Her ears strained for any sound of her sister. She was sure, even now, that Amberly would try to stop her from leaving. But she didn't. The yacht was empty and quiet.

"Keep moving," Kyle said. "I'll get in first. You follow."

She obeyed as if in a trance. Her feet left the dark

mahogany and found the steps of the ladder.

The minor jolt of the final descent barely shook Claire out of her reverie as she felt Kyle's hands on her waist, helping her down. Amberly's pain-stricken face and broken body felt as if it was burned in her memory. Kyle started the motor moments later and turned on the searchlight. It shone through the foggy waters ahead, revealing rocky jetties sticking out like wicked spikes. Waves broke against them and jostled the raft.

"I can't believe she saved me." Claire wiped her wet hair from her face. Cold steel hit her in the forehead. Looking down, she saw Amberly's knife in her hand. Tears sprang into her eyes.

Kyle reached over and took her hand, just as Amberly had. He opened his mouth to speak when a gunshot was fired from a distance.

Both Claire and Kyle whipped around to look back at the yacht. It was already several yards away from them, it's ominous stern disappearing between the waves that separated them. The gunshot rang out in her ears and echoed across the water as the fog swallowed the yacht completely. Claire squeezed her eyes shut, gripping Kyle's hand tightly.

EPILOGUE

Bright sunshine warmed her skin. Claire focused on it – anything to drown out the stares of the surrounding harbor patrons was welcomed as she left the dock. Pedestrian tourists on the street were just as intrigued. One of her police escorts showed her a crisp fold of a paper. It was her own face staring at her. *Tourist Missing* was all she could catch as she was ushered along. She shifted uncomfortably under the flash of a bright photo bulb. She would look drained when the picture was put to print. That much was certain. The notice flew away in the wind when the flash of another camera caused her to blink, leaving a bright orange yellow imprint in her vision.

"Stop that, please, move along." The officer sounded annoyed as the man drew the camera slowly from his head, positioning it instead near his waist before snapping one more shot at Claire.

That irritated the police further and kept them busy until rows of tourists ended at a beautiful black wrought iron gate. Her bare feet ascended the small hill as the gate creaked open. They passed neat rows of palm trees and walked inside an architectural feat of a building. The rotating golden doors of the hotel whooshed closed behind her and revealed a long marble hallway leading to the concierge. The air conditioning caused Claire's loose strands of greasy hair to flutter about her face. The room was open and large, festooned with glossy paneling and crystal chandeliers.

The officer smoothed the front of his uniform, as if to impress someone. He placed his hand delicately behind Claire as if she were made of fragile glass. The front desk was an elongated extension of the marble floor in which several beautiful women and men smiled at their guests. The officer guided her to a pretty blonde woman, her long polished nails resting serenely on the marble top as she *stretched out a smile and winked at the officer.*

"Room one-zero-zero-four, hon." The red lips of the blonde spoke pleasantly. Claire followed her eyes to the long golden hallway and froze in shock.

Amberly stood there, dripping blood onto the marble. Her hair whipped about her as if in a powerful ocean gale. Within seconds she crossed the floor to meet Claire, raising her arms and pointing her knife.

A sense of dread engulfed Claire as if the world was closing in. She drew ragged, shallow breaths, but her airways seemed to constrict with the building panic. The officer grabbed the back of her neck.

"What are you —" Claire jerked her head towards him, then gasped.

It was Svante.

Claire tried to push away, dropping her room card to the floor, seeing that it was a knife covered in blood. Amberly laughed.

"I told you I'd never let you go."

Claire sat up in a cold sweat. She looked around, afraid that her sister was waiting for her in the shadows of the small cabin. Kyle emitted slow, deep breaths beside her, still lost to sleep. A gentle breeze passed over the water outside. The slivers of light on the floor told her that it was just after daybreak. She glanced at the nightstand and opened the drawer slowly.

Amberly's knife slid slightly with the drawer's movement. Claire ran her hand along the familiar worn hilt.

"You okay?" Kyle woke and traced his hand along her bare back gently. It sent tendrils of pleasure and relaxation down her spine. She nodded and closed the drawer. "Just the same bad dream." She rubbed goose bumps out of her arms and covered her legs with the sheet. "It's the uncertainty that I can't stand. Sometimes I think just knowing she was alive would be better than this."

Kyle sat up next to her and placed his arm about her waist.

"We have to move on."

"I know," she whispered, "but they still haven't found her boat or her body. It's been a year."

"Claire," he whispered, tracing his finger against her own scarred cheek. "We'll keep getting through this. You brought me peace. Save some of it for yourself."

"I know," she whispered back. "I think it'll just take me more time."

Claire gently moved his arm from her waist and swung her legs over the side of the bed. She walked naked across the tiny room to open the porthole window. A warm ocean breeze blew across her face and she breathed deeply, clearing her head. Buoys bobbed in the distance, and she heard the sound of flags rustling quietly in the sunrise. A note fluttered on the table below.

She ran her hands along the crème-colored invitation and re-read it.

Hey island lovebirds!

This is your formal invitation to our anniversary celebration. You'll both stay at the inn, as long as you want, in my nicest room overlooking the sea. Business has boomed thanks to Claire's reinvention of my website. It was the best wedding gift – can't thank you enough. Also, Henry is done with physical therapy! Now we all have scars from the White Sand Isles, which should really be the slogan for your business, ha-ha! Besides, Justine and Henry would love to see you again, too. I won't take no for an answer! Try not to sink another boat if you sail.

Best – Paul

Claire laughed, almost hearing Paul's lighthearted voice say the words before turning back to Kyle. He was lying down, watching her closely, a look of concern etched across his brow and reflected in his handsome brown eyes.

"I've been thinking after reading Paul's note." Claire sat

back on the bed and scooted closer to Kyle. "We *should* sail to Scotland next month instead of fly."

Kyle looked at her in surprise. "We've already talked this through, Claire. We have customers lined up since your website's been taking online orders, and we—"

Claire put her hand over Kyle's, and he paused. "We can block the time off. I already checked, and it's only a handful of locals at that time. I know them, and we can work it out, Kyle. The busy season is still a couple months away, and we're booked for it. We'll make up more than the cost."

Kyle gave her a slow smile. "Thanks to you. But going out to sea after everything that happened . . ." He trailed off.

"Maybe it will bring closure," she said gently.

"We make our own closure," he said firmly. "I think we've learned that. Searching for her won't help. What brought us pain isn't going to bring us healing."

"I know," she whispered.

"Are you sure?" he pressed. "I want you to want to sail for the right reasons. Our brains want endings and answers, but we're responsible for finding our own peace."

"That's what I'm saying. This can be a positive trip, Kyle. A new beginning. We can still get reservations to sail, and we can do this as part of finding our own peace." Claire intertwined her hands absentmindedly. "I feel more connected to her when I'm out on the open sea."

"I understand," Kyle replied quietly. He ran a hand causally through his hair, and Claire watched his bare chest flex with the movement. She blushed slightly. Even after a year, she still felt excited twinges when watching him. He caught her looking, and with a small smile, nodded. "Okay. Let's do it. A new beginning would be a nice way to start the season."

Claire beamed at him. "You'll keep teaching me to navigate?"

"I'll keep teaching you everything I can, boss." He winked.

Claire laughed and blushed. "Stop calling me that. It's so weird."

"Not a chance, especially since it's true."

"Fine. I'll rearrange the charter trips today."

"Perfect," Kyle replied.

Claire brushed some of Kyle's curly hair from his shoulder and unintentionally touched his long scar, the first one Amberly had given him years ago. She traced it gently before his hand caught hers, and he held it there, gazing at her with what was now a familiar earnest glow.

"No second thoughts?"

Claire shook her head.

"No. I know we can do this." Clare paused. "I know I can find peace, but will you stay by my side as I keep working through it?"

He winked again and drew her down on the bed with him. "Always, Claire. Always."

ABOUT THE AUTHOR

White Sand Secrets is Catherine Hazen's debut novel. It was one of many storylines constructed when Catherine was a teenager, daydreaming of various adventures. Catherine lives in Minnesota with her family. You can follow her on Instagram @catherine_hazen22.